# FRAIL BARRIER

# FRAIL BARRIER

Edward Sklepowich

**Severn House Large Print**
London & New York

This first large print edition published 2009
in Great Britain and the USA by
SEVERN HOUSE PUBLISHERS LTD of
9-15 High Street, Sutton, Surrey, SM1 1DF.
First world regular print edition published 2007 by
Severn House Publishers Ltd., London and New York.

British Library Cataloguing in Publication Data

Sklepowich, Edward.
    Frail barrier -- (The Urbino Macintyre series)
    1. Macintyre, Urbino (Fictitious character)--Fiction.
    2. Americans--Italy--Venice--Fiction. 3. Venice (Italy)--
    Intellectual life--Fiction. 4. Detective and mystery
    stories. 5. Large type books.
    I. Title II. Series
    813.5'4-dc22

    ISBN-13: 978-0-7278-7787-1

Printed and bound in Great Britain by
MPG Books Ltd, Bodmin, Cornwall.

You fear not to place so frail a barrier
between yourselves and the wildness of the sea.

Cassiodorus, regional official, 523

# Prologue

## Death at the Feast

Once again, Urbino Macintyre and his friend Barbara, the Contessa da Capo-Zendrini, were in happy possession of their accustomed table at Caffé Florian.

On this afternoon in late July, however, the elegant Chinese Salon with its mirrors, maroon banquettes, bronze *amorini*, gilded wood, paintings under glass, and burnished parquet floor was less the refuge that it usually was for them. The doors between the salon and the wide arcade, closed in the cooler months, had been thrown open. The room seemed more of an extension of the piazza than a secluded vantage point, and had lost some of its charm for the two friends.

In the piazza, in what Napoleon had called the finest drawing room of Europe, tourists were jammed together, competing for space and their share of the hot, humid air that hung around them like wet sheets.

If any of them were foolish enough to pause for more than a few seconds to take in the domes of the Basilica, the redbrick Campanile, and the clock tower, with its zodiacal figures, or to angle for a photograph, they did it with considerable risk to limb if not actually to life. For the procession of admiration was not for the weak or the timid.

Even the ubiquitous pigeons seemed afraid of being trampled on the stones. Avoiding even the few unencumbered parts of the pavement, they settled on heads and shoulders, and looked down from the roofs and windowsills of the surrounding buildings. A screaming child spun in frantic circles as two pigeons tried to alight on her blonde head.

A man helped a dazed woman, who held her hand against her head, to the relative safety of Florian's arcade where a cream-colored curtain had been partly lowered past the high arches to block the sun. A father grasped his young son tightly as they plunged into the crowd. Outside the Chinese Salon a frail, elderly woman with a cane dropped into an empty chair at a table occupied by a young couple, took out a handkerchief, and patted her face.

Two tour groups approached each other beneath the pale blue sky like opposing armies. They parted the human sea and created waves that encroached on the edges of the outdoor tables, the orchestra platform, and the arcade. To guide their forces to the next spot to be conquered by eye and camera, one leader brandished a furled red umbrella decorated with yellow ribbons; the other held aloft a German flag, limp in the listless air.

A constant clamor echoed from the buildings. Urbino wished he could hear some of the expressions of delight on the lips of this surging mass. It would have compensated for seeing his beloved city inundated in a manner almost as destructive as that of the *acqua alta*, the storms, and the encroaching Adriatic.

The activity within Florian's was hardly less frenetic than that in the piazza. Tourists streamed through the salons of the café as if it were another exhibit of the lagoon city and as if patrons like Urbino and the contessa were wax effigies that bore a remarkable resemblance to the living. Boisterous groups sat around the marble-topped tables. Although they had long since finished eating and drinking, they had not yet satisfied themselves with all of the details of the establishment, nor taken enough photographs to prove that they had been within its fabled walls. White-coated waiters, a special breed at Florian's, negotiated everything with grace and a touch of haughtiness as they moved smoothly through the rooms, emitting kissing sounds to attract each other's attention.

Being played out again for yet another summer was the age-old spectacle of beauty and consumption.

The contessa found all this activity exasperating, but Urbino was enjoying it in his peculiar fashion. It was triggering pleasant memories. For it seemed as if it were only yesterday when he had been one of these same wide-eyed, open-mouthed consumers besieging the city in high season and risking an aesthetic headache or worse. And Vivaldi's 'Summer', whose lively strains now drifted across the square from Quadri's orchestra, was playing when he had first stepped on the piazza's stones more than twenty years ago.

In fact, the fresh-faced young man with an old *Baedeker* peering into the Chinese Salon reminded Urbino of his former self who had come to Venice from America that long-ago summer and never really left.

Urbino smiled at him. His younger self, however, moved away from the doorway and was swallowed by the throng.

'Have you heard from Habib?' the contessa asked.

Habib was Urbino's young Moroccan friend. Urbino had helped the painter, who was currently visiting his family in Fes, establish himself in Venice.

'Yesterday. He's fine. He'll be back at the end of September.'

The contessa reached for another one of the petits fours that had been placed on the table a short time before. Only one now remained on the plate.

'Too late for the regatta,' she said. 'He enjoyed it so much last year.'

The Historical Regatta, with its processions and boat races on the Grand Canal, would take place on the first Sunday of September. The contessa was giving a party at her palazzo on the grand waterway for the occasion. Five days ago she had abandoned her cool, quiet villa up in Asolo, where she retreated every summer, to celebrate the Feast of the Redeemer and to make preliminary arrangements for her party.

The contessa looked rested after two months in the hill town. She always managed to shroud her true age in vagueness, inspired by Coco

Chanel's philosophy that as one ages, youth must be replaced by mystery. Urbino suspected that she was two decades older than him, but the exact time she had passed the barrier reef of fifty, then sixty in their long friendship had gone unnoted by him and decidedly unremarked by her. He wouldn't have needed his skills as a sleuth, however, not to mention those of a biographer, to establish the minute as well as the year of her birth. But people should be allowed to keep their secrets if it did no one any harm. It was enough for him that the contessa was healthy and splendid at whatever age, her face aided by its bone structure and the make-up obvious only because of its apparent absence.

The two friends knew each other so well that there were hundreds of ways that they showed their feeling by the things they said and did, and didn't say and do. Some Venetians, not too kindly, referred to them as 'the Anglo-American alliance', which only amused the pair. In truth, each of them had acquired some traits of the other, and at times the contessa's speech was American-inflected as Urbino's carried echoes of the contessa's. When you added to all this the fact that they were both expatriates, and had a strong overlay of the Italian, you came up with a couple unusual in many ways.

On this sultry afternoon, the contessa was wearing one of the dresses that most became her. Sheer, with a pattern of marigolds on a wine-dark background, it suited not only her gray eyes and honey-brown hair but also the rich colors of the Chinese Salon – even the amber tones of the

11

first flush jasmine in her teacup and the sherry in Urbino's glass.

'A rather small group,' she said about her regatta party, eyeing the last of the petits fours. 'Small enough so that everyone can have a place on the *altana* and the loggia to see the procession and the races.'

From its position on the Grand Canal between the Cannaregio Canal and the Rialto Bridge, the Ca' da Capo-Zendrini would provide an excellent view of most of the races and a distant one of the water parade which ended at the great curve of the waterway.

'Romolo and Perla will be there, of course,' the contessa said, naming a voice teacher and his young wife. The contessa had met Romolo Beato when they were both students at the Venice Music Conservatory, where she had studied the piano before she had married.

'And there will be Sebastian's Nick,' she added.

This individual was an Englishman who came with the recommendation of the contessa's young cousin Sebastian Neville. Nick Hollander, whom neither the contessa nor Urbino had yet met, was planning to be in Venice through the Regata Storica.

She mentioned more of the invited guests. Most of them belonged to the contessa's social set or were members of the conte's family and her own. Some would be in Venice for the upcoming film festival as well.

Florian's orchestra, which alternated its musical offerings with those of Quadri's and

Lavena's, now launched into a Broadway show tune. A middle-aged man and woman arose from their table near the front of the white-canopied stage with its profusion of potted green plants and managed to find enough space, cramped though it was, to execute a few lively steps.

Urbino and the contessa watched the dancing couple.

'Poor man,' the contessa said after a few moments.

At first her comment puzzled Urbino. Why would she be saying that about the man who was so evidently enjoying himself on barely two square feet of the piazza's stones?

But someone else, from whom she looked away, had caught her attention. It was he who was the source of the sentiment and the sigh she now gave.

This individual was an extraordinarily thin, bald man in his early fifties, dressed impeccably in a well-cut light brown suit and flowing lemon-colored cravat. He pressed a handkerchief against his nose. The edge of the white cloth – though hardly more white than the man's face – was stained with blood.

A man in his early twenties with thick black hair and wearing a sea green cashmere sweater accompanied him. He guided the older man along the arcade in the direction of the Correr Museum, speaking close to his ear. The bald man, steadied by his companion, faltered a step or two.

'You can always recognize grave illness,' the contessa said. She took the remaining petit four,

13

less out of hunger than the need for its small dose of comfort.

'At least he has someone to look after him. An Italian, from the look of him.'

The contessa followed with sympathetic eyes the two slowly departing men until they were lost from sight, and cast another glance out into the bustle and merriment of the piazza.

'Death at the feast.' She gave a little shiver. 'A young man. Yes, young, *caro*, too young for this. And his fine clothes aren't any help to him, are they? Things never are.'

Urbino touched her hand.

'But money can make a difference when one is ill,' he said. 'In some cases it can even buy you better health. Would you like another pot of tea?'

'What I'd like is for life to be different but there's no chance of that, is there? Yes, I'll have more tea.'

When Urbino looked around for their waiter, he was already approaching their table.

Claudio was a tall, handsome man in his mid-thirties, with black hair threaded slightly with gray and deep-set, piercing eyes. Since he had started to work at Florian's ten years ago, he had become their favorite waiter. Claudio was an opera enthusiast, and had an excellent operatic tenor. The contessa had arranged for him to take voice lessons from Romolo Beato.

Claudio was also a champion rower. He had been training, with Urbino's gondolier Gildo as his partner, for the *gondolini* qualification races next month. The *gondolino* competition, involving the small gondola designed specifically for racing, was the highlight of the regatta.

'You know what I want even before I do, Claudio,' she said.

'What is that, Contessa?'

Claudio spoke English well but with a heavy accent.

'Another pot of tea, please.'

'Of course, Contessa. But your opinion is too high.' He flashed his bright, healthy smile. 'I came over to give you this.'

He opened his palm.

In it was a bracelet in an elegantly simple design of three gold strands and the intertwined letters *B* and *A* in gold. One of the contessa's most treasured possessions, it was a gift from her late husband Alvise on their last wedding anniversary.

'But I don't understand.' She looked at her bare right wrist and back at the bracelet, as if she expected to find that Claudio held only a replica and that she was still wearing the original.

'Albina found it, Contessa.'

This was Albina Gonella, the restroom attendant. The contessa was fond of her, and occasionally visited her and her sister Giulietta, a seamstress, who lived in the Dorsoduro quarter near Campo Santa Margherita.

'But I didn't even notice that I had lost it. However did such a thing happen? How careless of me! Poor Alvise!'

'Albina found it on the carpet in the foyer outside the restrooms.' Claudio placed the bracelet in her hand. 'She's seen you wearing it. You should have the clasp strengthened. You may not

15

be as lucky if it happens again. I'll get your tea.'

'Thank you, Claudio. And thank Albina – but no,' she interrupted herself. She got up from the banquette. 'I need to see her myself. Is she still upstairs?'

'Yes, Contessa.'

While Urbino waited for the contessa to return, he looked out into the piazza.

He took in the animated scene with appreciation but without focusing on anything or anyone in particular until he noticed two young men standing at the edge of the crowd under the arcade near Florian's. They were eating sandwiches and passing a bottle of mineral water back and forth. They listened to Florian's orchestra and appreciated the glowing mass of the Basilica until the two bronze figures atop the ornate clock tower caught their attention. The figures struck the fifth hour.

They were so obviously delighted with it all that Urbino felt a peculiar and unexpected pang of envy. It was followed by the urge to invite them into the Chinese Salon for drinks and some of Florian's small sandwiches.

But of course he didn't. How presumptuous of him, not to mention condescending. As if it could add to their enjoyment of the Venetian scene if they were perched as he was in the Chinese Salon with a whole menu to command.

And yet if the two young men need not envy him, he need not really envy them either.

Contentment surged through him. How fortunate he was! No, not because he could indulge himself at the Caffè Florian whenever he might want to, alone or in the contessa's company. No, his contentment came from the realization that his love for the city hadn't dimmed over the years. He was still very much a man in love.

When Claudio brought the contessa's tea, Urbino ordered another sherry for himself and a celebratory plate of scones.

Some of his euphoria left him, however, when the contessa returned. Tired sadness stamped her face.

'Dear marvelous Albina!' she said. 'If she weren't so marvelous, where would I be? Where would my Alvise's bracelet be?'

They glanced at the gold ornament, restored now to its proper place on her wrist.

Looking around a bit furtively at the other patrons, the contessa said, with intensity in her voice, 'Anyone in here might have had it stashed away in his pocket or purse with no idea of how precious and irreplaceable it is to me!'

'Why not have a scone, Barbara? Let me put some marmalade and cream on it for you.'

He took her silence for assent and attended to the soft tiny cake. When he offered it to her, she was staring absently at her bracelet, lost in thought. He waited a few moments, and then ate the scone himself.

'How disturbing, *caro*.' The contessa spoke musingly, looking up. 'How easy to lose something precious and not know it! Not until it's much, much too late.' She reached out and patted his hand. 'Let's try not to forget that. There are so many precious things to lose.'

But then a puzzled look came into her eyes.

'Where's my scone? Didn't you say you were preparing one for me?'

'I—'

He moved his hand in the direction of the plate.

'No. Let me give *you* one. You're one of my precious things. I enjoy taking care of you.'

The contessa spread the marmalade over the scone and added a dollop of clotted cream. She was much smoother in her movements than Urbino had been, and considerably more generous in the dollop.

'If I ever start to lose *you* in the slightest way,' she said as she held out the freighted morsel, 'I would know it immediately.'

'I have no doubt of that, but we'll have to take it on the deepest faith. There will never be any risk of losing me.'

'And neither will you ever lose me.'

A shadow crossed the contessa's attractive face. Her eye drifted to the spot under the busy arcade where the gaunt man with the bloody handkerchief had passed earlier with his young companion.

Urbino, knowing the melancholy train of her thoughts, introduced the topic of Asolo, which never failed to cheer her, and from this they passed on to other pleasant subjects.

For the next hour, there in the Chinese Salon, the two friends dwelled on things not lost and on those happily anticipated: the regatta, the contessa's party, the city in all its beauty and madness, and the love and friendship that was theirs to share for what they hoped would be many more long and full years to come.

# Part One

## Storms

# One

Despite its splendid palaces and lively squares, its sun-washed Zattere and corridors of art, its oleander gardens and jewel-like courtyards, Dorsoduro is a quarter of death on this afternoon in early August.

Beneath the high dome of the Church of the Salute an old woman stares at the Black Madonna over the main altar. She petitions her for deliverance from the plague of age eating away her body. *Maria, salute degli infirmi, prega per noi.* Light spills on the woman's head from the windows piercing the dome, but she shivers.

In a vegetable barge in the canal by the Campo San Barnabà a man in the prime of health slices a melon in half to display its rich orange color. He cuts into one of his fingers. He laughs, sucks the blood, and jokes with a pretty young housewife. In two weeks he'll be dying in a hospital bed on the other side of Venice.

On a bench in the Campo Santa Margherita, a thin, pale woman watches her son licking a cone of mulberry *gelato* and wonders whether she'll be alive next year to see the dark fruit ripen in her courtyard and stain her windowsills.

An old man is being pushed in his wheelchair along the Zattere beneath rose brick walls and

21

cascades of honeysuckle. A sleek white liner, sparkling in the sunshine, makes its way down the Giudecca Canal toward the Adriatic. The man twists his head for a tear-blurred view of the island of the Giudecca where he fell in love for the first time. By the next low tide, when the city's rats emerge, he'll be dead.

In a darkened room near Ca' Foscari a woman who visited the Accademia Gallery once every week for thirty-five years is about to stop breathing. Her life is now reduced to memories, becoming dimmer and dimmer. The last vision before her eyes isn't the face of her granddaughter by her side. It's Giorgione's *La Vecchia*.

How far away she had thought this day would be when she had first seen the painting of the old woman. How little she had understood the warning on the scrap of paper in the woman's hands: *Col Tempo*. With time.

In a small, stuffy apartment not far from the splendors of the Ca' Rezzonico where Robert Browning died, a father kisses the still warm – the too warm – cheeks of his infant son.

In a bedroom of a palazzo on the Grand Canal across from the Gritti Palace Hotel, a white-faced man lies in an eighteenth-century bed with St. Ursula painted on the tester. Another man, wearing a peacock blue sweater, sits beside the bed. A third man, bald and dressed in a cream-colored suit, paces the Turkish carpet.

'He's dead,' says the man at the bedside.

The other man stops his pacing, stares at the body.

It's what they've been waiting for, but not in

the same way.

And before too long, they too will be dead this summer, and Urbino and the contessa's serene world will be shaken up once again.

A week later the city was attacked by its most violent storm of the summer.

Until three in the afternoon the sky over the city and the lagoon was bright blue. Then, within moments and as the Moors were striking the hour in the Piazza San Marco, the blue turned deep purple with swirls of bright red. It was a canvas worthy of the Peggy Guggenheim Museum. Tourists marveled at the beauty of the sky. But the Venetians knew that chaos was on the way.

Jagged shards of lightning split the sky over the narrow strand of the Lido. A gale-force wind turned the glassy waters of the lagoon into high peaks. Sheets of rain slashed against everything and everyone exposed to the sudden onslaught. Boats were forced to take different routes, avoiding vulnerable stops where the landings rocked violently or were flooded.

The sirens warning of *acqua alta* sounded, barely audible above the clamor of the storm. The Piazza San Marco, with its orchestra platforms and chairs, looked like the abandoned deck of a sinking ship.

The storm lashing Venice was the kind that threatened its frail existence more than barbarian hordes, rival empires, or Napoleon's troops ever had. The strongest defenses that the city could construct would be too fragile if storms like these became more frequent than they already were.

And on this day in early August the storm was devilishly twinned.

Shortly after ten o'clock, lightning illuminated the *campi* and bridges like stage sets under the fiercest day-for-night lamps. The thunder was so deafening that when windows broke from the force of the wind, it was as if the thunder had done it.

It all ended around midnight, abruptly. The malicious hand that had been testing the limits and the bulwarks of the lagoon city, built on marshes and mudflats, released its prey. And in its quick release it showed its power more than it had during all the previous hours of rage.

Three days afterward, in the late morning, the black coffin-like craft that was Urbino's gondola glided down a small canal in the Dorsoduro district.

It was a bright, sunny day, but traces of the recent storm marked the scene.

An occasional piece of rubbish, swept into the canal by the wind and rain and still not carried off by the tides, brushed the sides of the gondola and sometimes clung to Gildo's oar. The offensive odor of backed-up drains lingered in the air. The *ferro* of a gondola had been snapped off, and a fragment of the decorative prow floated in several inches of water in the boat.

Perspiration beaded Urbino's forehead. The air inside the *felze* was damp and heavy. The occasional breeze that entered the small, closed

24

cabin with its shutters was not quite fetid, but certainly far from the fresh and invigorating air the contessa was enjoying in Asolo. Despite these discomforts, however, Urbino preferred the covering of the *felze* to being in plain view, and it did provide shelter from the sun. In fact, he seldom had Gildo remove the structure, even though sitting inside it only increased curiosity since gondolas had long since dispensed with the *felze*.

But Urbino couldn't bear all those eyes on him – nor, if the truth were told, being mistaken for a tourist who insisted on being floated by his gondolier beneath the Bridge of Sighs during his allotted minutes on the water.

It might seem strange that although shy about being seen, he indulged in such an ostentatious form of transport. But Urbino had long since stopped worrying about his inconsistencies or even being aware of many of them. As for good friends like the contessa, who had given him the gondola to mark the twentieth anniversary of their relationship, they regarded them as perpetual sources of amusement.

Although he was an energetic walker and loved roaming the city on foot, the craft's suggestion of invalidism and indolence suited another part of his temperament, as the contessa well knew. Rowed by the young, vigorous Gildo, Urbino could reduce all effort to lifting his finger to turn the page of a book, moving his head to gaze through the shutters, and rearranging his cushions.

Nor was Urbino unaffected by the gondola's

old-fashioned associations. When he was drifting along, concealed in the *felze*, it was as if the clock had been moved back to some late Victorian year and he was on his way to have his portrait painted by Sargent.

Perhaps an even stronger appeal in the craft than these, however, was the marvelous way that it provided a floating post from which he could observe the world outside while not being observed himself.

There could be no better example of this latter advantage than what he was experiencing now. For something in the scene outside drew his attention. He put his volume of Goethe down in his lap, marking his place with a postcard reproduction of Tischbein's portrait of the writer.

The gondola was approaching one of those bridges typical of Venice; small, stone, single-span, and with a low parapet. Water steps, slick with green, descended to the water on either side. Prominent on the bridge against the brilliant blue sky was the figure of a woman in late middle age. She wore a green dress. Around her pale, thin face was a fiery crown of red hair, obviously the result of art and not nature. She stood beside an easel with a paintbrush in her hand.

Urbino immediately identified her as a distinct type. She was one of the amateur painters – almost always either English or German – who descended on the city with their easels, watercolors, and collapsible stools to render the Venetian scene with varying degrees of skill.

On the surface of the canvas Urbino could

vaguely discern the form of a campanile. It resembled the one rising above the tiled rooftops beyond the bridge in the direction of the Campo Santa Margherita.

Two nuns were examining the woman's work from a respectful distance. Standing closer and engaged in spirited conversation with her was a short, stout man. He pointed at the canvas and the campanile in the distance, and nodded with approval. The woman clapped a straw gondolier's hat with a red ribbon on her head and smiled.

The gondola passed beneath the bridge. When Urbino regained his view of the figures on the bridge through the slats of the shutters, the scene had drastically altered.

The stout gentleman appeared to have accidentally knocked down the easel in one of his lively gestures. He was all red-faced and apologetic as he helped the woman reposition the easel. The woman minimized any damage or inconvenience with a warm smile and a touch on his shoulder. Her soft laughter drifted down the canal to Urbino.

For Urbino it was all a pleasant little scenario. There was order and calm one moment, then their interruption, and then a return to order and calm. It was like Venice after the terrible storm. It was like so many other things in his life.

But order and calm could not always be restored. As the gondola moved away from the bridge, the contessa's words at Florian's, about how easy it was to lose precious things, echoed through his mind.

Urbino reopened his Goethe. He examined the Tischbein portrait of the writer. Goethe was in semi-profile. Dressed in a flowing white traveler's cloak and a dark hat with a round, wide brim, he was reclining on a bench, looking intelligent and meditative. The antique, ivy-adorned ruins around him contributed to his noble air. In the distance the hills of the Campania unrolled beneath a cloud-filled sky.

Urbino was struggling through Goethe's *Italian Journey* in the original German. His German was far from as free and as fluent as his Italian and French.

At the beginning of the summer he had embarked on a new writing project. It was an addition to his 'Venetian Lives', a series that combined his interest in biography and his love for his adopted city. *Goethe and Venice* would focus on the role that the city had played in the writer's life and art, concentrating on his visit to the lagoon city in the autumn of 1786. It would have reproductions of paintings and photographs of Venetian scenes that had been important to Goethe during his stay.

Goethe's sentiments about Venice struck strong responsive chords in Urbino. He had been reading his Goethe for the past weeks with almost as much interest in finding parallels to his own experience as in gathering material. When Goethe had come to the crowded city, he had observed that he could now enjoy his cherished solitude even more since nowhere was more conducive to being alone than a large crowd.

This was exactly how Urbino had felt when he had made Venice his home. It also gratified him that Goethe could be as contradictory as he was, and praise the city's incomparable light and gleaming palaces one moment, and the next moment recoil from the refuse dumped in its canals and the sludge underfoot after rainstorms. Goethe seemed to be the kind of person, like Urbino himself, who could appreciate beauty even more by acknowledging all the faults not only surrounding it but also, in some strange way, contributing to it.

But Urbino warned himself now, as he did so often, about the dangers of identifying too closely with his subject. He preferred to think that his tastes and temperament, his likes and dislikes, seldom complicated his biographical portraits or his sleuthing, one of his other passions. In truth, they very often did. In the pages of one of his books, the potential damage was only professional. But in the conduct of one of his cases it could be a matter of life and death – his own or someone else's.

For the moment no case occupied his attention. They were not something he sought out, but something that, for reasons different with each one, he could not ignore with a clear conscience.

It was much better to devote his time these days to Goethe, who after a long and productive life, had died, quite naturally and peacefully, in a corner of his big armchair in Weimar.

With this consoling thought, Urbino lost all sense of time and exterior scene, except when he became momentarily distracted whenever Gildo cried out a warning *'Hoi!'* as he turned from one canal in to another.

He buried himself in the volume for the rest of the ride home, carried on the wings of Goethe's words back to the days of a former century when the city had been, nonetheless, very much the same as it was now. Whenever he looked out of the *felze* at the canals and the buildings and the bright blue sky, appreciation and satisfaction surged through him, made more intense by the fact that Goethe, centuries ago, had felt the same things Urbino was feeling today.

When the gondola came to a gentle bump at the water entrance of the Palazzo Uccello, Urbino closed the book and refreshed his eyes with the sight of the worn stones of his Venetian home, his only home.

He would often remember this feeling of contentment as, in the coming weeks of high season, death entered his perfect little world again and asked him to make some sense of it.

Everything, in fact, was set in motion a few minutes later when the contessa called from Asolo.

'I have distressing news, *caro.*'

The contessa must have been out in the gardens of the Villa Muta. The repeated *'Ciao!'* of her brilliantly plumed parrot that she kept in a brass cage on the pergola was a counterpoint to the serious tone of her words.

'What is it, Barbara?'

'It's that poor man we saw under the arcade outside Florian's, the one who looked so ghastly, the one with the bloody handkerchief. He's dead!'

Urbino was somewhat taken aback. It was indeed disturbing that the man had died, whoever he was, but as far as he was aware, the contessa hadn't known him. Neither had he.

'I'm sorry to hear that, Barbara.' He paused. 'But you didn't say that you knew him.'

'I do now. I mean I know who he is – or was!' A trace of exasperation rasped her voice. 'I know because of Sebastian. I was going to call you about it today but then – then I found out he died, Konrad Zoll.'

She wasn't making much sense.

'Is that his name, the man we saw?'

'Yes, Konrad Zoll. A German. He had been living in Venice for a year. Strange that our paths only crossed that one time at Florian's. Last week I got a letter from Sebastian with an article about him. It had his photograph. That's how I identified him, although the poor man changed so! He was an art collector.'

'But why did Sebastian send the article?'

'Because of Nick Hollander. Since Sebastian asked me to invite Hollander to the regatta party, he thought it might be nice if I invited Zoll, too. Hollander is Zoll's stepson – rather he *was* his stepson. No, not because Zoll is dead,' she said before he could ask for clarification. 'Hollander's mother and Zoll divorced five years ago.'

'His ex-stepson, then.'

'Yes. The way you have an ex-brother-in-law from your divorce. And I assume they must have been close the way you and Eugene are. Sebas-

31

tian would never have suggested that I bring them together if they hadn't been.'

Urbino, who knew the contessa's young cousin was capable of this and more, remained silent. He had traveled through Morocco a few years before with Sebastian. The trip had turned out to be disastrous. They had parted company in Fes.

'But I still don't know how you found out that this Zoll is dead.'

'Sebastian called this morning. Hollander told him. And that's where you get involved.'

'Me? How?'

'By going to see Hollander and offering our condolences. He's staying at the Gritti Palace. I would do it myself if I weren't up here.'

'He didn't leave after Zoll died?'

'Not according to Sebastian.'

'I guess the dark young man with Zoll was Hollander.'

'Apparently not. He's not dark and he has hardly a hair on his head, according to Sebastian. Try to see him later today or tomorrow. Perhaps he can come up to Asolo this weekend. The both of you. I'll ring him. He could use a change of scene. Venice in August isn't the best place to be when you're grieving. He'll be welcome here.' Once again, this time as if on cue, the parrot uttered its remarkably human-sounding *'Ciao!'* in an even more welcoming tone. 'And even if he doesn't come, I'd like you to come. I'll show you the article Sebastian sent.' The contessa sighed. 'Poor man. He was so vigorous-looking such a short time ago.'

\* \* \*

Urbino was reviewing his conversation with the contessa when a knock sounded on the library door. It was Natalia, his housekeeper and cook.

'Gildo would like to speak with you, Signor Urbino.'

The smile on Natalia's round face was not for Urbino, although she liked him well enough. It was for Gildo, who was her pet. Ever since the young man had started to work as Urbino's gondolier a year before, she had taken him under her wing. She delighted in bringing meals to his self-contained apartment by the water entrance and looking after him in every other way she could.

The young man stood behind her. He was slim but muscular from his exertions at the gondola oar. His good-looking face, glowing with health, was open and ingenuous.

The plump Natalia reached up to tousle his reddish-blond curls before she returned to the kitchen.

'I was wondering if you will need me for the rest of the day, Signor Urbino.'

'You know that I didn't even want to go out in the gondola this morning.'

Urbino spoke in Italian, as he did in most of his dealings with Italians. He seldom ventured for long into the Venetian dialect, however. He hadn't mastered it as well as the contessa.

'Yes, but, as I told you,' Gildo said, 'it was good exercise, with the qualifying competition coming up tomorrow.'

The next day, in the waters off Malamocco on the Lido, the *gondolino* rowers who had applied to the municipality would be having the last of the rigorous competitions that would determine which teams would participate in the regatta.

'Nonetheless, Gildo, after tomorrow I want you to give all your attention and energies to practicing for the regatta itself.'

'We must take one thing at a time, Signor Urbino!'

'Well, whatever happens tomorrow, Natalia and I – and the contessa – are already proud of you and Claudio. You tell him that for us.'

'You can tell him yourself. He's downstairs. He wants to see you about something anyway.'

Claudio was sitting by the window that opened on to the canal, looking through a boating magazine.

After the three of them had chatted about the upcoming competition, Claudio said, 'I was wondering if I could borrow Callas's Hamburg Concerts. They'd be a good way to relax before tomorrow.'

'That's a good idea,' Urbino said. 'No problem.'

Gildo made an exaggerated frown.

'You're strange, Claudio. All that opera stuff – oh, excuse me, Signor Urbino,' Gildo added quickly. 'I didn't mean that *you're* strange.'

'What a disappointment!'

This only discomposed the young gondolier more. He looked back and forth between Urbino and Claudio.

'I'm sorry, Signor Urbino. Of course you are different. Everyone knows that. But – but you are strange in a good way! Yes! In a good way!'

Urbino laughed. He patted Gildo on the shoulder. 'Now you'll have to explain to Claudio how he's strange in a bad way! I'll get the Callas for you, Claudio.'

After giving Claudio the recording, Urbino went to the kitchen. Natalia was bustling around preparing lunch. He was pleased to see that it was something light, an *insalata mista* and *prosciutto crudo* with melon.

'I hope you're not putting too much pressure on those two boys.' She gave him a quick look over her shoulder as she washed a plate. 'You know how much Gildo wants to please you, and Claudio is always doing things for other people and not himself.'

'Don't worry. I've made it clear that even if they don't get selected for the regatta, they've already succeeded in my eyes. They don't have to win anything.'

Natalia made a sound that sounded suspiciously like a harrumph.

'Sometimes you say things without saying them,' she observed.

Urbino, who couldn't dispute the truth of this, remained silent. He smiled to himself. Here, within less than a quarter of an hour, Gildo and Natalia had pinpointed two of his qualities: his eccentricity and the way he often communicated both more and less than his spoken words.

'And who knows?' Natalia pursued. 'If Gildo strains himself, he won't be able to ferry you around like a doge in that gondola.'

Natalia had never approved of the contessa's gift, although she didn't seem to realize that her beloved Gildo would never have come into their lives without it.

'And how would you feel if you were responsible for spoiling Claudio's beautiful voice?' she threw in for good measure.

Urbino started to slice the melon. Natalia took the knife out of his hand.

'Thank you very much, but remember how you cut your finger with the zucchini last winter and had blood all over my kitchen. If you want to help, just let me do what I have to do.'

She sliced the melon with a few deft strokes of the knife.

'And if anything happened to his voice, you can be sure that Albina Gonella would be angry with you, gentle soul that she is. He goes to her house and sings for her and her sister.'

'That's very kind of him. By the way, do you know what café Albina works in in addition to Florian's? I'd like to stop by tonight and see what her working conditions are. I might be able to find her a full-time position somewhere.'

'That would be wonderful. Her boss at the café keeps asking her to do more and more work. You'll see with your own eyes what she has to put up with. She cleans up at Da Valdo. She starts around ten thirty.'

The café was in the Campo Sant'Angelo not far from the Fortuny Museum. It would make a pleasant walk this evening. Urbino thanked Natalia and left her to her work.

\* \* \*

36

A few minutes later Urbino called the Gritti Palace and asked for Nick Hollander. He was connected with him in the bar.

'Yes? This is Nick Hollander.'

It was a precise British voice.

'Hello, Mr. Hollander. This is Urbino Macintyre. I'm a friend of the Contessa da Capo-Zendrini, Sebastian's cousin.'

If it hadn't been for the murmur of voices, the tinkling of glasses, and the light music in the background, Urbino might have thought they had been cut off.

'Ah, yes, Mr. Macintyre. Sebastian speaks of you often.'

'How is he doing?'

'Very well. He's in Scotland for the summer with Viola.' Viola was Sebastian's twin sister. 'They so much would like to be here for the contessa's party.'

'It's unfortunate they can't make it. Barbara would love to see them. It's been almost four years.'

That had been on the occasion of another of the contessa's parties, during which there had been a murder at the Ca' da Capo-Zendrini. Sebastian was sure to have mentioned this to Hollander.

'I hope I can compensate a little for their absence,' Hollander said after a few moments. 'I'll tell her what they've been doing these days.' He gave a strained chuckle. 'Well, not quite everything. You know Sebastian and Viola.'

'Not as well as I'd like to.'

37

This was far less than truthful, for the Neville twins hadn't particularly impressed him, least of all Sebastian. But if Urbino knew one thing, it was that our world would crash down around our heads if we didn't lie half the time. Social lies. Little white lies – whatever you called them, they were necessary. But if they made his social life easier, they made his biographies and his sleuthing much harder. He had to spend many long hours sorting out the white lies from the much darker ones.

'How is the contessa? I look forward to meeting her.'

'She's well. She's looking forward to meeting you, too.'

Urbino was about to mention the contessa's invitation to Asolo when embarrassment rushed through him. He hadn't mentioned the death of Hollander's ex-stepfather! It should have been one of the first things he said. He rectified his oversight immediately.

'But forgive me for going on like this about relatively trivial things, Mr. Hollander. I meant to give my condolences on the death of Konrad Zoll as soon as I got you on the line.' It seemed best to refer to Zoll by name rather than by his former relationship to Hollander. 'It was thoughtless of me.'

'Not at all. Thank you. Did you and the contessa know my stepfather?'

Urbino, grateful to Hollander for having settled the issue of how to refer to Zoll, wondered whether his dropping of the 'ex' indicated the closeness of their relationship.

'We never had that pleasure. We only recently learned that a man we saw walking past Florian's in July was your stepfather. He was with a young man who was very attentive.'

Urbino waited for Hollander to identify his stepfather's companion, but there was silence.

'He made a deep impression on us,' Urbino continued, 'especially on the contessa. He looked so ill. We admired him for being out, considering his condition.'

'Leukemia. He was diagnosed only six months ago.'

Urbino, whose greatest fear was illness, contemplated what it must have been like for Zoll.

'This might not be appropriate, Mr. Hollander, considering your recent loss,' he said, 'but perhaps we can meet for a drink tomorrow or another day – at your convenience, of course.'

Hollander assured him that there would be no problem. They arranged to meet the day after tomorrow at five in the afternoon on the terrace of the Gritti Palace.

After lunch, a tenor voice singing one of Mozart's *lieder* filled Urbino's library as he lay on the sofa. Serena, the cat he had rescued from the Public Gardens several years ago, was nestled between his legs and giving a low, deep purr.

One particular song got Urbino's attention because of his interest in Goethe. It was Mozart's musical version of Goethe's poem 'Das Veilchen', the story of a violet that fell in love with a shepherdess only to be trampled beneath her feet. It was a delightful piece, beautifully put to music and nicely interpreted by the tenor.

When the Mozart ended, he went to the dark-wood ambry in the corner. The small, enclosed cupboard contained neither alms nor chalices, however, although one of the latter stood on a nearby table, draped with a seventeenth-century lace cover. The ambry had a secular function these days that nonetheless bore a similarity to its original ecclesiastical purpose since it served as his liquor cabinet. He withdrew a wine glass and poured himself some chilled Prosecco.

When he stretched out on the sofa again, Serena promptly found her previous spot. He opened his Goethe to where Tischbein marked his place. He reread Goethe's initial impressions of Venice during his negotiations of the labyrinth of the city. Like Urbino, the German writer had enjoyed finding his way in and out of the maze by himself, believing that his manner of experiencing things personally was the best. After a while, Urbino put the book down on his chest.

One of Goethe's ideas lingered in his mind as he lay on the sofa.

Goethe, whose vision had been renewed during his weeks in Venice, believed that the eyes are educated by the objects it is accustomed to look at from childhood onwards. According to Goethe, Venetian painters had enjoyed the great good fortune, because of the glories that their eyes had been formed on since childhood, to see the world as a brighter and happier place than most people did.

As for his own eye, Urbino thought, hadn't it

been formed – or rather re-formed, reconfigured – since moving to Venice?

He arose from the sofa and went to one of the windows from where he was accustomed to refresh his eye with the Venetian scene. He leaned on the broad marble sill, being careful not to disturb the pots of red geraniums.

It might be a small portion of the whole Venetian scene but it was representative. A *calle* led into a small open area where bright sunshine cut oblongs into the dark shade.

A covered wellhead with its worn relief of cherubs and garlands, which had belonged to the Palazzo Uccello in the seventeenth century, stood in the middle of the little square. A brindled cat sat on the well, soaking up the sunshine.

A bridge raised its humpback over a narrow canal on the other side of the square where a low-lying *sandolo*, recently repainted bright blue for the upcoming regatta, rocked in the wake of a passing delivery boat. Steps, green with moss, led from the side of the bridge down to the water.

The surrounding buildings were rose-colored and in that state of dilapidation that is graced by being called picturesque.

One of the buildings had an inverted bell chimney emerging from its tiles and curved, wrought-iron balconies with rows of flowers and ivy. On the roof of another building perched a wooden terrace, an *altana*, where in former years Venetian women would sit to bleach their hair, aided by a concoction of powdered Damascus soap and burned lead. Now the structures, like the one on the roof of the Palazzo Uccello, were used for far different purposes, such as drying laundry and airing clothes and blankets, although Urbino's own *altana* was also a welcome retreat made almost pastoral with its abundance of plants.

As he remained at the window, shouts and laughter echoed against all the stones, magnified somehow by the water. They could have come from a few feet away or from a greater distance, so unusual are the acoustics of the city. A few seconds later two children raced down the *calle* and over the bridge with a soccer ball, followed at a more sedate pace by their mother pushing a baby carriage. Walking backward when she reached the bridge, she pulled the carriage up the steps as she was obliged to do dozens of times a day as she went about her errands. An elderly man coming from the opposite direction helped her negotiate the steps down the other side.

Two women emerged from the *calle*. Their dark gray dresses and scarves identified them as nuns from the nearby Convent of the Charity of Santa Crispina. They leaned down to admire the baby and chatted with the mother before continuing over the bridge.

Neighborhood figures drifted into the square, stopping to exchange greetings and gossip. Two tourists half carried, half dragged suitcases from the *calle* beneath Urbino's window. Bewildered and exhausted, they accosted a white-haired woman, a vendor at one of the kiosks along the Lista di Spagna. After they showed her a piece of paper, she pointed in the direction from which they had just come.

Urbino could spend hours looking out of the library window or, in fact, any of the windows in the house. The contessa had once joked that one of his next presents would be a very modest one. It would be nothing more than a little pillow, though nicely embroidered, she promised, the kind that elderly women leaned on from their windows as they watched and gossiped and dozed.

He was about to turn back into the room when a thin woman in a green dress and a gondolier's hat, from which wisps of metallic-looking red hair escaped, emerged from the *calle* on the other side of the canal. She was struggling with a bag over her shoulder, a pack on her back, and a case in her hand. She was the woman on the Dorsoduro bridge whom he had observed earlier from the shelter of his *felze*, the painter who had been so good-natured with the man who had accidentally knocked down her easel.

That she was now in the Cannaregio district was not unusual. One of the delights of Venice was its smallness, hardly bigger than Central Park in New York City, and you were always meeting people you knew or strangers who soon became familiar figures.

The woman paused in the middle of Urbino's bridge – for so he thought of it – and looked along the length of the canal, first in one direction, then in another. She proceeded down the steps into the little square, and started to divest herself of her burdens. When they were all on the ground around her, she stroked the cat.

She surveyed the buildings that enclosed the square, giving a few moments of attention to each in turn, until her gaze fell upon the Palazzo Uccello. Urbino drew back from the window so as not to be seen, but not so far that he could not continue to see.

The woman stared at the building. Urbino had become accustomed to the attention that the Palazzo Uccello, with its stilted arches, marble facings, and pointed extradoses, received. Its seventeenth-century imitation of the Veneto-Byzantine style was often pointed out by tour guides and sketched by architecture students. He had once heard one of the tour guides explaining to a small group gathered on the bridge that not only had the building been built by an eccentric, reclusive bachelor in the seventeenth century but it also was now owned by one.

From his concealed position, Urbino smiled as the memory crossed his mind. The woman seemed to be absorbing the details of his building with an intense expression on her face that bordered on a frown. Could she be going to make the Palazzo Uccello the subject of one of her paintings?

But if she was, it wouldn't be today, for she slowly and a bit wearily gathered together her paraphernalia and went down the *calle* beneath Urbino's window.

# Two

At nine that evening, soon after Urbino went over the humpbacked bridge and down the *calle* toward the Grand Canal, he regretted it.

Not that he regretted his ultimate destination – the café in the Campo Sant'Angelo where Albina Gonella worked – but instead the route he had set out upon to get there.

It had him almost immediately encountering rowdy groups that were merely the eddies of the strong current of people he would soon be fighting against. At this hour the tidal flow of the summer crowd moved away from the Piazza San Marco in the direction of the train station and the car park at the opposite end of the Grand Canal.

Lightning flashes sharpened the night sky with knives of light, but no thunder rumbled. When he approached the Rio Terrà San Leonardo, a sudden gust of hot, damp wind blew drops of rain against his face.

He became caught in a group of Spanish tourists who were passing around a bottle of wine. When he pulled close beneath a shuttered shop to let another group pass, he took advantage of his knowledge of the city – the mixed blessing that never allowed him to lose himself anymore – and went off the main route.

45

He first backtracked in the direction of the Palazzo Uccello, skirting the Ghetto. The crowd started to thin. By the time he reached the neighborhood of the Church of the Madonna dell' Orto, and in fact long before, he was meeting tourists who had lost the main route or who, like him, were wisely seeking out the indirect way to their destinations.

He plunged deeper into the quieter reaches of the Cannaregio, where it approached the lagoon and gave views of the cemetery island and the causeway to Mestre and the mainland.

After several minutes he entered a small *campo* where local residents sat on benches and children played beneath a stunted tree whose lower trunk was imprisoned in a rusted iron cage. A tall building dominated the square not so much despite its state of dilapidation but somehow because of it. The shadow it cast seemed darker than any others in the open area.

It was the Church of San Gabriele, flaking from age, dampness, and the poisonous exhalations from petrochemical plants in nearby Marghera. It wasn't its early fifteenth-century Gothic pedigree that made Urbino pause to contemplate it. He was interested in its more recent history and for the role it had played in his life.

For the Church of San Gabriele was the site of a murder that had set him on his course of sleuthing.

Lying in one of the church's chapels was a glass coffin containing the preserved body of a female saint. It wore a white gown, crimson gloves and slippers, and its face was concealed beneath a silver Florentine mask. Snatched from Sicily by so-called sacred thieves of the Venetian Republic, the diminutive corpse had been at the center of his most macabre case.

Urbino shifted his gaze to the other side of the square where another building, with damp-warped shutters and chipped, leprous statuary and stones, seemed aloof despite its lighted windows and open doorway. This was the Convent of the Charity of Santa Crispina. During one carnival the mother superior had asked Urbino to use his discreet detecting skills to clear her house of suspicion following the murder of a guest of the convent's pensione. The frenzied festival, where nothing was what it seemed, had provided Urbino with a series of clues that led to the unmasking of the murderer at the contessa's ball only a few minutes before the clocks had started to chime the end of carnival.

He resumed his walk, pondering these two investigations that had followed each other in quick succession. He moved down the narrow streets, over the bridges, through the squares, and under the covered passageways of Cannare-gio. He didn't have to give much attention to where he was going, so familiar was he with the route. And yet details registered with great vividness – a flower-bedecked street shrine to the Virgin lit by a votive candle; a woman applying gold leaf to a harlequin mask behind the window of a closed shop; diners in the garden of a small restaurant; a brightly lighted window displaying eighteenth-century gowns, jackets, purses, boots, and trunks; and a death notice, affixed to a weather-beaten door.

But all the while Urbino was carried along on the stream of his thoughts about the occupation that seemed to have chosen him rather than the other way around.

The contessa called him a nosy parker. It was true that without his curiosity, whose intrusiveness was peculiar, considering how much he cherished his own privacy, he would never have gone far in any of his investigations.

But even more than curiosity, his passions for justice and order drove him. He had a strong need for due rewards and punishments, and an impatience with unanswered questions and untied strings.

Still harboring these thoughts, Urbino reached the lagoon where a vaporetto was making its way to the lace island of Burano. Considering the drift of his reflections, it was understandable that the figure of a lacemaker now appeared before him, an old, half-blind woman whose death had started him along another one of his twisting paths, motivated once again by curiosity and his love for order.

He stopped for a drink at a small café on the Fondamenta della Sensa. As he sipped the chilled white wine and watched the men playing cards at a table set up beside the canal edge, he realized what he would do when he left the café. He wouldn't go directly to Da Valdo. There was still enough time to catch Albina there. He usually allowed himself the luxury of having more time than he needed to get from one point in Venice to another, for he knew how little he could ever resist the temptation of wandering.

And wander a bit more he would do this evening as he visited some more spots where the dead had quickened him into motion.

Urbino frequently got into these states. Like a ghost, he thought to himself, or like a criminal revisiting the scene of the crime – except, of course, that in his investigations he only had to think like a criminal, not be one. Sometimes the line between the two seemed much too thin for his comfort.

He often heard the words of childhood priests in New Orleans come back to him: *Thinking of something bad is the same as doing it. You have already sinned.*

He reentered the bustling areas, and soon found himself among the strong flow of people again. As before, he was moving against the current as he went down the wide Strada Nuova lined with shops, over the Ponte Santi Apostoli where diners were finishing their meals under the *sottoportico*, and past the large, square mass of the Fondaco dei Tedeschi that housed the central post office.

In the Campo San Bartolomeo Venetians, most of them well-dressed in the latest fashions and colors, milled about or stood in small groups, smoking, laughing, talking. For this was one of the main meeting places of the city, presided over by the statue of the playwright Carlo Goldoni, who cast a bronze eye and a bemused smile over just the kind of activity and Venetian types that he had satirized centuries ago.

Urbino exchanged a few words with friends who were on their way to a wine bar near La Fenice. He declined their invitation to join them.

A few minutes later he paused in the middle of the Rialto Bridge to take in the view of the Grand Canal as it swept toward the Ca' Foscari. Soon, the Ca' Foscari, because of its position at the great bend in the Canalazzo where the regatta had its finishing point, would be the most watched place in Venice.

The pavements and the landing stages were crowded. A raft of gondolas laden with tourists passed under the high arch of the bridge in the direction of Ca' Foscari.

Urbino descended the steps of the bridge and went past the Church of San Giacomo di Rialto to a broad, open area along the Grand Canal. Scraps of lettuce and crushed tomatoes littered the stones. He proceeded slowly and carefully. A group of young people were at the far end, drinking, laughing, and dancing. During the daytime this was the city's main vegetable market. Late one November night it had been the site of a bloody double murder that had directly affected both him and the contessa.

After contemplating the scene, he continued deeper into the San Polo district. He moved away from the shops, most of them closed now, and entered a nest of alleys until he reached a remote corner of the quarter. There, he stood on a small, stone bridge. The odor of moldering stone and decaying vegetation hung in the air. Further along the narrow canal a lantern on the stern of a gondola glowed and rocked as the boat moved in the direction of the Grand Canal. The two gondoliers were singing verses of *'Torna a Surriento'* in turns, competing with each other in their powerful tenors as the song proceeded to the accompaniment of an accordion. The song became fainter as the gondola turned into another canal, and soon Urbino was surrounded by only the sound of water lapping against the stones of the bridge.

He gazed up at the crumbling façade of a palazzo with boarded-up windows. The building, with its eroded stone loggia, showed the ravages of a recent fire, a fire that could easily have claimed his life and that of the contessa if circumstances had been slightly different. The palazzo was not only a reminder of the undeniable pleasures of his sleuthing – for he had made some order here and triggered a grim form of justice – but also a warning of the dangers it could bring him and those close to him.

With his thoughts considerably more sober now than they had been when he had left the Palazzo Uccello, he set off in the most direct way for the Accademia Bridge.

Although this was one of his favorite walks, through the twisting lanes of San Polo and into Dorsoduro and the lively area around the Campo Santa Margherita, he enjoyed it less this evening than he usually did. The sight of the burned-out palazzo had dropped a chill over him that the humid air only made more uncomfortable.

He didn't stop until he reached the Accademia Bridge. Tourists lined both sides of the parapet, looking up and down the Grand Canal, taking photographs, pointing. Urbino managed to find a free spot at the wooden railing. On his left the rich marbles and carvings of the Palazzo Barbaro – actually the two Gothic buildings that went by that name – were brightly illuminated. He stared at the palazzo, trying to change his mood by thinking about Henry James, who had used it as a setting in one of his greatest stories.

But the chill that had dropped over him remained, for James's story was not only one of love but of death as well. So as not to risk making the chill any keener, Urbino avoided looking down the Grand Canal to a long, low white building on the right, which housed the Peggy Guggenheim collection. For near the palazzo's water steps one summer afternoon during the Biennale Art Exhibition the body of a lovely young woman had floated to the surface. Urbino, who had been on the terrace of the palazzo at the time, had realized that one of his investigations had turned deadly serious and that the contessa herself was under a dark shadow of suspicion.

He checked his wristwatch. He would have to hurry now if he wanted to catch Albina before she left the Caffé Da Valdo.

The night sky had become thickly covered with low clouds during the past half-hour. Thunder rumbled. It seemed that the city was going to get some brief relief from the heat and humidity, but the storm that would bring it was certain to come with a price.

Urbino left the parapet of the bridge, made his way slowly through the crowd, and moved toward the steps that would bring him down into the San Marco quarter. Before he reached the steps, however, he bumped into a couple. It was Romolo and Perla Beato.

'Urbino!' Perla said with a bright smile. She was a slim, blonde woman in her mid-thirties with smoky brown eyes and high cheekbones. 'There must be better ways to meet each other. We haven't seen you in ages. But excuse us. It was our fault. We're trying to catch the boat.'

Romolo was a portly man in his early sixties with thick hair that had been snow-white ever since Urbino had first met him fifteen years before. He was dressed in a well-cut suit. Since marrying Perla five years ago, he had shown a much greater interest in his appearance.

'No, it was my fault,' Urbino said. 'I wasn't looking.'

'Either you do not look because you are always in your own world,' Romolo said with a smile, 'or you are always looking. A man of extremes.'

Both Romolo and his wife preferred to speak in English with Urbino.

'Are you going to Harry's?' Urbino asked.

Romolo and Perla were regular patrons of the bar. The vaporetto from the Accademia stopped in front of Harry's Bar.

'Harry's in the month of August!' Perla cried. 'Have you lost your wits? With all those tourists sticking their heads in to have a quick look, not to mention the ones taking their time and nursing Bellinis?'

Perla's English, perfected as she had studied

alternative medicine in London, was much better than her husband's, although she strained too hard for idioms.

'I'm going to Santa Lucia now,' Romolo explained. Santa Lucia was the name of the train station. 'To see Rocco for a week.'

Rocco, his son, lived in Padua where he taught art history at the university.

'Don't forget the business that goes with the pleasure,' Perla reminded him. She planted a kiss on his cheek, bending slightly from her greater height.

'I won't. I'm having problems with one of my tenants,' Romolo explained to Urbino with a frown. 'He hasn't paid the rent in three months.'

Romolo owned buildings in Padua that he had inherited from his father, an industrialist. His income from the buildings supported his love for music – and for Perla. What he earned from his voice lessons could barely pay for their frequent trips and her clothing bill.

'Romolo is much too gentle for a businessman, but that's one of the reasons I love him. I had to insist that he go to Padua.'

Perla gave him another kiss and put her arm around his shoulder.

'Yes, you certainly have been insisting, my dear.'

Urbino thought he detected a slight edge in his words, but Romolo looked up at his wife with what seemed a warm smile.

'You should also be happy, Romolo dear, that you're getting away from another one of our storms,' Perla said.

54

'My dear, storms can come anywhere and any time. If I – or you – try to avoid one, we will only find another.'

'True, my dear. But don't forget *"O Sole Mio,"*' Perla said with a slight tremor in her voice. *'"L'aria serena, dopo la tempesta!"'*

She half spoke, half sang the words of the old Neapolitan song that gondoliers had appropriated as their own. Her face looked strained.

*'Brava*! You show your husband's expertise,' Urbino complimented her. 'By the way, Romolo,' Urbino said, 'how is Claudio doing with his voice lessons?'

'Very well. He's a young man of many talents. In fact, he—'

'But we must hurry,' Perla broke in. 'The boat is coming.'

The *diretto* was about to pass beneath the wooden bridge.

'See you soon, Urbino,' Perla said as she took Romolo's arm.

Urbino fought his way to the railing at the opposite side of the bridge and waved at the couple before Romolo boarded the boat. After blowing her husband a kiss, Perla went down the Calle Gambara in the direction of the Beato apartment near the Zattere.

One dim light illuminated the interior of Da Valdo. Most of the tables had chairs turned upside down on their surface, exposing loosely intertwined wooden slats beneath the seats. The table legs cast a twisted net of shadows around the walls.

Da Valdo, popular with tourists and locals, was in a corner of the Campo Sant'Angelo on the route to the Rialto from the Accademia Bridge and the Piazza San Marco. Its outdoor tables provided a clear view of the tilted bell tower of the Church of San Stefano.

Inside, steins and green and purple plastic grapes hung from the wooden beams of the low ceiling. Behind the bar were an Italian flag and photographs of footballers and of Valdo, the owner, with friends and clients. One wall held a calendar and posters. Another had a collection of photographs. They were of the *acqua alta* of 1966 and the collapse of the Campanile in San Marco in 1902. Other photographs, of carnival and the Regata Storica, were much more recent.

The café was empty at this hour except for the solitary figure of Albina Gonella. She was slowly removing upturned chairs from the tables, having finished cleaning the floor. She paused to catch her breath. She held two legs of a chair as if she were waiting for strength to return to take it down.

'Let me help you, Albina,' Urbino said, coming up to the woman.

She started but brightened when she saw who it was.

'Signor Urbino! What a surprise! Thank you.' She stepped away from the table. 'I am a little tired tonight.'

Albina was a small woman in her late fifties with lively eyes and graying hair that she usually preferred to keep beneath a bright green knit cap, even on hot nights like this one. She was

56

usually charged with energy out of proportion to her physical size, but tonight her face looked worn. She wore a yellow shirt dress, much too small for her. The hem was stained with bleach marks.

'Maybe we should try to find another job for you, Albina. Only one place where you would have regular hours.'

The woman stood up straighter and went over to another table. She took down a chair and placed it on the floor.

'Don't worry about me. I'm fine here and at Florian's. My heart is stronger than the doctor says. If I feel a little tired tonight, it's not because of work. It's because of Giulietta.'

The two sisters, both unmarried, lived together in Dorsoduro.

'I hope she isn't ill.'

Urbino took down another chair and put it in an upright position.

'As strong as a gondolier. But that doesn't mean that she helped me for one second with the boxes she made me carry up to the apartment today. Her fingernails, she says. All long and painted. She'd chop me into little pieces if she broke one of them. Easier for me to tote a hundred boxes up ten, twenty flights than to deal with her when she's angry!'

Giulietta was as different from Albina as two sisters could possibly be. The seamstress expected Albina to wait on her hand and foot, and seemed to give little in return except for her cast-off garments.

'Let me take care of the rest of the chairs,'

57

Urbino said as he went over to another table. 'Do whatever else you need to do. I'll walk you home.'

'It'll be nice to get back earlier than usual. There's something I want to watch on television.'

While Urbino replaced the chairs, Albina made a few adjustments around the café, neatened glasses by the sink, emptied a bucket of sudsy water into the sewer grate, and closed the window behind the bar.

'I don't want to keep you waiting, Signor Urbino. Let's go.'

'There's no need to rush.'

'I'm finished.'

Urbino pulled down the metal shutter with a pole, wondering how the woman managed to do it herself. Albina took two keys on a ring from her dress pocket and locked the shutter with one of them.

'This is nice,' Albina said as they headed toward the Accademia Bridge. 'If you hadn't helped me, I would have got caught in the storm that's coming.'

A strong, damp wind blew against their faces as they entered the Campo Santo Stefano. What shops and cafés were still open on this summer's night were closing. Awnings were being rolled up and merchandise taken inside. Tourists looked apprehensively at the dark sky. Some stood immobile on the stones of the square as they tried to decide what to do. Others hurried back to their hotels or the shelter of an open café.

'But I don't think it will be as bad as what we had two nights ago,' Albina said.

Urbino, who had developed the Venetian sensitivity to the weather, agreed with her.

'Were you caught in that storm?' he asked her.

'I was at the restaurant when it started. I thought the walls were going to come down around me! A neighbor's son came to rescue me and walk me home, just like you're doing. We probably didn't get blown away because we were holding on to each other for dear life.'

Urbino took her arm as they went up over the Accademia Bridge.

'You don't have to take me all the way home. Here comes the *diretto*. You'll be in Cannaregio before the rain comes.'

'I like the rain.'

'Not the kind this one is going to be. But as you wish.'

Urbino and Albina soon entered the Calle Gambara down which Perla Beato had slipped an hour earlier, but in a few minutes their steps diverged from those which would have taken Romolo's wife to her apartment. Albina and her sister lived in the unfashionable part of Dorso-duro – or at least it was considered unfashion-able by residents like Perla and members of the large expatriate community who favored Dorso-duro above other areas in Venice.

But it was one of Urbino's favorite quarters, and he had been frequenting it a lot of late. He enjoyed the liveliness of the Campo Santa Margherita and its proximity to the university at Ca' Foscari. Although nothing could shake his devotion to Florian's, on many afternoons he could be found at one of the small cafés in Santa Margherita. He had become acquainted with some of the students, and often got involved in discussions with them about art and politics that went on for hours.

Although it would have been a few minutes quicker to Albina's apartment if they went over the bridge by the Church of San Barnabà, Albina suggested they pass through the Campo Santa Margherita.

'I go that way whenever I can,' she said. 'I like to see the people, especially the young ones.'

Urbino guided her through the Campo San Barnabà and over the Ponte degli Pugni.

By the time they reached the Campo Santa Margherita the branches of the trees in the square were twisting in the wind. Groups of students congregated outside the cafés and pizzeria, unconcerned about the approaching storm. Several elderly people greeted Albina, but showed no inclination to stop for more than a moment. The woman kept up a flow of conversation, mainly about her work at Florian's and about Claudio. The two of them looked out for each other in whatever way they could. She was praying that he and Gildo would qualify for the *gondolino* competition.

'He's such a good boy,' she said. 'Like the best of sons. Last October he took Giulietta and me to see *Così Fan Tutte*. It was at the Scuola Grande dei Carmini.' She inclined her head in the general direction of the guildhall originally associated with the Church of the Carmini.

Decorated by Tiepolo and located right off of the Campo Santa Margherita, it was sometimes used these days as a venue for innovative opera productions. 'I thought it was very funny, but Giulietta just sat there like a statue. And she kept criticizing the costumes.'

They turned into a *calle* that led away from the square and that eventually, after connecting and intersecting with other alleys, would have brought them to Ca' Foscari and near the Grand Canal. But they didn't go that far. They took a few turnings down empty alleys where plastic bags of refuse were set on the stones in front of the building entrances.

They entered an alley with a *sottoportico* at the end. A footstep scraped the pavement behind them. In order to give the person more room in the narrow passageway, Urbino drew Albina closer to one side. They were now moving slowly. Albina seemed to have lost whatever remaining energy she had had as they approached her building.

When Urbino glanced over his shoulder, he saw no one. A television started to blare from an open window above them, drowning out any other sounds.

They passed through the *sottoportico* and turned right. Albina's apartment building was at the end of a cul-de-sac a short distance away. The light fixed to the side of her building was not working.

'Here we are, Signor Urbino. Thank you so much. Let me get my key and I—'

She broke off.

'How stupid of me!' she said, looking up at him. 'I forgot my house keys at the café!'

'It's my fault.' A wave of anger at himself swept over Urbino. 'I interfered with your usual routine.'

'I forgot because I'm becoming an old woman. But it doesn't matter. Giulietta is home. And this old door can be pushed in by a child – probably our apartment door too!'

'That's not safe.'

'Safe enough. And Giulietta can protect us. I don't like it, but she has—' She broke off. 'She has a very bad temper,' she continued. 'I suppose I shouldn't say it. But she can scare anyone!'

Albina gave a nervous laugh, and looked up at the second floor. Lights showed behind the curtains of an open window. She pushed one of the bell buttons beside the door. She paused before pushing it again. The curtains at the window were thrust aside. A head with curly, short-cut blonde hair appeared.

'What's the matter with you ringing the bell like that?' Giulietta's harsh voice spewed out in almost impenetrable Venetian dialect. 'Oh, it's you as well, Signor Urbino,' Albina's sister added in more gentle tones. 'Good evening!'

'Good evening, Signorina Giulietta. Excuse us for disturbing you. Because of me Albina forgot her key at Da Valdo.'

'Do you think this is the first time she's forgotten something? It's been happening for years now. Just a minute.'

They waited until Giulietta's head reappeared at the window.

'Here, you!' she shouted. She threw the key down to the ground. It barely missed hitting Albina. Giulietta pulled the curtains back in place.

Urbino picked the key up and fit it in the door. He noted that the door was damaged, as if from repeated attempts – successful or not – to push it in. Even the key didn't fit easily into the lock, but needed some maneuvering.

'You should speak to the owner and get this door repaired.' He held the door open for her and handed her the key.

'A lot of good that will do! Good night, Signor Urbino. Thank you for your care. Sleep well and give my best wishes to the contessa.'

She gave him a bright smile as she closed the door behind her.

Urbino walked down the deserted *calle* and back through the covered passageway. The wind, which had been strong only a short time before, had completely abated, but the air was heavy and dank. He looked up at the sky above the buildings. Stars were brightly visible.

By one of those strange weather patterns characteristic of Venice the storm that had been about to descend on the city had moved away. But Urbino knew that it would fulfill its threat sooner rather than later, and before the coming of the dawn.

He reached the Campo Santa Margherita. A group of young Venetians was gathered around a *gelateria*. One of them, a history student, called out to Urbino. Urbino waved but didn't stop.

He went over a bridge and past the Church of San Pantalon. Soon he was on the Crosera. Noisy groups of young people stood outside the cafés, leaving only a small space for others to get by. Tourists, most of them probably from the small hotels in the area, walked slowly along, looking in shop windows.

Urbino quickened his step. He was eager to get home now. It had been a long day. The San Tomà boat landing was only a few minutes away. From there a vaporetto, after only two stops, would bring him to Cannaregio.

As he was about to enter the Calle della Madonna, three black women stopped him to ask directions to the train station. They spoke in French and carried large cloth bags. They needed to catch a train for Bologna.

Urbino consulted his watch. It was a few minutes past eleven. The last train for Bologna, or for anywhere else, left in an hour. If the women missed it, they would have to wait until about five in the morning. He began to give them directions for walking to the station, but feared they would lose their way. He advised them to take the vaporetto with him. The stop for the station was the one after his. They would get to Santa Lucia in plenty of time to catch the last train.

'The landing is near here,' he told them. 'But follow me. It's easy to miss.'

As they neared the *calle* to the boat landing, Urbino recognized the lone figure of Claudio walking toward them from the direction of the Campo San Tomà.

'*Salve*, Claudio!' he called out.

Claudio seemed startled. He took in Urbino and the three women.

'*Buona sera*,' he said.

'Out for a walk?'

Claudio lived only a short distance away near the Campo San Tomà.

'Yes, a walk. The storm has decided not to come.'

'We'll have to see about that. How are you enjoying the Callas?'

'I was listening to it before I left the apartment. I'll play it again when I get back. It soothes me. So do my walks.'

Claudio appeared on edge. It was understandable, considering that tomorrow, the day of the final qualifying competitions, would be an important day for him and Gildo.

'Don't worry. I'm sure you and Gildo will do fine tomorrow. And you know my philosophy. The essential thing is making the effort. By the way, I just saw Romolo Beato. He said you're doing well with your singing. Congratulations.'

'When did you see him?'

'An hour or so ago. With Perla. He was on his way to Padua. But excuse me.' The women were looking at him nervously. 'I'd talk to you longer, but these ladies are on their way to Bologna. I want to be sure to get them to the station. Enjoy your walk. Good luck tomorrow. I'll be there to cheer you on.'

An hour later the storm broke. Urbino was dry in the Palazzo Uccello and the three women had

65

caught their train to Bologna.

But the city was exposed. This storm, coming so soon after the one of only three days ago, put the vulnerable city in great danger again.

The rain was torrential. It poured off roofs, ran through alleys like rivers, and spread in sheets across squares. Rubbish, from plastic bags that burst and overturned bins, was swept into the canals and washed into the drains, which were soon choked. In some areas the stench was over-powering from the backed-up sewers. Many boats, unwisely left uncovered, sank. Even most of those covered with plastic and tarpaulin couldn't bear the volume of water, which pulled loose the protective coverings and flooded the boats. People living in ground-floor apartments regretted that they had been seduced by the much lower rent, for they spent the whole night moving furniture and bailing out their rooms. The gondolas and motorboats moored along the Molo rocked violently, and the Molo itself was a deep sheet of water. At one point visibility became so poor at the tormented mouth of the Grand Canal that a water taxi almost collided with a vaporetto, crammed with passengers and riding dangerously low in the water.

Once again the city, built as it was on thous-ands of sand and clay islets of the lagoon, was being destabilized.

It would survive this storm, and the next, and the next, but it couldn't go on forever exposing its frailties to the forces of nature.

Two French tourists suffered through it. Blessedly, the most vicious salvos were now over. The man and the woman, trapped in Dorsoduro, were soaked to the skin and desperate to reach the train station. They thought that the last train of the night, the one that would take them across the causeway to Mestre where they were lodging, left at one fifteen, but it had pulled out of Santa Lucia almost an hour ago.

'If you didn't want to save a measly twenty euros a night, we'd be in our beds by now,' the wife said. She pulled up against a building.

'And if you didn't want another drink, we'd have got to the station before this storm,' her husband shot back.

'Do you know where we are?'

'You have the map.'

'This pathetic thing?'

She held up the map. It was falling apart at the folds. She thrust it into her husband's hands.

'It's useless,' she said. 'No, don't throw it on the ground!'

'As if another piece of rubbish is going to make a difference!'

Some of the plastic bags that had stood beside the buildings only a short time ago had been tossed around by the wind and split open. Refuse littered the *calle*.

'Let's try this way.' The husband indicated the entrance of a *sottoportico*. He threw the map on top of a plastic rubbish bag. 'Maybe we'll find a sign.'

'And maybe it'll be pointing in two different directions like the ones we saw on the other side of the Grand Canal!'

They entered the covered passageway. No light showed.

'Watch yourself,' the husband said. 'Give me your arm.'

'It's so dark in here.'

They groped their way slowly. Fifteen feet ahead a sheet of rain marked the end of the *sottoportico*. The husband took out a small flashlight attached to his keychain and directed its small but strong beam on the pavement.

'This puddle is almost a foot deep,' the husband cried. 'Don't they have sewers that work in this city? Watch out. You—'

He stopped short.

'What's that?' he said more quietly.

He redirected the flashlight beam to illuminate a dark form in front of them.

It was an unmoving figure. It was sprawled on the flooded stones, face down in the puddle. One arm reached toward the head. The other was twisted beneath the body.

Two sodden, half-smoked cigarettes floated on the water near the body. Each of the cigarettes was smeared with bright red lipstick, which had the appearance of blood.

The French couple had no doubt that the person was dead. Why should they have? This was Venice, wasn't it?

# Part Two

## Into the Maze

# Three

Urbino spent part of the next day at the final qualifying competition for the regatta in Malamocco. Since the Lido town wasn't easy to get to, he had arranged for Pasquale to bring him in the contessa's motorboat. The contessa was still up in Asolo.

Back in Venice the evidence of the ravages of the monstrous storm was all too evident. Even the Palazzo Uccello, which was protected because it stood almost midway between the Grand Canal and the lagoon, had suffered broken windows and damage to the supports of the *altana*. A flowerpot on the *altana* railing had become dislodged by the wind and crashed down near the water landing, narrowly missing the gondola. Fortunately, Gildo had secured the gondola well to the mooring and tightly covered it.

As soon as Urbino had awakened, he had called Vitale, the contessa's major-domo. He was relieved to learn that the Ca' da Capo-Zendrini had received only minor damage, mainly to the plantings in its garden and to a mooring pole that had been splintered when a water taxi had hit it.

Malamocco had escaped the major brunt of the

71

storm, however, even though it was at one of the three points on the Lido where there was an opening into the Adriatic. The opening was the site of one of the ingenious – and controversial – dikes that were under construction to protect Venice from the devastating floods that threatened the city, and of which they had just got a disturbing preview.

Malamocco had put on a festive air for the competition. Perhaps because of the storm the usually sleepy town wanted to celebrate even more, and the residents seemed particularly spirited. Malamocco, which had once been the capital of the lagoon government before it was moved to the area of the Rialto, might not have seen much devastation from last night's storm, but it had a history of destruction from the sea, though not recent. A tidal wave had obliterated the original settlement a thousand years ago.

Urbino was part of the large crowd gathered along the waterfront in the sunshine. He cheered on Gildo and Claudio as they rowed their *gondolino* past in the shallow waters. The two men were in fine form, and although they were evidently not the best among the competitors, they weren't among the weakest.

The chronometer that made the eliminations was in their favor. Gildo and Claudio were selected as one of the final nine teams. Barring some unforeseen disqualification or illness, they would run in the *gondolino* regatta.

Urbino made his apologies to the two men when they invited him to celebrate with them and their supporters in Venice. He wanted to wander around the Lido.

Before having Pasquale take him to the Piazzale Santa Maria Elisabetta, Urbino had a panino and a glass of chilled white wine in a garden trattoria. From his table under a grape arbor he had a good view of the expanse of water in which the competition had taken place. The lagoon off Malamocco was still lively with boats. Many of them were private craft – motorboats, sandolos, rowboats, and gondolas – most of them staying close to shore and filled with merrymakers. People strolled along the wooden pier or sat on the grass and benches.

The waters immediately off of Malamocco were notoriously dangerous because of mudflats and currents. Wooden poles in the water marked the safe boat routes. Supposedly when Pepin asked an old local woman the way to Rivo Alto, the high bank of the Venetian islands that became known as the Rialto, she pointed across the exact point of the lagoon where she knew there were treacherous waters. *'Sempre dritto,'* she said, 'Straight ahead,' directing him and his men to their destruction by the Venetian forces when his fleet became mired. Today you could hear Venetians offering the same directions without any malevolence as they pointed out the way to some building or square or bridge. The irony, of course, was that in the confusing maze of Venice nothing could ever be 'straight ahead'.

When Pasquale brought him to the busy Piazzale Santa Maria Elisabetta where the boats came in from Venice, Urbino walked down the Gran Viale toward the Adriatic. Although he

73

loved Venice, he sometimes enjoyed escaping from it for a few hours on the Lido and taking in what seemed to him to be, after months in Venice, the distinct anomalies of bicycles, Vespas, cars, and buses. But August was not the time to do it, for it was crammed with tourists, bicycles, and cars. He was jostled by the crowd, most of them in shorts and bathing suits although some of them – these he suspected being early arrivals for the film festival – were dressed in the height of fashion and sometimes quite outlandishly. A child ran into him with a cone of chocolate *gelato* that made a stain on his trouser leg. He was almost run down by two teenagers pedaling furiously on a tandem.

After stopping for a mineral water in a café, for the day had become increasingly hot, he eventually reached the Old Jewish Cemetery, where he knew he would be able to find some peace and quiet. Other than himself, there was only an elderly couple, who returned his greeting politely and continued their slow circuit of the cemetery.

The cemetery was a small area that had recently been restored, although not to the best effect. Many of the old tombstones had been moved and regrouped together, and the place had lost some of that melancholy charm that appealed to Urbino, especially in cemeteries.

After walking around and examining the inscription on the obelisk that proclaimed the cemetery to be the 'House of the Living', he sat on the ground near a cypress tree. It seemed an appropriate place to take out his Goethe, which he had slipped in his pocket before leaving the Palazzo Uccello.

For the next half-hour, surrounded by the tombstones with their images of upraised hands, urns pouring water, lions, and coats of arms, Urbino lost himself in Goethe's impressions.

The next afternoon Urbino, on his way to meet Nick Hollander at the Gritti Palace, sat in the stern of a vaporetto as it passed down the Grand Canal. This was his preferred place in the boats, with his back to the prow. He enjoyed looking out at the scene after the vaporetto had already passed it.

What has been called the finest street in the world was also one of the busiest. To an eye less practiced than Urbino's it would also have seemed to be one of the most chaotic, but not because of any ravages of the recent storm.

Wasn't his vaporetto about to capsize the rocking gondola only a short distance away? From the look of alarm on the faces of the tourists in the black craft, they certainly seemed to think so. And how could the fireboat, speeding from the station near Ca' Foscari, possibly make its way among all the water traffic without a collision? Surely stretches of the Grand Canal would soon be filled with sinking crates of wine and mineral water, plastic bags of refuse, and splinters of sleek, polished wood?

But despite all the activity and all the craft going about their business, there was order. Everyone kept to his proper place on – or rather *in* – the liquid pavement, even the three bright yellow kayaks that hugged the Cannaregio shore.

Urbino saw only this harmony in the scene. It was a harmony of green water and bright blue sky; of old stone buildings and their mirror images; of white seabirds and creamy boat wakes; of motion and stillness; of sound and silence.

The harmony was all the more remarkable, considering the chaos of the other night. But Venice was licking its wounds, pushing the water out of the front doors, repairing the windows, drying out the carpets, clothes, and furniture. It had done it before. And it would have to do it again.

Urbino was filled with admiration for the city. The traffic on the Grand Canal was like a procession of thanksgiving for having escaped the latest assaults. It was a procession that took the form of normal coming and going, of everyday business and entertainment.

Urbino's vaporetto, loaded with passengers it had picked up at the Piazzale Roma and the train station, rode low in the water. From his position beside the doors that led into the cabin Urbino felt as if he were level with the waters of the Canalazzo. Middle-aged American women occupied the other six seats in the stern. They were in a convivial mood, and kept snapping photographs as the boat proceeded in the direction of the Piazza San Marco.

Urbino gave himself up to the play of light and color and the marble walls of buildings that were austerely classical one moment and fancifully Gothic the next. He wondered how much more he might have enjoyed the palaces if they had been cleaned of the patina of age and weather and if their original frescoes and bright golds, blues, and reds had been restored. One thing would have been gained, something else lost.

Urbino would have remained in a ruminative frame of mind if some chance words in the conversation of his fellow passengers hadn't drawn his attention.

'That palace there,' a woman's voice said, 'that's where the Queen of Cyprus was born.' She held a guidebook in her hand. 'You remember Cyprus, Laura. All those orange trees?'

'The Queen of Cyprus! Where, Darlene? Oh, it's beautiful.'

Laura stood up and took a photograph of the building that Darlene, her friend with the guidebook, pointed out. But the building receiving her attentions was the Ca' d' Oro and not the palace on the opposite side of the Grand Canal where Caterina Cornaro, whose memory would be honored in the upcoming regatta, had seen the light of day in the late fifteenth century.

'Excuse me,' Urbino said, 'but that's the Ca' d' Oro. The one we just passed, the one over there' – he indicated the considerably more plain building on the San Polo side – 'is the one where the Queen of Cyprus died. It's the Palazzo Corner della Regina and it's—'

'Oh, I understand!' Darlene interrupted. 'Regina means Queen in Italian, doesn't it? I had a girlfriend named Regina in Schenectady. This book here has got me all confused. I'm looking at things backwards and upside down!' She gave

77

him a broad smile. 'You're an American!'

Urbino admitted to it.

'I could have sworn you were an Italian,' Darlene said with a laugh. She took in his Italian linen suit and Italian shoes. 'What about you, girls?'

They all vigorously assented.

Urbino soon realized what he had got himself into. They started to assail him with questions. He explained that he had been living in the city for twenty years and was a writer. He wasn't even tempted to reveal that he was also an amateur sleuth.

'I can't believe I'm really here!' Darlene said.

'But only for one night,' Laura lamented. 'I'm glad it's not raining. Someone told us in Rome that it always rains in Venice.'

'Not every day, obviously,' Urbino said, 'but we get more than our share. You're lucky you weren't here the other night.'

'It was bad enough in Florence,' Laura said.

'It's so romantic,' Darlene enthused. 'We should be here with someone special. Not with a bunch of other girls, right ladies?'

Her companions turned their eager smiles on Urbino and away from the glories of the Grand Canal.

Urbino knew that the best way to avoid any further personal questions was to assume the role of a cicerone.

For the next fifteen minutes, he provided a running commentary on the buildings, squares, and bridges they were passing. He informed them that the *altane* were not fire escapes,

78

assured them that the big stone bridge was not the Bridge of Sighs but the Rialto Bridge, and explained that the canal that ran beside the Ca' Rezzonico was the one that Katharine Hepburn fell into in the movie *Summertime*. He told them about the upcoming regatta, commiserating with them that they would miss it.

They soon passed under the Accademia Bridge. Urbino provided some statistics about the wooden bridge, surprising even himself with the way the information about the city was flowing effortlessly. He then told them about the newest bridge being built over the Grand Canal by the Piazzale Roma, the first one in over a hundred years, one to be made out of Murano glass.

'At least two years behind schedule. They put up an arch from each side of the Grand Canal, but they collapsed.'

The women gave murmurs of surprise and regret.

By this time Urbino was thoroughly enjoying his new role.

He was about to launch into a description of the Palazzo Guggenheim which they were approaching, complete with anecdotes about the flamboyant Peggy Guggenheim, when Laura, who had been pushing her camera button almost constantly, said, 'How I wish I could do what that woman over there can do instead of just taking these pictures!'

She pointed toward the Campo San Vio that fronted the Grand Canal. It wasn't difficult for Urbino to determine whom Laura was talking about.

A tall, thin woman in a gondolier's hat stood in front of an easel. It was the red-haired woman he had seen twice on the day of the second big storm.

'Keep on at it, girl!' Laura shouted.

She waved her arms wildly. She caught the attention of the woman, who waved back at her.

Urbino continued to impart odds and ends of information to the women, pacing himself so that he came to the end of his description of the plague and the Salute just as the vaporetto approached the Maria del Giglio landing. There were so many thank-yous and kisses and handshakes that he almost missed the stop.

Coming out on to the terrace of the Gritti Palace Hotel from the bar, where he had spent several minutes talking with an acquaintance, Urbino's eyes were initially dazzled by the sunshine glancing off the Grand Canal. As he searched for Nick Hollander among the other patrons under the blue-and-white-striped awning, his eye fell on two women. Perla Beato and Oriana Borelli were sitting at a table against the wooden railing above the hotel's private boat landing. With their blonde heads bent together, they seemed oblivious of not only Urbino but also the splendid scene beyond the terrace.

'Isn't this a surprise,' Oriana said in a voice that had been made hoarse from cigarettes. She was an attractive woman who, rumor had it, had just celebrated – or rather concealed – her fiftieth birthday. 'I didn't know the Gritti was one of your haunts. I keep learning more about you.'

'I'm glad to know I'm not completely predictable.'

'Nothing like that at all!' In a characteristic gesture she pushed her large-framed sunglasses up on her nose. 'Wouldn't you say "ditto" to that, Perla?'

Perla had applied more make-up than usual today but not enough to conceal a slightly weary look and a purple bruise on her left cheek. 'Ditto, Oriana. Dependable but not predictable,' she responded. 'As good as his word, but not as ... as...' She stared at Urbino with her brown eyes as if appealing to him to help her come up with the right expression. Oriana smiled, but then Perla finished: 'But not as regular as clockwork! Yes, that's it!'

She glanced triumphantly at Oriana.

Whenever Perla and Oriana spoke English in each other's presence, their competitive spirit asserted itself, sometimes with amusing results.

'Take a load off your feet, Urbino dear,' Oriana now said.

'Yes, we'd love to shoot the breeze with you,' Perla put in.

'It would tickle us pink,' Oriana said without missing a beat.

Urbino decided, for his own sake, to put an end to their idiomatic skirmish.

'It would be lovely to join you but I have a rendezvous.'

He looked around the terrace and saw a tanned, bald man in his early thirties sitting alone at the end of the terrace by the screen of green plants. He seemed to be regarding Urbino with curiosity, although when he saw that Urbino was looking at him, he turned his gaze to the row of palaces on the opposite side of the Grand Canal. He met the description the contessa had given Urbino – or rather the description that her cousin Sebastian had passed on to her – at least in the sense that he was completely bald.

'If it's with that stunning woman with the auburn hair drinking Dom Pérignon,' Oriana said, 'I'm going to let the cat out of the bag and tell Barbara.'

'You'll have to keep the feline in the sack,' Urbino said with a smile. 'It's with that man by the railing.'

'Him!' Oriana said. 'We were wondering who he was waiting for. We assumed it was a woman.'

Oriana, although married, always had her eye out for available – and even unavailable – men. Urbino often wondered whether the competition between her and Perla extended beyond the linguistic into affairs of the heart.

'You'll have to excuse me,' he said. 'I should not keep him waiting.'

'What's his name?' Oriana asked.

'Nick Hollander, and don't worry, you'll get your chance to meet him yourself. He's coming to Barbara's party.'

Urbino went over to the man

'Excuse me,' he said tentatively. 'I believe you're Nick Hollander.'

The man gave a slightly strained smile and

stood up. He was dressed in a well-cut, stylish suit in a shade of pale yellow with subtle gray stripes. He wore no tie.

'Please sit down, Mr. Macintyre,' he said after they had shaken hands.

'Thank you. Call me Urbino.'

'Nick, please.'

'Let me give my condolences again.'

Urbino's seat provided a view of the Salute farther down the Grand Canal.

'Thank you. Would you join me?' He indicated a bottle of Soave in a bucket of ice. It was half filled. 'I had the waiter bring two glasses.'

Hollander poured him a glass.

'To health,' Urbino said.

'Yes. *Salute.*'

Involuntarily both men looked across the water to the church of the same name, with its associations with the plague and death. A somber look fell over Hollander's weather-beaten face. There were dark smudges beneath his blue eyes. The two men took in the scene silently.

'A lovely view, isn't it?' Hollander said after a few moments. 'And I have a front room. I see all this when I get up.'

'You're fortunate.'

'Not as fortunate as you. I'm only staying in a palazzo. Sebastian tells me you live in one.'

Urbino gave an embarrassed laugh.

'It might be called a palazzo but it's a very small building – though more than big enough for me,' he added quickly, in case it might sound as if he were complaining. 'And it doesn't have a view that even begins to compare with this

83

one. I inherited it about twenty-five years ago from my mother's side of the family. She was Italian. It was in terrible disrepair when I got it.'

Urbino provided more details about the Palazzo Uccello. When he had finished fifteen minutes later, with some intelligent interventions by Hollander, he didn't feel as if he had indulged himself. What he felt was that he had helped put his companion at ease. Hollander seemed more relaxed. They finished the Soave and ordered another.

'It was unfortunate that Barbara and I never got to meet your stepfather.'

'He was an interesting man, and a good one. You would have enjoyed knowing each other.'

'Regrettable that our paths never crossed – except that one time, most indirectly, in the Piazza San Marco.'

'My stepfather was on the shy side. And during the past several months he kept to his apartment much of the time, because of his illness.'

'I understand. Where did he live?'

'In one of the palaces over there.'

Hollander gestured across the Grand Canal toward the noble line of buildings to the right of the *traghetto* stop.

'Which one?'

'The one with the row of pointed windows.'

Hollander's reference to the Gothic windows identified the palazzo as one of the most elegant on the Grand Canal and one of the most storied.

'He bought the apartment last year. He thought it would be his pied-à-terre for a lot longer than

84

it was.'

Hollander forced some brightness into his face as he added, 'So you aren't the only one with your own piece of Venice, though mine is more modest. But I doubt if I shall keep it. It has bad memories. Perhaps you can help me with an estate agent? The one that brought the apartment to my stepfather's attention retired a few months ago.'

'I'd be glad to, but it might not be a good idea to do anything in haste.'

'I understand what you mean. But I've thought enough about it.'

'Were you staying with your stepfather?'

Hollander took a sip of his wine before answering.

'Not this time. In the hotel, as I said. I stayed with him last November. He wanted his privacy this year. But I was right across the canal.'

'Even if you weren't just across the canal from each other, you would have been close one way or another. Venice is such a small town.'

'Too small for me, actually. I prefer London. I have a house in Chelsea, but I travel much of the time. My mother has a tour company. I'm the president.'

From here it was logical for the two new acquaintances to pass on to the topic of travel. They shared their impressions of various destinations and discussed travel literature, about which Hollander was knowledgeable. In the process they discovered that they were in agreement on almost every point except mass tourism. Hollander quite understandably defended it since, without it, Hollander Tours wouldn't exist.

'But it's destroying so much,' Urbino insisted. 'Look at these boats! Filled with tourists. I remember not too long ago when the city was almost quiet by six in the evening, even at this time of the year.'

'Oh, for the days of the grand tour, trunks, and transatlantic voyages!'

'Something like that. I know it's not very democratic.'

'And you the American!'

The waiter poured the last of the Soave into their glasses. The two men fell into a comfortable silence. Each was lost in his thoughts as he contemplated the scene spread out before them.

'It *is* a beautiful city,' Hollander emphasized, breaking the silence. 'I'll certainly grant you that. I understand why my stepfather loved it. He said that he never wanted to leave, and I guess that in a sense he never did leave, did he? Oh, I see that your friends are about to go.'

Urbino turned around. The two women came over to their table. Urbino made the introductions.

'We look forward to seeing you at Barbara's party,' Oriana said.

'They are very attractive,' Hollander said after the two women had left. 'And married, I see.'

'Yes, married,' Urbino said without any further clarification.

Hollander consulted his wristwatch.

'I'm on my way to the apartment. I need to check on a few items. Would you like to come with me? See it for yourself? You might be able to give me some idea of what I can expect from a sale.'

'I'll leave that to the estate agent. But yes, I'd love to see it.'

The landing stage for the *traghetto* that would take Urbino and Hollander across the Grand Canal was next to the terrace of the Gritti Palace and only a few feet from a statue of the Blessed Virgin Mary, who smiled benevolently down from her street shrine.

'The poor man's gondola,' Hollander observed as he stepped into the boat from the small wooden landing stage.

The Santa Maria del Giglio *traghetto* was one of several placed along the Grand Canal at strategic points. Like the others it was a convenient ferry to the other side as well as an inexpensive, if all too short, gondola ride. Usually, it was Venetians who used them, not tourists.

'I'll stand like the rest of you,' Hollander said when Urbino advised that he sit down.

There were three other passengers, a man in blue work clothes and two women with shopping bags that bore the names of fashionable shops in the San Marco district.

'It can get a bit rocky with all this traffic,' Urbino warned.

But when the boat moved into the canal, was washed by the wake of a vaporetto, and then had to avoid a delivery boat, Hollander was steady on his feet, as steady as Urbino and the Venetians.

'I'm accustomed to it,' Hollander said. He stared straight ahead at the buildings on the other bank. 'I do a lot of boating. It's my passion. I was in the regatta at Capri last year. We didn't win but we did pretty well. My stepfather came. What about yourself? Are you into boating?'

'Only as a spectator sport – or as a passenger. There are a lot of opportunities for that in Venice. And I have a gondola, but my gondolier does all the rowing,' Urbino added with a smile.

'Your own gondola? I didn't think anyone had his own private one anymore. Sebastian didn't mention that.'

'I'm not sure he knows. It was a recent gift from Barbara.' This was offered as a way of distancing himself from the extravagance and eccentricity as well as giving his good friend her proper due. 'The gondola and some cruises on Barbara's yacht are the closest I've come to the sport. If it counts, I'm helping to sponsor one of the regatta races.'

'Which one?'

'The *gondolino* race. My gondolier and a friend of his are the rowers.'

'The *gondolino*.' Hollander nodded. 'I met some men from the San Giorgio Yacht Club a few weeks ago at Harry's Bar. They were talking about the *gondolino*. They had a lot of inter-esting things to say about it.'

As their *traghetto* came to a brief halt to let a boat with an outboard motor pass, Hollander spoke about the racing craft with a great deal of accuracy.

'I've been looking forward to the regatta,' he

said when he finished. 'It will be my first in Venice.'

'It's unfortunate that the circumstances couldn't be better.'

Hollander might have given a sigh but Urbino couldn't be sure because of the sounds of the water and the boats. The two men remained silent as the boat approached the Dorsoduro landing where several people were waiting for the return trip.

'But as I told you on the telephone,' Hollander said as he prepared to get out of the boat, 'my stepfather loved life. He was keen on the regatta. He would have been able to see it right from his windows. Of course, I could do as well, but I'll enjoy it more at Barbara's with all of you – and without any sad associations.'

'But I'm afraid you won't have as great a view of the water parade that opens the competition as you would from here. The parade doesn't go as far as Barbara's place. But the great compensation will be that you'll see the *gondolini* go past both before and after they reach the turning point.'

Urbino and Hollander went down the narrow *calle* to where it joined a wider one, busy with a stream of people. It was the route between the two popular sights of the Salute and the Guggenheim Museum. The men went only a short distance along the *calle* and stopped at a high, wrought-iron gate. Beyond it was a small mossy courtyard filled with plants and a small tree. The broad staircase across the courtyard had pots of bright flowers and a large Murano chandelier.

Hollander took out a key, and they passed through the courtyard and up the staircase to the second floor. Large wooden double doors opened on to the painting-hung foyer of Konrad Zoll's apartment – or rather Hollander's, as it now was.

'This is it,' Hollander said as they went into the large, high-ceilinged *sala*. Beyond the balcony doors, which had delicate strips of wood embracing the glass, was the Grand Canal. The doors were closed but through them a bright, aqueous light washed the room.

For the next fifteen minutes Hollander showed Urbino around the apartment. In addition to the spacious *sala*, there were three bedrooms, a small study, and a kitchen and dining area. The apartment was appointed with Murano chandeliers, green marble, antique Venetian mirrors, decorative stucco walls and ceilings, silk wallpaper, Persian and Turkish carpets, tapestries, statuary, paintings and many fine pieces of gilded furniture that were either authentic or excellent imitations. Urbino expressed his admiration.

'The apartment came with most of the furnishings. I'm glad about that. It makes it a little easier to dispose of them. I'll have a harder time with his house in Munich. It's stuffed with things he lived with for almost his whole life, things he loved. He was a collector. His father was a banker. He left him a fortune. My stepfather spent much of his money on beautiful things. Like this.'

Going over to a small table, he picked up a

small, worn leather-bound book. He handed it to Urbino, who examined it. It was a breviary illustrated with Flemish miniatures that must have dated back to the eighteenth or even the seventeenth century.

'Lovely,' Urbino said.

'My stepfather wasn't religious. He appreciated the beauty of it. And he could see beauty in practical things, too, like this.'

He indicated an eighteenth-century carriage clock in a brass casing with a handle. It had a white enamel dial and black numerals.

'Isn't that an Abraham-Louis Breguet?' Urbino asked.

'I think that's the name. It has a leather traveling case in almost perfect condition. You and my stepfather would have got along well. Carriage clocks were one of the things he collected. I'll add it to the others in Munich. And I'll also take the Pietro Longhi on the wall by the door.'

They went over to examine it. It was a typical Longhi, depicting with great delicacy a seated Venetian lady in a *bauta* mask with a white cat at her feet and a cup of chocolate on a small marble-topped table.

'Exquisite. Barbara loves Longhi. She has a collection of them. By the way, she asked me if you might be free to join her in Asolo for a few days. I'm leaving early this evening on the train. Her car will pick us up in Bassano del Grappa.'

'She was kind enough to ring me and ask me herself. I have things that need doing here. Some other time perhaps.'

Urbino nodded in understanding.

91

'In addition to the breviary, the clock, the Longhi, and a few other things, I'll be taking this back with me to London,' Hollander said in a lower voice.

Hollander carefully, almost reverently, picked up an urn about a foot high from the mantel-piece. It was rather plain in comparison to every-thing else in the apartment. Urbino understood what it was before Hollander explained.

'My stepfather's ashes. He was cremated on the cemetery island. I'm not sure what I'll do with them. He left no instructions about whether they should be scattered, or where.'

He replaced the urn on the mantelpiece.

'I'm sure you'll do the right thing,' Urbino said, 'whatever it might be. Thank you for show-ing me around. It's a marvelous apartment. Your stepfather had excellent taste. I'll let you know about an estate agent next week. And here's my number and address.'

He handed Hollander a visiting card.

As Urbino was making his way back to the *traghetto* landing, he went over his impressions of Hollander. He found them to be positive. He had expected not to like him for the same reason that the contessa was predisposed to him – because he came with Sebastian's recommenda-tion. But Urbino found the man easier to talk to than her cousin. He had a greater fund of sym-pathy and intelligence.

Birds of a feather did not always flock to-gether.

After taking the *traghetto* back to San Marco,

Urbino went to one of his favorite bookshops. Recessed in a corner of a little courtyard off the Calle Lungo Santa Maria Formosa, it was bursting with books, both new and used, on long tables and high shelves in two rooms. People were sitting in the area behind the shop at round tables with plants and flowers on them, paging through books.

The owner, a genial bespectacled man, came over to Urbino when he finished with a customer.

'We just unpacked the copies of *Regate e Regatanti* this afternoon.'

He was referring to a history of the Venice regattas. It was filled with details about the races, photographs, and brief biographies of the rowing champions since the nineteenth century, both men and women. It had a gold register of the finishing teams and unusual pieces of information about the competitions. Urbino had ordered three copies, one for himself, and one each for Claudio and Gildo.

'I was going to call you,' the bookseller added. 'And here are your Goethe books.'

He indicated several volumes – most of them used copies – on a shelf behind him.

'Great. I'm going to look around awhile.'

'Don't forget to sign the copies of your books. Some came in last week.'

Urbino browsed the shelves looking for a gift for the contessa. He was beginning to despair of finding something suitably festive to mark the occasion of another visit to La Muta when he came upon a book in French on treasure hunts organized in houses and gardens. The contessa had long talked about arranging a treasure hunt at the Ca' da Capo-Zendrini or the Villa La Muta.

As Urbino was signing copies of his books, Romolo Beato went by the shop in the direction of the Campo Santa Maria Formosa. He was too far away for Urbino to hail since the shop wasn't directly on the *calle*. At any rate, it didn't seem as if he was in a good mood. An angry expression tightened his usually friendly face. Urbino was puzzled. Two nights ago he had said he was going to spend a week with his son and do some business. Obviously he had cut his visit short.

Urbino had a second item in mind for the contessa.

Just as she knew him so well as to be able to give him the perfect gift, even when it was as outlandish as a gondola, he knew what would please her. He turned his steps to a nearby *legatoria*.

The shop, selling various kinds of paper goods and other small items, most of them handmade, was a little farther down the Calle Lunga Santa Maria Formosa in the direction from which Beato had just been coming. It had opened a year ago but Urbino had not yet patronized it, since he was a regular customer at a more established shop in San Marco. But he liked to encourage new businesses, especially ones devoted to the traditional Venetian arts and crafts, and his visit to Legatoria Foppa was overdue.

A young saleswoman smiled at him from

inside the large front window where she was re-arranging items in the window – address and appointment books, notepads, notebooks, stationery, letter holders, lampshades, wrapping paper, picture frames, and pill boxes, most of them made with marbled paper in various designs. There were also pens and inkwells in Murano glass.

A gentle bell tinkled as he opened the door. The shop had a clean smell. An area at the rear was set up as an artisan's workshop. A woman stood at a long table. She was in her early thirties, with large brown eyes, black hair feathered around a small oval face, and a well-shaped mouth emphasized by bright red lipstick. She was demonstrating the marbling process to five customers.

The woman, who wore a dark purple dress with restrained red embroidery around the neck, explained that the technique was more than a thousand years old and had originated in Japan.

'Arab culture brought it to Europe in the fifteenth century,' she said in accented English. 'After years of neglect Venice gave it a new birth when I was a child. We have many craftsmen who marble paper now – and craftswomen,' she added with a smile.

She nodded at the marbling tray on the table. Urbino drew a little closer. The entire liquid surface was spotted with yellow, red, and blue colors.

'Earlier I dropped the colors in with a brush, each color separately. Now I pull the colors into different lines with this.' She indicated a pointed instrument that had the desired effect when she used it on the surface of the liquid. The spots became transformed into wavy lines from the top of the tray to the bottom. 'Very carefully I bring this comb across the surface and – as you see – the marble appears.'

The tourists gave appreciative murmurs as the lines became marbled.

'And I place a sheet of white paper on top of the liquid – like this – but I must be attentive not to let any air stay beneath.'

The small woman had muscular arms, as if she were a sportswoman or worked out regularly. And yet she placed the sheet of paper on top of the liquid with delicacy and care. After doing this, she lifted the sheet slowly. One side was completely marbled. She hung the sheet from a cord near the back wall.

After the demonstration the customers went around the well-stocked shop selecting various items. The young saleswoman was helping them. The *cartaio*, the owner of the paper shop – for this is whom Urbino assumed the woman in the purple dress was – started to clean and neaten her implements.

Urbino examined a display of notebooks. Between each empty page of heavy gauge paper was an onion leaf. The covers were in various patterns of marbled paper with strong cotton corners and bindings. He selected a small notebook in the old Venetian red flame pattern. The *fiammato* had touches of gold. During the past few years the contessa had taken up the habit of jotting down thoughts and impressions from time to time. She had filled three books of a similar size. Urbino had noticed that she had only a few pages left in her newest notebook. Urbino, who was seldom without a notebook, selected one in peacock green for himself.

The *cartaio* was at the cash register.

'It's a very nice shop,' he said in English.

'Thank you. It's mine. I'm Clementina Foppa.'

Urbino introduced himself and mentioned that he lived in Venice.

'I'll tell my friends about your place,' he added.

'Thank you. It isn't on one of the main routes. I'd be grateful for any help of that kind. Word of mouth is the best advertisement.'

The woman had a soft, melodious voice. It seemed touched with sadness.

As Foppa's assistant was wrapping the gift, Urbino's attention was drawn to an oblong sheet of paper, encased in clear plastic, tacked on the cluttered board behind the counter. It was the size of a sheet of typing paper and not marbled. It was one of the death notices that were customarily displayed in the city by members of the deceased's family. They sometimes had a photograph of the deceased, as did this one. The notices usually appeared on the front door of the dead person's residence, at points throughout the neighborhood, and at his or her place of work. He had noticed one in Cannaregio the other night during what he had called his corpse tour.

The person in the photograph looked familiar. Confusion coursed through Urbino. Surely it was a photograph of Claudio! This was impossible of course. He had just seen Claudio yesterday, alive and well in the final qualifying competition.

The photograph was a black-and-white one of a handsome young man with thick dark hair and deep-set eyes. He did indeed resemble Claudio. With some effort Urbino made out his name. Luca Benigni. He couldn't read the rest of the notice but he knew it would contain appropriate sentiments about the deceased, a list of survivors, the date of death, and the place and time of the funeral.

Sometimes photographs of the dead were taken years, even decades before, but this photograph was not one of this kind. For it looked as if it had been taken as recently as three and a half weeks ago when Urbino and the contessa had been at Florian's.

For the man in the photograph was the one who had been so solicitous of the ailing Konrad Zoll as the two men had walked under the arcade.

# Four

Urbino's scrutiny of the death notice had not gone unobserved by the *cartaio*.

'Did you know Luca?' she asked in Italian. She looked at him sharply as if she were accessing him just as he had been doing with the death notice. 'Are you one of his university professors?'

'No, I didn't know him. But his face is familiar. I saw him recently in the Piazza San Marco. You have my condolences, signorina. Was he a relative?'

'My half-brother.' Her face relaxed. 'We had different fathers.'

She looked at the photograph. Her eyes filled with tears.

'Your brother was young. And he seemed to be kind.'

'I thought you said you didn't know him?'

'I didn't, but I saw him helping a sick man that day. Right after the Feast of the Redeemer.'

'A German man. Luca's friend.' She lowered her gaze and picked up one of the pillboxes that were on display. She absently removed and replaced the lid. 'He's dead, too. He died about a week before Luca.'

'Yes, I've heard about that. May I ask how

your brother died?'

'An accident. A parapet stone hit him. It hadn't been properly secured and became loosened from a building under renovation. In Dorso-duro.' She named the *calle*. It was between Zoll's apartment and the Zattere. 'During the storm, the first one.'

The assistant handed Urbino his package. After giving Clementina Foppa his condolences again, he left.

As Urbino walked to the Rialto vaporetto station, he couldn't help but reflect on the unusual circumstance of the deaths of Konrad Zoll and Luca Benigni within such a short time of each other. One by natural causes, the other by a freak accident. But Urbino had long ago become accustomed to the unusual and had discovered that coincidence played a much larger role in life than one would like to ack-nowledge.

His experience as a biographer and a sleuth had taught him that it was the apparently normal that more often needed an explanation.

By the time Urbino reached the Rialto every-thing he had purchased was beginning to feel twice as heavy. A quick look in the direction of Ca' Foscari indicated that his boat was not yet in sight. He sat down on the landing platform and put the two bags on the empty seat beside him. He extracted one of the Goethe books.

He was immersed in a poem when a woman's voice said in English with a British accent, 'Are those packages yours? I must sit down.'

100

'Excuse me.'

Embarrassed, Urbino removed them. The woman dropped heavily into the seat. She took off a straw gondolier's hat with a red ribbon and fanned herself with it. The hat was slightly battered and was starting to unravel on the brim. It also appeared to be damp. She put it back on her head. Urbino recognized her as the tall, thin woman with red hair who painted watercolor scenes of the city. She had her black leather case and her backpack with her. Her pale face was shining with perspiration. She was wearing the same green dress.

'Are you all right?' he asked. 'Would you like some water?'

'I'd love some. Oh, no, please, don't trouble yourself,' she added when he got up. 'I thought you had a bottle with you.'

'It's no problem. Just watch my packages.'

Urbino went to the nearby kiosk and bought a large bottle of chilled mineral water.

A few minutes later, after the mineral water and the shade of the landing stage had had their beneficial effects, the woman was looking better, although she was breathing shallowly.

'I love this city,' she said, 'but the heat and the crowds! Not to mention the smells! I should have come when the weather is milder. Nice English weather, if they ever have it.'

'It doesn't help having to carry things around. I've been having a hard enough time with what I have.'

'And you're much younger than I am. By the way, my name is Maisie Croy.'

101

'Pleased to meet you. I'm Urbino Macintyre.'
The woman extended a cold, damp hand.

'As I was saying, this is a marvelous city, but I'm feeling all the heat and humidity today. And up and down the steps of the bridges! There's no end to them, is there?'

'They do get fatiguing.' Urbino looked down at her case and backpack. 'You paint.'

'Watercolors. Mainly for my own pleasure, though I sell one now and again, even here.' She was breathing more normally now. 'I thought that I might be able to give one to my hotel as payment but they looked at me as if I were dotty. I remember reading somewhere that they do that in Venice.'

'I don't think they do it much anymore. It was a nice custom.'

'You know Venice?'

'I live here,' he explained.

'How nice! I just met a group of Americans in the Piazza San Marco but they were on a tour. Since you know Venice so well, maybe you can help me. I'm looking for an inexpensive hotel. I've been going from one to another and they're either full up or too expensive.'

'Where are you staying?'

She named a hotel in Dorsoduro not far from the Accademia Gallery. 'I'm on my way there now,' she said.

'How much longer do you plan to stay in Venice?'

'Another three weeks, if possible. I've already been here for two weeks. There's so much to paint! There's something about Venice that makes you want to stay here forever once you get here. I guess you know what I mean by that!'

Urbino smiled. 'Yes, I do.'

'But I'll have to leave soon if I can't find a cheaper place to stay.'

Urbino asked her how much she was paying at her hotel. She didn't name an exorbitant amount, but he knew there were far less expensive hotels in town.

'Maybe I can do something,' he said. 'I can't promise, but I know some places that might have more reasonable rates, though they're not as well located as Dorsoduro. I can contact you at your hotel?'

'Until the middle of next week. That will probably be my limit.'

'I'm going out of town for a few days, but I'll try to find something more suitable for you as soon as I get back.'

'Are you always a good Samaritan?'

Urbino laughed. 'Far from it. But I've noticed you a few times in different places in the city. I feel as if I know you a little. Venice can have that effect. One time you were good-natured when a man knocked down your canvas.'

'I remember that. No damage done.'

'And another time you even walked past my building. I was looking out of the window. I live near the Ghetto.'

'What a coincidence! Right past your house!'

She shifted uncomfortably in the seat.

'Here's my card.' Urbino handed it to her. He stood up and picked up his package. 'My vaporetto is coming. Yours will be arriving from the opposite direction.' He pointed toward the Rialto Bridge.

'I'll let you know if I change my hotel before you contact me, Mr. Macintyre. Thank you very much.'

As the vaporetto was on its way to the San Marcuola stop, Urbino realized that he now had two favors to do: find an estate agent for Nick Hollander and an inexpensive room for Maisie Croy. He started to run various possibilities through his head.

On the train to Bassano del Grappo, where the contessa's car would meet him to take him up to Asolo, Urbino tried to concentrate on his Goethe, but thoughts about Konrad Zoll and Luca Benigni distracted him. The deaths in rapid succession of the two men, so different in age, health, and other circumstances, made him feel vulnerable with their reminders of what could happen to anyone at any time.

He forced his mind to think about the contessa and the Villa La Muta. He always enjoyed being with her in Asolo. One of these years he would stay with her for an extended period of time instead of these brief visits.

One of these years, he repeated silently to himself. One so easily assumed that there would be other occasions, other opportunities to do the things one had always wanted to do.

Konrad Zoll, with his fortune and his liberty, had been able to do whatever large or small things he desired, but disease had come along to smash everything. Now he was dead, reduced to ashes in an urn in a lavish apartment on the Grand Canal. And the younger Luca Benigni, who must have pitied the fact that his wealthy friend was nearing the end of his life, was dead, too.

These thoughts fed Urbino's melancholy temperament. He usually told himself that he enjoyed his melancholy and wouldn't want to be any different. But other times he suspected that he had only become accustomed to it and was afraid, for reasons he couldn't understand, of being bereft of it.

When he got off at Bassano del Grappa and went to the waiting Bentley, he was disappointed to learn that the contessa had decided not to come with the car. He was eager to see her and had hoped they might indulge themselves in a grappa at the Nardini distillery on the timber Alpine Bridge in Bassano. On the drive to Asolo, he decided he would spend a few weeks at La Muta with the contessa in September after the regatta. The days would be beautiful then.

The sight of the Villa La Muta, in the gently rolling hills beneath the arcaded town, lifted his spirits. When he got out of the car, he breathed in the fresh air gratefully and looked beyond the villa across the wide Trevisan plain to the Alpine foothills. This was a place where you could easily forget your cares for a while.

Giorgione had lingered with his lute in its rose gardens and the Queen of Cyprus had held fabled court in its lambent air. In fact, Urbino reminded himself, it had even bequeathed its name to an Italian verb of indolence. Pietro

Bembo, a Renaissance satirist who had used Asolo as the setting for his dialogues on love, had coined the verb *asolare* to describe spending one's time in pleasurable, mindless inactivity and irresponsibility. Yes, the relatives of the contessa's husband had chosen their retreat well in the eighteenth century. Instead of following the custom of other Venetians who had made their summer *villeggiature* on the banks of the Brenta Canal, the Conte Paolo had gone to Asolo, twenty-five miles northwest of Venice, where he had taken over a villa designed by Palladio's follower Scamozzi.

The villa's name – *La Muta*, or 'The Mute Woman' – originated from a seventeenth-century woman who had retired to the hill town after witnessing a bloody murder in Florence and who had never been known to speak again.

Understandably enough, the contessa – of a far less melancholy turn than Urbino – had been disturbed by this rather Gothic association. After some troubled thinking, she had ingeniously found a solution by commissioning a copy of Raphael's painting of a gentlewoman, known as *La Muta*.

In fact, Urbino was soon embracing the contessa below the painting itself on the stone staircase in the front hall.

'Here,' he said, handing her the two gifts.

'Thank you, *caro*. And I have something for you as well. A few days of blessed rest away from the madness of Venice.'

'Sad,' the contessa said half an hour later as the

two friends walked through the puzzle maze behind the villa. Urbino had just told her about the death of Luca Benigni.

It was dusk. The lights had come on a few minutes earlier. But the contessa didn't need light to find her way to the center of her maze. Urbino was convinced she could do it blind-folded.

As for him, although he had negotiated it a dozen times, he needed the contessa to guide him through its devious twists and turns and cul-de-sacs. It was either her guidance, that is, or the indignity of uncovering one of the signs that said 'LIFT IF LOST'. He remembered one summer afternoon ten years ago when he had ventured into the maze on his own and become lost. He had been too proud to uncover any of the signs. Trying a trick he had read about, he had kept his left hand in constant contact with the hedge wall, but it had done no good. He had eventually found his way to the center by exhausting trial and error, and had waited sheepishly for the contessa to join him with a bottle of Prosecco.

'It's the fine line, *caro*,' the contessa said when they stopped at a spiral junction.

'The fine line?' Urbino repeated.

He waited for the contessa to take one of the paths, which she did without any hesitation. All he could see above the hedges were the upper stories of La Muta, the darkening sky, and the top of the viewing tower in the center.

'It's a painful truth,' the contessa responded. 'The fine line between life and death. Remember what happened to Gildo's friend last August?

107

Out in the lagoon and hit by a bolt of lightning in the middle of his forehead. Dead, dead, dead. If it's not a storm of one kind or another that gets us, it's something that sneaks up on us until...' She trailed off.

Urbino, whose sentiments were similar to the contessa's, said nothing.

She sighed and patted his arm.

'Ah, but here we are, *caro*!' she cried.

The contessa meant that they had reached, without the slightest confusion on her part, the center of the maze. The tower rose above them into the purple evening air.

But her words held another meaning for Urbino. Here they were, he said to himself, this moment now, together.

They seated themselves on the scrolled marble bench.

'It's a good time to read this,' the contessa said.

She withdrew a piece of folded newsprint from the pocket of her dress and handed it to him.

'There's still enough light. It's the article about Konrad Zoll that Sebastian sent. Read it while I climb the tower. No, I'll be fine. I like the exercise. I do it once a day.'

Urbino unfolded the article. It was clipped from an edition of the *International Herald Tribune* of two years ago. Urbino, who read the newspaper a few times a week, had no memory of having read the article.

It gave an account of an exhibition in Munich of ancient Egyptian objects from Konrad Zoll's private collection. The exhibition had been arranged to coincide with a new production of *Aida* in which Zoll's friend, the tenor Zacharias Kellner, sang the role of Radames. Zoll, who, according to the article, had inherited a fortune as the only child of the banker Richard Zoll of Frankfurt, was described as a philanthropist and art collector who traveled widely and had special interests in ancient Egyptian, Islamic, French, and Venetian art. He had organized a campaign to come to the relief of an earthquake-stricken village in Algeria and had endowed a chair in art history at the University of Munich. In addition to his native German, he had been fluent in Italian, French, and English. The rest of the article described some of the items in the exhibit and their provenance.

The photograph accompanying the article showed a smiling, healthy-faced Zoll in black tie. He was holding up an agate bowl as the stout Kellner looked on. In the background were several men and women. One of them was the bald, tanned Nick Hollander. He stood close to a woman in her sixties who bore a striking resemblance to him. Urbino assumed that she must be his mother. Zoll and Hollander's mother had divorced five years ago. It would seem that the divorce had been more or less amicable since she had showed up at the exhibition.

Urbino started to reread the article. He held it at an angle to catch the illumination from one of the lanterns on the tower. He was interrupted by a loud voice that carried over the tops of the hedges. It was Gervasio, the contessa's major-domo.

'Signor Urbino, there is an urgent telephone call for you.'

Urbino went inside the tower. He looked up the spiral of the stone staircase. The contessa had turned on the light switch.

'Barbara?'

'I heard him. I'm on my way down. I—'

A scraping sound echoed against the stones.

'Are you all right?'

'I'm afraid I twisted my ankle. But I'll be all right.'

Urbino went up the narrow staircase to help the contessa down. He supported her as she guided him out of the maze. Gervasio was waiting for them at the entrance.

'Go ahead and take the call. Gervasio will help me. Take it in the *salotto verde*.'

It was Natalia.

'Thank God, Signor Urbino! What took you so long?'

'What's the matter?'

Her voice was choked.

'It's Albina Gonella! She's dead!'

Urbino was stunned. He couldn't say anything for a few moments.

'Dead?' His heart was racing. 'But I just saw her two nights ago!'

'She's dead just the same. Heart attack, they say. And not just that, but the way it happened.'

Urbino heard her take a deep breath.

'All alone she was. In a *calle* near her apartment. And in the middle of that storm we had.

What are things coming to? Albina Gonella dying like an abandoned dog in the street! Who would have thought such a thing?'

'This is terrible news. Poor Albina. She didn't complain about feeling ill but she did look tired.' He was silent for a moment, then added, 'I helped her with her work that night.'

His sadness and shock were joined now by a stab of guilt. Apparently, Albina must have died only a short time after he had seen her to her door. Tears filled his eyes.

'Didn't I tell you that slave driver at Da Valdo was working her to death? Why couldn't you have found some other job for her? I have to hang up now. I wanted to call you as soon as I learned, seeing as you're all the way up in Asolo with the contessa.'

Natalia gave a slight emphasis to 'Asolo'.

Her meaning couldn't have been any clearer if she had used the verb of indolence itself.

The contessa, with Gervasio supporting her under the elbow, came into the *salotto verde* as Urbino was putting the telephone receiver down. Catullus, the contessa's Doberman, had joined them and was looking up at his mistress with an almost human solicitude. The contessa seated herself in one of the carved chairs and Catullus settled at her feet on the Aubusson.

'What is it, *caro*? You look knackered all of a sudden.'

Urbino dropped into a chair.

'Albina Gonella is dead.'

'Dead?' the contessa repeated hollowly in a

111

low voice after a few moments.

'The night of the storm. Apparently of a heart attack. That was Natalia.'

'Holy Mother of God! Albina!' Tears welled in her eyes and spilled on to her cheeks. 'May she rest in peace.'

As she took out a handkerchief to wipe her eyes, her gaze strayed to the easel portrait of the Conte Alvise painted at the time of their marriage. The portrait captured him at his prime, around forty, handsome, vigorous, with black hair, blue eyes, and fair Venetian skin.

'A fresh death brings back all the others,' she said in a low, choked voice.

'I must have been with her right before she died.'

'What do you mean?'

Urbino explained how he had met Albina at Da Valdo and walked her home.

'She forgot her house keys at the restaurant. Giulietta let her in.'

He picked up one of the hand-painted ceramic *fischietti* on the marble ormolu-mounted table beside his chair. The whistle was shaped like a dove. He looked at it from several angles as if he was obliged to study it, but for what reason, he had no idea. He returned it to the table with the other bird and animal whistles.

'You feel guilty because you were with her before she died,' the contessa said. 'I understand. But what does that signify? You shouldn't feel that way, no more than I should have when Alvise died half an hour after I left his room.'

'But you did.'

Instead of responding the contessa looked down at her gold bracelet with the intertwined letters *A* and *B* that Albina had so recently restored to her.

They remained in silence. Urbino got up and went over to the small bar concealed in the top of a Hepplewhite bureau bookcase. He poured out a sherry for himself and the contessa.

When he was seated again, the contessa said, 'You couldn't have prevented her death. She had a heart attack.'

'So it appears. No,' he added when the contessa gave him a surprised look, 'I have no reason to doubt that she did, although I have every intention of finding out more. It's because of the keys that I feel the way I do. If I hadn't gone to Da Valdo, if I hadn't helped her, if I hadn't changed her routine, she wouldn't have forgotten them.'

'And you think that's why she went out again? To get her keys?'

'It seems logical. And when she went out she got caught in the storm, she might have lost her way, become frightened and ... and then she died alone.'

But even as he worked this scenario out it didn't seem quite right.

'Don't torture yourself,' the contessa said gently. 'You're not responsible. You could just as much blame Giulietta for having opened the door for her. If she hadn't, you both would have gone back together for the keys, if that's why she went out again. Or blame the storm or the fact that she had to have a job that took her out at that hour of the night. Or blame life itself!'

They both became absorbed in their own thoughts. They sipped their sherry. The contessa patted Catullus's head. Urbino stared blankly at the pastels and miniatures by Rosalba Carriera on the opposite wall, seeing none of their delicate beauty.

The contessa gave a sigh and got up. She took a few steps, limping slightly.

'I don't think I did much damage. It should be all right if I put some ice on it.'

She blessed herself with the holy water from the *acquasantiera* by the door.

'Poor, precious Albina,' she said. 'I can't absorb it. I'll call Giulietta. She would appreciate some help with the funeral. They only had each other.'

Albina Gonella's funeral was celebrated in the Church of the Carmini between the Campo Santa Margherita and the Zattere only a few steps away from the Scuola where she had enjoyed *Così Fan Tutte* last October with Claudio and her sister. The ornate and somber interior of the Gothic church, with its wooden sculptural decorations and dark frieze of paintings high on the walls, made a contrast to the woman's simple coffin and drew even more of the mourners' attention to it.

Urbino sat in the same pew as the contessa, Giulietta, Oriana, Natalia, and Gildo. There were many others who had come to pay their final respects as well as some tourists who had wandered into the church with their guidebooks but were refraining from walking around. They stood quietly observing the ceremony from the small chapel with Cima da Conegliano's *Nativity* over the altar, probably secretly thrilled that their visit coincided with an authentic Venetian funeral.

Many of Albina's colleagues from Florian's were present as well as a waiter from Da Valdo, although Valdo himself was absent. Neighbors from Albina's quarter occupied two whole rows of pews. Or rather not quite two rows, for wedged in the middle of one pew were Romolo and Perla Beato, who lived in the much more fashionable part of Dorsoduro. Perla had once used Giulietta's services as a seamstress in the days before she married Romolo and worked as a nurse.

Giulietta, ashen and wearing a black dress trimmed in cream-colored lace, sat stiff and dry-eyed throughout the service.

Only two things surprised Urbino about the mourners. One was how few Gonella relatives were there, a mere three elderly aunts and uncles with one cousin, all from Treviso.

The other thing was the presence of Clementina Foppa. The *cartaio* had arrived after the Mass began. She sat by herself. From the way she kept staring at Claudio, who sang the *Ave Maria* and other hymns from one of the carved and gilded singing galleries, it was as if she had come for his performance alone. Perhaps she was taken with his resemblance to her dead brother, as Urbino had been when he had seen the death notice.

Claudio seemed oblivious to everyone and everything around him. The quality of his voice was not good this morning, but he more than made up for it in the depth of his emotion. The darkness of the church and Claudio's distance from the other mourners concealed what Urbino was sure were tears in his eyes, for he could hear them very distinctly in his voice.

After the service, during which the elderly priest delivered a short but eloquent eulogy to Albina, the priest and the mourners followed Albina's coffin to the funeral gondola.

As they neared the doors that opened on to the little square and the canal, they passed a wooden statue of the Madonna and Child on a throne decorated with cherubs. The figure of Mary, veiled and robed in white, looked like a bride. A scapular hung from one of her hands.

Claudio, his face drawn, had descended from the singing loft to be one of the pall-bearers. Silently, somberly, and wreathed by the fog drifting up from the canal, Claudio and the other men carried the coffin to the funeral gondola. They placed it on a canopied platform with black curtains.

The barge-like vessel, much larger than a regular gondola, was adorned with figures of a grieving angel and a lion and with an ornate double garland around the hull, all the details carved and gilded.

Claudio and Gildo, with their oars, took their positions immediately in front of the casket, with two other rowers behind it. The two friends could little have imagined that their rowing

116

skills would have been required for this sad duty. The funeral gondola started to move slowly through the light fog drifting above the canal toward its destination on the cemetery island.

Two hours later Urbino and the contessa were walking down one of the paths of the cypress-clad cemetery island in the lagoon between Venice and Murano. It was a hot day with a gray overcast sky and an uncomfortably damp wind from the lagoon that blew wisps of low-lying fog against them. Urbino felt both overheated and chilled. The contessa walked without any problem, the injury to her ankle having proven to be minimal, as she had predicted.

'At least we spared her this,' the contessa said.

She nodded toward rows of disinterred graves, surrounded by mounds of dirt, broken pieces of concrete, and withered flowers.

They were skirting the edge of a field where the graves were in the grim process of being dug up now that the dead's twelve-year tenancy was over. Many families rented burial space for only this brief period. They were usually less grieved by the inevitable exhumation than one might think. Most dead were soon forgotten, and space for them was a precious – and expensive – commodity.

The contessa had arranged for Albina to be buried in a perpetual grave with a space next to her for Giulietta, whenever her day might come. Their parents' graves had long since been dug up and their bones placed on one of the lagoon's ossuary islands used for this sad purpose.

After Albina had been buried, Urbino and the contessa had visited the Da Capo-Zendrini mausoleum. She had deposited a bouquet of flowers and spent half an hour unnecessarily neatening the area – unnecessarily because she made sure that it was well tended to once a week.

They were now going to make a visit that had become a ritual for them. It was to the grave of Diaghilev. The contessa's mother had been Diaghilev's friend and had always regretted being unable to pay her last respects to a man she had loved and admired. In memory of her mother the contessa visited the ballet impresario's grave whenever she was on the cemetery island.

Urbino and the contessa passed graves where men and women were cleaning the stones and tending to plants and flowers. They walked through an area of loculi where the dead were buried in walls. There was a movable ladder to give access to the higher graves. They paused at one tier of loculi. The contessa gazed up at one of the burial niches and said a silent prayer for the soul of a former maid who was buried there.

They then entered the Orthodox compound and went down the path to the brick wall. The fog was thicker here. A rusted iron gate opened on to marshland and the bluish-gray expanse of the lagoon, where boats were making their way to Murano in the near distance. To the far left and out of their sight was the Dead Lagoon, where the tides never reached.

'As if we didn't know what we'd find.' The

contessa looked at Diaghilev's simple memorial stone. 'There's another one.'

She didn't mean the bouquet of purple and white carnations with the yellow ribbon at the base of the tombstone, but the ballet slipper on top of it. It had lost little of its color and hardly any of its shape. It was very different from the twisted, faded, and moldy one they had seen on the stone in June. But like the other slipper, this one too had a spider's web spun across its opening.

'We never see anyone leave a slipper, but there's always a new one,' the contessa mused.

'One of Venice's many mysteries. One of its benevolent ones.'

On their way out of the Orthodox compound, the contessa said, with a sidelong glance at Urbino, 'You want some answers about poor Albina, don't you? Isn't what Salvatore Rizzo told us enough?'

Rizzo had been Albina's physician. After the burial, he had explained that Albina had indeed had a weak heart.

'Not completely,' Urbino said.

'He said that it was perfectly consistent with her condition that she could have died suddenly.'

'And he also said that she could have lived for many more years.'

The contessa gave a little sigh.

'Fate, *caro*, fate and circumstances. Not the kind of philosophy that a supposedly good Catholic should have, I know.'

'But I was part of Albina Gonella's circumstances on that night, Barbara. If it was her fate,

I had some role in bringing it to her. I need to know what happened to her.'

'I don't know what you think you'll learn and however it might comfort you.'

A slight edge of impatience sharpened the contessa's tone.

'If Albina went out for something other than her keys,' he explained slowly, 'then I'd be a little comforted.'

'But she would still be dead.'

'And,' Urbino pursued, ignoring the truth of the contessa's comment, 'if I learn that she didn't die naturally even if she did go back for her keys, then I might have the satisfaction of finding out who *is* responsible.'

'And you'd be off the hook.'

'I'll never be off the hook with this one.'

The two friends didn't return to the subject until they reached the contessa's motorboat by the bone-white church of San Michele.

As he was helping the contessa settle into her seat, Urbino said, giving her some of the fruit of his thoughts since they had left Diaghilev's grave, 'Konrad Zoll, Luca Benigni, and Albina Gonella. All dead.'

'You're not thinking there's some kind of connection? It doesn't make sense.'

'Many things don't. Not at first.'

# Part Three

## The Recently Dead

# Five

At a few minutes past seven the next morning Urbino was awakened by the telephone.

'Signor Urbino? Is it you?'

The low voice, a woman's, was unrecognizable. It sounded muffled in tears.

'This is Urbino Macintyre, yes.'

'It's Giulietta Gonella.'

Albina's sister had never called him before. He sat up and propped a pillow behind him.

'Giulietta? What's the matter?'

Albina's sister had remained calm throughout the funeral and the burial, even a little cool and distant. The more the other mourners had become emotional, the more she had withdrawn into herself. But Urbino was aware that a bereaved person's demeanor was an unreliable indicator of the depth or sincerity of emotion.

'Someone broke into our – my – apartment,' Giulietta explained in a stronger voice.

'When?'

'Yesterday. No one was in the building. Everyone was at the funeral. Most of the people in the *calle*, too. When I got home last night from staying with a friend in Castello, my door was open. The apartment is upside down.'

'You have to call the police.'

123

'I did, as soon as I realized what had happened. And I had to wait a long time for them to come! They asked a lot of questions and wanted to know if anything had been taken.'

'Was there?'

A silence fell across the line.

'I don't know,' Giulietta said after a few moments. 'Maybe some of Albina's things. Not anything of mine. No, not any of my things,' she repeated. 'None at all.'

Urbino was a little skeptical. It often took someone days, often longer, to determine that something was missing unless it was a large item or a valuable one that they quickly checked on.

'Money? Jewelry?'

'What I have, I keep in the pockets of an old coat no one would ever want to steal or think of searching. It was all still there. But I'm afraid, Signor Urbino. Afraid that whoever broke in will come back. Please, could you help me? I don't want to stay in the apartment with the door broken.'

'Of course you don't.'

Urbino, who knew how long it took owners of buildings in Italy to make repairs, even with the intervention of the police and the municipality, told her he'd be there as soon as he could.

Urbino was sitting in Giulietta's living room shortly after nine, to the obvious relief of the frightened woman. She was wearing the same black dress she had been wearing yesterday. It was wrinkled, and a piece of the cream-colored lace trimming had ripped.

The living room had a musty smell, but it seemed clean. Some things were out of place. A bonbon canister was overturned, a small rug was doubled up against the side of the sofa, and romance novels and crossword puzzle books were scattered across the floor. The base of a porcelain lamp was shattered in a corner. A dressmaker's dummy stood in a corner, tipped against the wall. Scraps of flowered blue material draped one shoulder of the dummy. Beside the window were three cardboard boxes that carried the name of a Tuscan winery. Brightly-colored garments with brocade and sequins spilled out over their open flaps.

The furniture, although of good quality, was worn and old. As Urbino sat next to Albina's sister on the sofa, an exposed spring pressed into him from beneath the piece of green material that had been thrown over the sofa.

'Don't worry, Giulietta. I'll arrange to have your door fixed right away. And the one downstairs too. It's in bad shape. Is there a locksmith near here that you and Albina used?'

'She brought someone back a few years ago when we had trouble with our lock. But I don't know who he was. She took care of those things.'

'There's one near the Carmini. I'll go directly from here.'

The woman's small thin face was gaunt, and its tiny black eyes were rimmed with dark circles. She periodically bit a corner of her brightly-rouged lower lip.

'Are you sure you wouldn't like a glass of

water?' she said. 'I'd offer you coffee but I couldn't even make one single cup for myself these past few days. We ran out of coffee, and I've been too busy to get some. Albina took care of it. Or maybe a glass of Cynar? That would be nice, wouldn't it?' she asked with eagerness.

The thick, brownish liqueur made from artichokes was far from Urbino's favorite drink.

'I'm fine, thank you.'

Giulietta looked disappointed

Urbino stood up.

'Are you sure that the person broke in your door? Maybe you left it open. You've had a lot to deal with.'

'I locked it when I left. I've never forgotten to do that. Albina was the forgetful one. And the lock is broken. I told you that!' she added petulantly.

Urbino went over to the door and moved the slide bolt that Giulietta had shot into place as soon as he had come in. He opened the door and examined it but could find no evidence of a forced entry. However, the door was so old and the lock so worn and rusted that it was possible that a person without much strength could have been responsible for the damage. And when he had entered the building, he had noted that the entrance door, which had Albina's obituary notice on it, could be opened with a slight push although he had waited until Giulietta had released the lock to let him in so as not to frighten the woman any more than she already was.

'What did the police say about the door?'

taken advantage of her condition to take them.'

'But why would someone break into our apartment?' Giulietta persisted. 'I just don't understand.'

'There are people who read obituaries to find out when relatives will be out of the house for the funeral. It's a time when they know they have a better chance of not being interrupted. It's a good time for robbery.'

But Urbino believed there was more to it than that.

Fifteen minutes later Urbino was at the locksmith's shop. The locksmith was familiar with the building although he wasn't the one Albina had once engaged. He knew the owner of the building, who lived in Mestre.

'Let me give him a call,' he said. 'Can't just go and change the locks of another man's building.' He softened his words with a smile.

The owner had no objections after the locksmith explained that a friend of the Gonella sisters would pay for all the work and supply keys to him and all the tenants.

The locksmith promised to take care of things as soon as his assistant returned. He would put in the best locks he had.

Urbino set off toward the Caffé Da Valdo. It was the kind of hot, cloudless day that would become much hotter and more humid as the hours passed. Urbino felt a little fatigued, even slightly dizzy, perhaps because of the way he had been abruptly awakened and had hurried out of the

'Bah, the police! They said nothing. They did nothing.'

'May I see Albina's room?'

'Why?'

Giulietta gave him a stern-faced expression.

'Whoever broke in might have taken something of hers, you said. They didn't take any of your things, right?'

She stared at him.

'If we can figure out if they took something specific from Albina's room,' he went on, 'there might be a chance of finding the person or persons who broke in.'

Giulietta considered this for a few moments.

'I suppose you're right,' she said with what seemed reluctance. 'You know more about these things than someone like I do, the way you like to investigate. As you wish. Her room is this way.'

She led him down a narrow, dark hallway with four closed doors. She opened one at the far end.

Albina's room had a frayed dark blue carpet. Its one window was covered with thin, semi-transparent blue curtains through which the brick wall of an adjacent building was visible. Crowding the small space were a single bed with a wooden headboard, a plastic chair, a chest of drawers, a dark armoire, and a corner bookcase.

Being in Albina's room was one thing. Searching it, which is what Urbino wanted to do, was something else entirely. He realized that he was going to have to be content with not much more than a quick visual survey. All the drawers of the chest had been pulled out. Garments gaped out.

Shoes lay in a jumble on the carpet. The doors of the armoire were wide open. Clothing made a disorderly pile on the floor in front of it. The bedclothes were in disarray and the mattress didn't seem to lie properly on its frame.

'My room looked the same, but I straightened it up. I haven't had the energy to do it in here. I don't even know if I'll keep all her things.'

'Natalia can come over and help you. But I wouldn't throw anything away, not yet. Just put things back as best you can. We'll figure out what to do with them later.'

Giulietta didn't question his advice. She bent down and picked something up from the floor. It was a brightly-colored birthday card. She put it on the dresser. Urbino noticed that two of the fingernails on her right hand were broken.

'From Claudio,' Giulietta said. 'He brought it over and sang songs. In July. Albina was five years older than me.' Then she added, mechanically, 'My poor sister.'

'Your sister was well loved. Look at all the people who came to her funeral. I'm sure she didn't have an enemy in the world.'

He tried to make this last observation casually. Giulietta stiffened slightly and looked at him, her eyes rounder.

'Why do you say that? Is it because you think someone came into our apartment because of Albina? Because they didn't like her?'

'Were any of the other apartments broken into?' Urbino asked, without responding to her questions.

'No.'

'Albina left the apartment a short time after I walked her home, right?'

Giulietta bent down and picked up a worn shoe. She searched for its mate, found it, and put them both neatly beside the bed.

'She went back for the keys,' she said.

'But why would she go out again so late, and with the storm that was coming?'

'It made no sense to me either.' Giulietta stood up. 'The keys would keep, I told her. But she was determined to get them. She was afraid someone might take them, and then she'd have to spend money to have new ones made.'

'Were any keys found with her?'

'The keys to Da Valdo. In her pocket. With some money. Thank God no one robbed her while she was lying there dying or already dead!'

'Do you know if she got her keys from Da Valdo before she died?'

'All these questions, Signor Urbino! I have no idea. I never asked her slave driver if her keys are still in the café. I didn't even think of it.' She gazed out the window, and then turned back to Urbino. 'Oh, I see what you mean. Someone could have used the keys to get into the apartment. And – and that could mean that someone might have attacked her. For the keys? Yes, someone could have attacked her for the keys.'

The possibility seemed to please her. Or perhaps, Urbino thought, she was trying to encourage him in this line of thinking.

'Possibly,' Urbino said, a bit cautiously given Giulietta's reaction. 'Or someone could have

'Bah, the police! They said nothing. They did nothing.'

'May I see Albina's room?'

'Why?'

Giulietta gave him a stern-faced expression.

'Whoever broke in might have taken something of hers, you said. They didn't take any of your things, right?'

She stared at him.

'If we can figure out if they took something specific from Albina's room,' he went on, 'there might be a chance of finding the person or persons who broke in.'

Giulietta considered this for a few moments.

'I suppose you're right,' she said with what seemed reluctance. 'You know more about these things than someone like I do, the way you like to investigate. As you wish. Her room is this way.'

She led him down a narrow, dark hallway with four closed doors. She opened one at the far end.

Albina's room had a frayed dark blue carpet. Its one window was covered with thin, semi-transparent blue curtains through which the brick wall of an adjacent building was visible. Crowding the small space were a single bed with a wooden headboard, a plastic chair, a chest of drawers, a dark armoire, and a corner bookcase.

Being in Albina's room was one thing. Searching it, which is what Urbino wanted to do, was something else entirely. He realized that he was going to have to be content with not much more than a quick visual survey. All the drawers of the chest had been pulled out. Garments gaped out.

Shoes lay in a jumble on the carpet. The doors of the armoire were wide open. Clothing made a disorderly pile on the floor in front of it. The bedclothes were in disarray and the mattress didn't seem to lie properly on its frame.

'My room looked the same, but I straightened it up. I haven't had the energy to do it in here. I don't even know if I'll keep all her things.'

'Natalia can come over and help you. But I wouldn't throw anything away, not yet. Just put things back as best you can. We'll figure out what to do with them later.'

Giulietta didn't question his advice. She bent down and picked something up from the floor. It was a brightly-colored birthday card. She put it on the dresser. Urbino noticed that two of the fingernails on her right hand were broken.

'From Claudio,' Giulietta said. 'He brought it over and sang songs. In July. Albina was five years older than me.' Then she added, mechanically, 'My poor sister.'

'Your sister was well loved. Look at all the people who came to her funeral. I'm sure she didn't have an enemy in the world.'

He tried to make this last observation casually. Giulietta stiffened slightly and looked at him, her eyes rounder.

'Why do you say that? Is it because you think someone came into our apartment because of Albina? Because they didn't like her?'

'Were any of the other apartments broken into?' Urbino asked, without responding to her questions.

'No.'

128

'Albina left the apartment a short time after I walked her home, right?'

Giulietta bent down and picked up a worn shoe. She searched for its mate, found it, and put them both neatly beside the bed.

'She went back for the keys,' she said.

'But why would she go out again so late, and with the storm that was coming?'

'It made no sense to me either.' Giulietta stood up. 'The keys would keep, I told her. But she was determined to get them. She was afraid someone might take them, and then she'd have to spend money to have new ones made.'

'Were any keys found with her?'

'The keys to Da Valdo. In her pocket. With some money. Thank God no one robbed her while she was lying there dying or already dead!'

'Do you know if she got her keys from Da Valdo before she died?'

'All these questions, Signor Urbino! I have no idea. I never asked her slave driver if her keys are still in the café. I didn't even think of it.' She gazed out the window, and then turned back to Urbino. 'Oh, I see what you mean. Someone could have used the keys to get into the apartment. And – and that could mean that someone might have attacked her. For the keys? Yes, someone could have attacked her for the keys.'

The possibility seemed to please her. Or perhaps, Urbino thought, she was trying to encourage him in this line of thinking.

'Possibly,' Urbino said, a bit cautiously given Giulietta's reaction. 'Or someone could have

129

taken advantage of her condition to take them.'

'But why would someone break into our apartment?' Giulietta persisted. 'I just don't understand.'

'There are people who read obituaries to find out when relatives will be out of the house for the funeral. It's a time when they know they have a better chance of not being interrupted. It's a good time for robbery.'

But Urbino believed there was more to it than that.

Fifteen minutes later Urbino was at the locksmith's shop. The locksmith was familiar with the building although he wasn't the one Albina had once engaged. He knew the owner of the building, who lived in Mestre.

'Let me give him a call,' he said. 'Can't just go and change the locks of another man's building.' He softened his words with a smile.

The owner had no objections after the locksmith explained that a friend of the Gonella sisters would pay for all the work and supply keys to him and all the tenants.

The locksmith promised to take care of things as soon as his assistant returned. He would put in the best locks he had.

Urbino set off toward the Caffé Da Valdo. It was the kind of hot, cloudless day that would become much hotter and more humid as the hours passed. Urbino felt a little fatigued, even slightly dizzy, perhaps because of the way he had been abruptly awakened and had hurried out of the

130

Palazzo Uccello.

The streets were congested with tourists who seemed in a convivial mood despite the heat. Venetians, surrounded by their heavily laden baskets and carts from the morning shopping, stopped and talked with each other. The cafés were filled, both inside and at the pavement tables. Children wove and bumped through the crowd on their scooters and tricycles.

An anachronistic element in all the gaiety was a tall, thin figure walking down the Calle Toletta toward Urbino. It wore a black tunic of gauzy cotton, a wide-brimmed black hat over its ears and hair, large black-framed glasses, and a gold-painted mask with a long pointed beak over the nose and the mouth. The figure carried a wooden stick in his gloved hands and moved slowly.

Someone was choosing the height of summer to parade around in the carnival costume patterned after the protective uniform worn by plague doctors in the Renaissance. A piece of medicinally soaked cloth, whose fumes supposedly safeguarded the doctor, had been customarily placed in the cone of the nose. The stick was used to examine the victim's sores at a safe distance.

Most of the tourists around the figure found it a source of amusement and enjoyed being tapped by the stick. Two children ran around the figure, teasing it to tap them, but always dodging away when the stick started to descend. As the grim figure passed Urbino, it tapped his shoulder three times in quick succession. A group of Spaniards burst into laughter.

Urbino smiled although he felt a rush of irritation. Despite all his commitment to logic, he had been infected by superstition at an early age. He had never been able to eradicate it and doubted he ever would. And since moving to Italy it had gained in strength. It was yet another one of his many inconsistencies.

As Urbino watched the plague doctor move at a somber pace past him toward the Campo San Barnabà, the image of Konrad Zoll walking slowly under the arcade past Florian's appeared before his eyes – Zoll, the afflicted and dying man, being helped by his companion, Luca Benigni.

Urbino had said to the contessa on that afternoon that at least the sick man had someone to look after him. He wondered how many people had been reluctant to get close to Zoll because of his disease, even if it hadn't been a communicable one. How many of his friends and acquaintances, even his family, had treated him with the equivalent of the plague doctor's stick? Many people failed the sick, sometimes only because they didn't want to be reminded of mortality.

By the time Urbino approached the Accademia Bridge, the streets had become even more engorged. He fought his way over the bridge into the small Campo San Vidal and past the wrought-iron gates of the Palazzo Barbaro. He sought refuge for a few minutes in the main courtyard of the Music Conservatory. It was a large, open space beneath tiers of loggias. No aria or sonata spilled from any of its open windows as was often the case; this morning the building was silent. However, he remained for a few minutes and contemplated the stone statue of a robed and veiled woman, who clasped a book against her breast. For this was the reason he had stepped into the courtyard today, to look at the statue. Or was it to consult it? With Urbino's inexpugnable and, it seemed, ever-growing superstition, he had come to regard the mysterious statue as a kind of Sphinx. Except that this Sphinx did not propound riddles to him but instead seemed to encourage answers to ones that were troubling him. Nothing like this happened now, however, and, somewhat disappointed, he went into the Campo Santo Stefano.

The grand square, lively as usual, was a pleasant open space in one of the busiest parts of the city. Children played around the statue of Niccolò Tommaseo, atop whose head sat an immobile pigeon. A young couple stood by the statue devouring one pastry after another from a paper bag with the name of a well-known shop in the nearby Calle del Spezier.

By the time Urbino entered the *calle* that led into the Campo Sant'Angelo, he was beginning to feel the closeness of the air more than he had yet that summer. Ten minutes later, overheated and slightly nauseous, he was lucky to find an outside table at Da Valdo.

A waiter – one of those who had been at Albina's funeral – gave Urbino a warm greeting and took his order for a large bottle of mineral water.

The Campo Sant'Angelo had a lot to recommend it. Lined with lovely palaces and not over-

133

whelmed with shops and cafés, it was more peaceful than most other squares in this area. It was near a vaporetto stop of the same name, and the ornate Palazzo Fortuny, with its museum dedicated to the revolutionary Spanish couturier, was only a few minutes' walk away. In addition, it provided a good view of the listing campanile of Santo Stefano – and especially from the tables outside of Da Valdo.

Most of the other patrons around Urbino were tourists, enjoying the sunshine, snapping photographs, chatting on their mobiles, some of them enthusiastically describing the scene for family and friends back home. At one table a smiling, middle-aged woman sat methodically writing out postcards, and with a fountain pen, no less. Urbino's heart went out to her. Here was someone he could identify with.

Inside the café, a different crowd made up the scene. Except for a couple sitting by the entrance and paging through a *Guide Bleu* of the city, the clients were Venetians, and most of them older men. Some were playing cards in the back by the bar. Others were engaged in a loud discussion about the new glass bridge that the engineers were having such a hard time constructing over the Grand Canal.

A tall, dark-haired man in his early forties leaned against the bar near the cash register. Urbino recognized him as Valdo, the proprietor. Urbino's waiter said something to him. A few minutes later Valdo carried the bottle of mineral water and a glass out on a small tray to Urbino. He placed the glass on the table and poured some water.

'You're the American,' he said. 'The one who lives in Cannaregio. I've seen you around. Never in my place, though.' He gave Urbino a quick, short look from under his dark eyebrows.

'My loss so far,' Urbino said. 'You have a nice place. Very well-situated. It pleases both the tourists and the locals.'

'Thank you. Business is good.' He glanced around at the tables, all of which were occupied. 'You were Albina's friend.' He put the bottle of mineral water on the table. 'I couldn't come to the funeral. We'll all miss her.' Valdo stared at Urbino for a few moments. 'Not because of the work she did. She was a good woman.'

'She was.'

'Is there anything else you'd like? It's all on the house.'

Urbino thanked him and said that the water was all he needed at the moment. He excused himself to take a long, fatigue-lifting draft.

'I have a question or two, though, if you don't mind,' Urbino said as he set down the glass. 'About Albina. She forgot her house keys here the night she died. She either was on her way to get them when she died or she was returning home with them. I was wondering if you or one of your waiters found any keys. It's one of those details her sister would like to have resolved.'

'As a matter of fact, I did find some keys. The next morning. Wait a second.'

Valdo returned a few moments later carrying a nondescript metal ring with two large keys and a much smaller one.

'This must be them. I found them on the shelf by the door. I had no idea they were Albina's or I would have returned them. I figured a customer left them. I put them in the cash register for safe-keeping.'

Urbino took the keys and examined them. The big keys were old and scratched, and the small key, almost delicate, was slightly bent from twisting in a lock.

'Would you mind if I returned these to her sister? Assuming they're Albina's, that is. If they're not, I'll bring them back, and you can return them to the cash register in case their rightful owner shows up. Another thing,' Urbino said as he pocketed the keys, 'did Albina ever complain about being harassed by anyone – any passer-by or customer – when she was cleaning up at night?'

'That's a strange question. Albina told me that you investigate crimes. Do you think someone hurt her?'

'Someone might have robbed her after she fell in the *calle*. Her apartment was broken in to. That's why I asked about the keys. I thought that someone might have taken them from her.'

'Well, you see that the keys were here all that time. And to answer your question, signore, she never said anything about being bothered in any way while she was working here. My café has never had any problems. We're a peaceful little place. You see that woman over there?'

He indicated a short, stout woman in front of an easel. She stood about twenty feet away in the square. Urbino hadn't noticed her before. There

136

were so many amateur painters at this time of the year everywhere in the city that it was easy not to notice them after a while. They became part of the scene they were rendering.

'Women like her are always painting my place. It's very picturesque.'

Urbino agreed.

Feeling a little more energetic than he had earlier, Urbino went to Florian's after speaking with Valdo. Because of his familiarity with the city, however, he was able to avoid, at least for a little while, the main *calli* teeming with tourists being funneled into the Piazza San Marco.

He made a detour behind the Teatro La Fenice along a route which he seldom took. The small alleys and canals held an almost secretive, un-known look for him. As could so quickly and easily happen in Venice, he felt a dampness descend on him that, given his earlier and still lingering indisposition, had him shivering. When he reached the Campo San Gaetano, he stood in the sunshine to warm himself. He gazed up at the theater that had been carefully and lovingly restored after a recent, devastating fire. He reminded himself that he should arrange with the contessa to get opening night tickets for the new season for the two of them and Claudio.

Ten minutes later, after passing through the busy piazza, Urbino was standing at the bar in Florian's. He ordered a glass of mineral water with a twist of lemon.

Florian's bar was small and compact, and bustled with waiters. It provided him with a good opportunity to ask some questions about Albina.

But no matter whom he spoke with – whether it was the waiters, the manager, or one of the dishwashers who emerged from the kitchen for a few moments – Urbino got the same response. Albina had been a hardworking, cooperative woman who had won the hearts of the staff and been a favorite of the patrons. She would be missed.

After finishing his water, he climbed the staircase by the entrance to the foyer between the restrooms, with its little table, plate of coins, and chair. The attendant was tending to one of the clients in the ladies' room. Urbino had always thought that an establishment like Florian's should have finer restrooms than the small, cramped ones they had.

When the attendant, who had been at Albina's funeral, came out into the foyer, he asked her about Albina. She had only good things to say about her. And she assured him that Albina had never had problems with any of the patrons.

Most people were usually reluctant, at least at first, to speak ill of the dead, but Urbino didn't believe that this was the case with the attendant or with any of the other Florian employees downstairs. Perhaps some understandable idealization was going on, but what he was hearing about Albina was what he believed to be true, based on his own contact with the woman. But even a good woman – and perhaps, in certain circumstances, especially a good woman – could unintentionally provoke violence in someone else if her goodness, her very being, represented a threat.

After leaving Florian's, Urbino went about two errands unconnected to the dead woman.

The first took him to see a friend. This was Rebecca Mondador, an architect he had met when he was involved in the original renovations for the Palazzo Uccello.

He took the vaporetto from the San Marco stop to San Tomà. The boat was so full that he had little chance of finding a spot in the stern, and even if he had succeeded, he would have had to go through the closed cabin. On a day like this it would be stifling. He took a position on the port side by the pilot's cabin. Here he could get the benefit of the breeze made by the boat's movement up the waterway. He still didn't feel completely well.

Urbino was relieved to escape from the boat when they reached San Tomà. He couldn't help but wonder what Goethe would think if he had been dropped into the city today and seen the thousands who flocked to it; Goethe, the man who had spent three and a half weeks making his slow way here from Carlsbad. In those days travel was only for the privileged few, and a grand tour wasn't something accomplished in a whirlwind of mad consumption.

Urbino only hoped that the city, which Goethe had said could only be compared to itself, would survive all of the indignities and invasions its beauty encouraged, but on days like this, during high season, he had his doubts.

139

* * *

Rebecca's modern offices were off the Campo San Tomà.

'Of course I know the place,' she said after he had described Konrad Zoll's apartment. She spoke perfect, although accented English. 'That palazzo is one of the best on the Canalazzo, as you surely know yourself. It's been kept extremely well. I looked at the apartment once myself when it was on the market. Far, far beyond my means, even if I had five lifetimes. Yes, the estate agent who handled it back then has retired, like your friend said.'

'Could you recommend someone who could handle a resale?'

'With or without commission? For myself, I mean? Just kidding.' She gave him a bright smile. 'I think I know someone suitable.'

She mentioned an estate agent in San Polo and wrote her name on a sheet of headed stationery.

'She's very good,' Rebecca said, 'and she speaks pretty good English. That should be a plus.'

As he was leaving, Rebecca mentioned Albina's death.

'I regret I couldn't be at the funeral. I had an important meeting in Milan. Sad way for her to go, all alone like that in the middle of the storm. Heart attack, wasn't it?'

'That's what they say.'

A quizzical look came over Rebecca's small, pointed face. She knew Urbino's reputation as a sleuth. In fact, she had helped him in some small but vital ways. Before she might ask him any

140

questions, he thanked her and left.

At this early point he wasn't ready to confide his speculations to anyone other than the contessa, nor would it be wise.

Urbino had less immediate luck with his second errand.

He stopped in several small hotels in San Polo and Santa Croce to see if he could find a reasonably priced room for Maisie Croy, the watercolorist, but all the places were booked solid into mid-September.

As he stood outside a pensione near the Piazzale Roma, he decided that he would try some places in Castello, even though this meant that he would have to go to the farther end of the city. The Castello – or at least the working-class quarter of it, rather distant from the Piazza San Marco – was usually the last to fill up.

If there hadn't been some urgency in Croy's need for a room, he would have put off going until the next day. But after refreshing himself with a *granita di caffé,* he took the vaporetto, this one even more crowded than the one before, to the Arsenale.

From there he walked along the broad embankment along the lagoon to the Via Garibaldi, the broadest street in the city, lined with shops, cafés, and restaurants. Moving slowly from the Bacino in the direction of San Pietro di Castello on its own little island, he was turned away at one establishment after another. He was tempted to seek out a shaded bench in the nearby public gardens but kept pressing on.

When he was walking through the street market below the Canal of Sant'Anna he was becoming discouraged. He reminded himself again that this was the height of the summer season. But then he remembered a small pensione in an alley to the left of the canal. It was unlikely to be fully occupied, given its remote location. Few tourists ventured this far up the Via Garibaldi and access from the other direction was blocked by the mass of the Arsenale. Two elderly sisters owned it. In fact, it was called Le Due Sorelle. But the last time Urbino had had any contact with the pensione had been more than ten years ago. He had no idea if the place or the sisters were still in existence.

He was therefore pleased for himself, Maisie Croy, and, of course, the sisters themselves when he found the two women in the restaurant attached to their pensione, looking vigorous and not much older. One of them was preparing a lunch of tripe. The smell, particularly on a day like this and given the way that Urbino had been feeling, was far from appetizing. The other sister was sorting through napkins at one of the tables. She recognized him and responded to his enquiry enthusiastically.

'But of course, signore!' she said, standing up. 'We have a room, our best, for as long as your friend needs it. Breakfast is included, and as you see, we have a restaurant with home-cooked meals for a very reasonable price. Come.'

She collected a key from the desk in the entrance behind the dining room and led him up a dark, rickety staircase to the end of the hallway.

142

She had some difficulty unlocking the door of one of the rooms, and the door needed to be pushed slightly to open. The room held a double bed with a lithograph of St. Rita over the head-board, a chest of drawers, a small table and chair, a chipped sink, and a bidet. It was all rather drab and uninspiring, and certainly not what Croy was accustomed to in her room in Dorsoduro. The smell of the tripe had seeped into the room where it joined forces with a strong odor of mildew.

The woman, sensing Urbino's reaction, went over to the window, pulled aside the heavy drapes, and threw open the wooden shutters.

Light bathed the room. The effect was some-how not to reveal more of the room's drawbacks but to make it much more desirable.

The window provided a view of a narrow canal, a stone bridge, and an iron-railed balcony from which a profusion of flowers cascaded. An artist's eye would be unable to resist the charm of the scene.

When the woman quoted a price that was a fourth of what Croy was paying in Dorsoduro, he said that he would reserve it on behalf of his friend, starting with the next day. The woman insisted that he also engage it for that night since her chances of finding someone to take it for only one night would be slim. Urbino didn't argue. He left a deposit to cover three days. After getting his receipt and thanking the two sisters, he took a water taxi from the Riva dei Sette Martiri to Croy's hotel in Dorsoduro.

Croy wasn't there. He left her a note about the

pensione, telling her that she could take occupancy at any time today and giving her the address and explicit directions to reach it. He enclosed the receipt in the envelope along with the note. The woman at the desk assured him that Croy would get it as soon as she returned.

As soon as he got back to the Palazzo Uccello, Urbino called the Gritti Palace Hotel. Hollander wasn't in his room. Urbino left a message, with the necessary information about the estate agent.

After lunch, which was served by the morose Natalia, Urbino went down to Gildo's apartment. Natalia had told him that Claudio was with the gondolier. Urbino took two copies of *Regate e Regatanti* with him.

Claudio sat on the sofa watching Gildo repair an umbrella for Natalia at the table. Claudio's face looked more drawn today than it had yesterday.

'I thought I'd check and see how you two were doing. And give you these.' He handed them each a copy of the book. 'I think you'll find it interesting.'

The two men thanked Urbino. Gildo put aside the umbrella, dropped into the chair by the canal-side window, and soon became absorbed by the list of champions of the *gondolini* competitions. Claudio looked at the cover, which had a photograph of two stripe-shirted rowers in the *disdotona* race, and then opened the book at random to a photograph of the 1881 regatta. He stared at it for a few moments before putting the book down on the sofa.

'How are you feeling, Claudio?' Urbino asked.

'I'm fine. You don't have to worry.'

'I'm not.'

'Yes, you are,' Claudio stood up. 'You're worried about me because of Albina. But I'll tell you something. I have more energy than I did before she died. More energy to row in the race. Maybe even win it. Do you know what she told me before she died?'

'What?'

'She had a dream that Gildo and I were far ahead in the race. She was watching from the contessa's palazzo. She got so excited that she fell into the Canalazzo. We stopped rowing and went to help her and pulled her into the *gondolino*. But she was angry in the dream, she said. She wanted us to stay in the race.'

'You understand the dream, don't you, Signor Urbino?' Gildo asked, looking up from the book. 'Albina knew she was sick. She felt she was going to die. She was telling him to go on. She was telling us both to go on.'

Gildo put *Regate e Regatanti* down on a little table that held a large blue glass gondola. He went over to Claudio and threw his arm companionably around his shoulder.

'And we're going to do even better now, because of Albina, aren't we!' Gildo said.

Claudio gave his friend a weak smile.

Yet again that day Urbino felt the irrational pull of superstition. Albina's dream appeared to be both a veiled prediction of disaster and an encouragement to see beyond some calamity, depending on how you interpreted it.

145

'When did she tell you about the dream?'

'Three days before she died.' Claudio paused. 'The last time I saw her alive.'

'She was a good woman,' Urbino said. 'Everyone seems to have liked her.'

'Everyone *did* like her,' Claudio corrected him sharply. 'I never heard one bad word about her. Not from anyone. Everyone loved her at Florian's, the staff and every single customer.'

'Yes, she was good-tempered and kind. And generous. She didn't provoke anyone, and wasn't the type to complain, even if she might have had reason to.'

Claudio's face tensed.

'What do you mean?' he asked.

'Just that things may have been difficult from time to time with her sister and her other job at Da Valdo. And with problems that we might not have been aware of. Life doesn't always go smoothly for the good.'

Claudio seemed to consider this before saying, 'You're right that she never complained. Not to me, anyway. And as you see from her dream, she had no fears for herself, but only for other people.'

# Six

The next morning, after a long sleep, Urbino felt restored. He had been worried that he would fall sick. Illness was something that preoccupied him even though he enjoyed remarkably good health, except for the embarrassment of his gout.

He was in the habit of going up to the *altana* some mornings with his coffee, a book, and his thoughts, and he had hoped to spend some time doing that today with his Goethe, but a light, misty rain was falling. There had been thunderstorms overnight and prolonged periods of rain that had awakened him intermittently for a few seconds, until he had drifted back into a dreamless sleep.

After spending an hour in his library, he lost concentration on what the German writer had called his irresistible need to set out on his long, solitary journey to Italy. The death of Albina Gonella had given Urbino his own irresistible need and, in its own way, it was a journey just as solitary as Goethe's. He hoped that it would be just as fruitful.

He abandoned the Palazzo Uccello and set out at a brisk stride to San Marco. Deep puddles along his route, where no wooden planks were set up, made it necessary to backtrack. He soon

147

found himself among two sorts of tourists, the lost and the adventurous. The former he directed to the main streets or the nearest boat landing. As for the latter, he gave them what he hoped they realized were encouraging smiles, for he admired their spirit and imagination, and vicariously enjoyed their discovery of odd corners of the city, something that his long residency had deprived him of.

By the time he neared the Grand Canal, or more precisely the Bacino of San Marco, his pace was slackened by the *corso di gente* which he had been obliged to rejoin. Eventually, he reached the Riva degli Schiavoni and stood beside the Danieli Hotel.

The lagoon stretched before him beneath a sky not so much gray as opalescent. Vaporetti, motorboats, yachts, and barges criss-crossed the lagoon and moved in and out of the channels of the Grand Canal and the Giudecca. A tanker flying the Lebanese flag plied its way toward Marghera and passed a car ferry moving in the opposite direction toward the Lido.

At the mouth of the Grand Canal, the Dogana da Mare resembled the prow of a ship with the baroque whiteness of the Salute gleaming wetly behind it in the rain. Farther in the distance the Church of San Giorgio Maggiore, with its classical brick façade and bell tower, was in serene possession of its own little island, and the Church of the Redeemer rose chaste and dignified from the buildings clustered around it on the Giudecca Island.

Despite all the noise and activity on the water

and the Riva in front of him, Urbino felt a few moments of peace as he always did in contemplating this panorama. He hardly even heard the raucous song of a group of Turkish sailors dancing a few feet away from him. The balance and harmony of the two Palladian churches and the extravagance of the Salute created a marvelously unified composition. It encouraged him in the hope that the two different sides of his nature could be just as compatible.

A few minutes later, on the Riva degli Schiavoni, without much trouble, he found the person he was looking for. Giulietta had identified him for Urbino among the mourners at the Carmini. Maurizio, Albina's young neighbor who had sometimes walked her home from Da Valdo, was tending one of the souvenir kiosks close to the Ponte della Paglia. Tourists encumbered the bridge, gazing at the Bridge of Sighs and taking photographs.

Like the other kiosks, Maurizio's was bursting with guide books, T-shirts, fans, masks, prints of Venice, glass and plastic Rialto bridges and gondolas, postcards, straw hats, key chains, and other trinkets and souvenirs.

Maurizio was about nineteen, with short dark hair styled in spikes, an angular face, and clear blue eyes.

'Yes, I helped Signorina Albina get home many times,' he said in a low, quiet voice when he had finished with a customer. They stood under the plastic tenting of the kiosk. 'If I was passing that way, I'd stop by, sometimes help her with her work. She was a nice lady.' He looked

149

away toward San Giorgio for a moment. 'We were together during the bad storm before the one she died in. We had fun laughing and being pushed by the wind. She was like a little girl.'

'She told me about that night. She said you were a good boy.' Urbino turned the wheel of postcards idly, being treated to a kaleidoscope of the Bridge of Sighs, the Piazza San Marco, the Basilica, the Salute, the Rialto Bridge, the leaning campanile of Santo Stefano, and the Grand Canal. 'Do you know that her apartment was broken into on the day of her funeral?'

'My mother told me.'

Three French women approached the kiosk. Maurizio unfolded some T-shirts for them. He wished them good day when they left without buying anything.

'Albina's sister is very disturbed about the break-in,' Urbino said as Maurizio refolded the T-shirts. 'As I'm sure everyone in the area is. She's afraid that someone might have been angry with Albina and broke into the apartment because of that.' This wasn't exactly what Giulietta had indicated but it might serve Urbino's purpose to say it. 'Did Albina ever complain about anyone bothering her? Any of the customers?'

'Never. But after I heard about the break-in, I remembered something. How I was frightened the night of the storm.' He seemed embarrassed, and added, 'Not because of the storm. And not really frightened.'

'What do you mean?'

'I thought someone was following us. But it

150

was a crazy night. We both got home safely. It was probably my imagination. I had been drinking a little.'

'Did you notice if it was a man or a woman?'

'I just saw a dark figure, maybe more than one, different ones. Who knows? I didn't think about it too much at the time. At one point a gondolier's hat blew against us. One like these.' He indicated the hats with their red ribbons hanging from his kiosk. 'Signorina Albina got so scared because it hit her in the face, though it didn't do any damage. It just blew out of nowhere.'

'From the direction that you thought someone was following you?'

'I guess so.'

'Did Albina seem to be aware that someone might be following you?'

Maurizio shrugged.

'She didn't say anything. And, as I said, it was a crazy night. So much noise and confusion.'

An hour later when Giulietta led Urbino into her living room, he found Perla Beato on the sofa with a glass of Cynar. The bruise on her face had almost faded.

'Urbino!' she cried. 'Giulietta was just telling me how helpful you were with the locks and keys. Her guardian angel, she called you. Isn't that what you said, Giulietta? Your guardian angel?'

Perla gave a high-pitched laugh. In deference to Giulietta, whose knowledge of English was almost non-existent, she was speaking in Italian. She seemed charged with nervous energy.

151

Giulietta poured Urbino a generous portion of Cynar without asking if he wanted any on this occasion. As she handed him the glass, he noted again the two broken fingernails on her hand. Perhaps now that Albina was gone, she was obliged to endanger her manicures in doing more chores.

'I think it's wonderful when we can help each other in little ways as well as big ones,' Perla rushed on. 'Giulietta has enough food to open a restaurant, don't you, Giulietta dear? One woman brought her more *sarde in saor* than the Venetian sailors used to take with them on their voyages. No chance of you getting scurvy, my dear.' Perla stopped only long enough for a sip of the Cynar. 'And all I brought her was a basket of herbs and some bottles of aromas from the shop.'

Perla owned an *erboristeria* in Dorsoduro near the Church of the Carmini.

She began to describe the herbs and aromas. Urbino let her run on, wondering if her high level of energy this morning was the result of one of her concoctions. His eye wandered around the room. The dressmaker's dummy was now standing upright. The flowered blue material was neatly draped on it. The box of cartons had been neatened, the brightly colored garments refolded and placed inside. Natalia, who had helped Giulietta put the apartment in better order, had said that the boxes contained carnival costumes in need of repair. These must have been the boxes Albina mentioned the night she died, the ones she had carried upstairs for her sister to prevent her from breaking her finger-nails.

According to Natalia, although she and Giulietta had spent a lot of time on the rest of the apartment, they hadn't done anything with Albina's room. Urbino hoped that Giulietta hadn't thrown away anything from it as he had advised her.

The basket of herbs and aromas that Perla had brought lay on the end table beside his chair. The dark green bottles had identifying labels in elegant handwriting on the *erboristeria*'s violet paper with a wheat sheaf logo.

Giulietta had a blank look on her face as Perla spoke. She seemed to be somewhere else, and she was staring at the dressmaker's dummy. She had applied a lot of make-up, and bright coins of rouge on her cheeks made her look almost clown-like. Her lips were vivid red.

Perla brought her description to an abrupt end. She put down her glass of Cynar and stood up.

'If you need anything at all, Giulietta, don't be shy. Just ask Romolo or me. We don't live far away and the shop is even closer. Why don't I take this into the kitchen?' She picked up the basket. 'If you leave it in here, you might think it's a decoration and forget it has things for you to use every day. Things that will keep our dear Giulietta fit. But from what I saw you doing outside the apartment, you're very fit.'

Giulietta looked embarrassed.

'Do you know what I found her doing as I was on my way here? She was under the *sottoportico* sweeping and washing away. You would think the municipality had employed her. She had a bucket, a broom, a brush, rags, and a little shovel, and the most terrible smelling liquid. I hope you didn't inhale much of it, Giulietta.'

'I – I was only trying to clean the place where Albina died.'

'And bless you for that, but don't you think you were overdoing it? You need to take the best care of yourself. Well, as I said, my gift will help you. You stay right where you are, Giulietta, and keep Urbino company. I'll be back as soon as I find a good place for this in the kitchen.'

After Perla left the room, Urbino mentioned that he had seen Maurizio.

'He's a nice young man,' he said.

They spent a few minutes talking about Maurizio and his kindness to Albina. Giulietta told him that he was now doing errands for her before he went to work in the morning. She kept looking in the direction of the kitchen. She was starting to get up when Perla reappeared.

'I found the perfect spot for it on the little table under the window. I'm afraid I had to move a few things. Take care of yourself, Giulietta. See you soon, Urbino. No, Giulietta, I'll find my own way out.'

When Perla left, Giulietta thanked Urbino again for his help with the locks, but she struck him again as being abstracted. Perhaps she was starting to feel the full force of her sister's death and what it meant to her, being all alone.

After declining some more Cynar, Urbino withdrew the two keys on the chain from his pocket.

'Valdo found these at his place.' He held them out to Giulietta. 'Are they Albina's?'

Giulietta took the keys.

'They're hers, but the ones for the doors are no use any more, now that you had the new locks put in. Should I keep them or throw them away? I only ask because you said that I shouldn't get rid of any of her things for a while.'

'Just put them in her room with all her other things. We can decide what to do with everything later.'

'As you think best, Signor Urbino.'

'By the way, Giulietta, during the past few weeks have you noticed anyone unfamiliar, someone who isn't from the neighborhood, lingering around your building?'

'Tourists are always coming into the *calle* and turning around because it's a dead end. Some stay long enough to take a picture, but that's it. Once in a while painters will come for a few hours, cluttering the way with all their stuff. There was one a few weeks ago, a big, fat man. They're a nuisance. They should leave us alone.'

'Wish you were here, *caro*,' the contessa said on the telephone that evening. She had returned to Asolo after the funeral. 'We haven't had any rain. The air is delightful.'

'I'd love to be there. The rest would be nice.'

Urbino filled her in on most of what he had accomplished yesterday and today. When he finished, the contessa, who had allowed him to recount his activities with only a few clarifying questions, said, 'You're feeling guilty.'

155

'Guilty?'

'Yes, guilty because of those keys. You can't let it go that if you hadn't gone to Da Valdo that night, Albina would still be alive.'

'But—'

'It's guilt that's driving you,' she interrupted. 'All of these questions, all of these good deeds, all of this running around the city from one end to the other! You're doing penance. I hope you feel the burden lifted. Giulietta has her locks, Hollander has the name of an estate agent, and your new friend has a room with a view at a reasonable price. You've even returned to the scene of your crime and retrieved the keys from Valdo and given them to Giulietta. Bravo, my son. You don't even have to say fifty Ave Marias! Do you feel better now?'

'Not in the sense you mean. Of course I'm happy to have accomplished some things, but I've also learned a lot. The Gonella apartment was broken into and although Giulietta says nothing of value was taken, she's either not being honest or she doesn't realize what *has* been taken. Because surely something must have been, or at the least the person was looking for something of value. Why else break in? Maurizio suspected that someone was shadowing him and Albina when they walked through the storm from Da Valdo. I had the same sensation the night I walked her home.'

The contessa didn't respond at once. When she did, she asked, 'Is all that so much to have learned?'

'It's a beginning. One step leads to another.'

'Each step can take you further astray, especially in Venice! The way it is for you in my maze.' He detected a smile in the contessa's voice. 'My dear Urbino, would you feel better if Albina didn't die naturally? But she was still out in the storm because of the keys, and you feel responsible for that. I don't mean to be cruel, but that's the sense of it. We have to accept these things. Konrad Zoll's disease. His friend's accident. I hope you're still not bothering yourself about their unfortunate deaths. Life, *caro*.'

'Something doesn't seem right. We have three deaths, all so close together. And Zoll and Luca were friends. Is it too strange to think that Albina could have had some link to Zoll and Luca? After all, she worked in Florian's. No, something just isn't right.'

'But don't you see?' the contessa said. 'You *want* there to be foul play. That way you can console yourself by wearing yourself out, trying to find a murderer, and bringing him or her to justice in the way we know you can do so well. But you can do it only when there *has* been a murder. There hasn't been any. There hasn't!'

Urbino didn't respond.

'If there *was* a murder,' she went on, more calmly, 'then how do we explain what Salvatore Rizzo said about her heart?'

'There wasn't an autopsy, was there?'

'None was required, and Giulietta didn't request one. Why should she?'

'I understand that. And I'm not saying that Albina didn't die of a heart attack. Even if she did, she could still have been the victim of foul play.'

'You mean someone could have scared her to death?'

Her words were more than a little charged with ridicule.

'Something like that. It's not impossible.' He paused. 'Or someone could have induced the heart attack. Drugs exist that would do that.'

'To be honest I don't feel easy about Albina's death myself. But don't lose your clear way of thinking. Just because Albina died after Zoll and Benigni doesn't mean that she died because of them.'

'"*Post hoc, ergo propter hoc*,"' Urbino said. 'The logical fallacy: "After this because of this." But nonetheless I feel there's some connection. If there is, I'm determined to find it.'

'I understand. And I know how much you want to do the right thing. You and your good deeds! Look at all the ones you've been wrapping yourself in. I tell you what, *caro*, why not do another good deed? Oh, it has nothing to do with Albina! Why don't you invite your watercolorist to my regatta party? What's her name again?'

'Maisie Croy. That would be a kind gesture on your part, Barbara,' he said in an encouraging tone, despite a small cloud of uneasiness that drifted across his consciousness. 'From one countrywoman to another.'

'I don't know what my country is anymore, and neither do you! But the more the merrier, as they say. By the way, I'm having lunch tomorrow with Nick Hollander.' She named one of their favorite restaurants in Dorsoduro that was

158

attached to a little hotel. 'I made a reservation for one o'clock. If you'd care to, you could join us for dessert. I know how much you like their *tiramisù*!'

'That might be a good idea. And would you do me a favor?'

'What?'

'Would you try not to mention Benigni's death to him? Or Albina's? I'd like to be the one to do it.'

The next morning Urbino found Maisie Croy behind Le Due Sorelle. It was an overcast, humid day that threatened rain. Croy, surrounded by a group of neighborhood children and sporting her battered straw gondolier's hat, was making a watercolor rendition of the stone bridge.

'This is bridge number seven,' she said. She put down her brush and smiled. She looked worse than she had a few days ago. Her skin had a grayish pallor. One eye was bloodshot. 'I wonder how many more I have?'

Urbino made a quick mental calculation.

'There are about four hundred in the city. In a few years there should be four hundred and one.'

He mentioned the glass bridge under construction by the Piazzale Roma.

'So unless you stay here until they work out the problems with that one,' he said, 'you have approximately three hundred and ninety-three bridges left to paint.'

'You know such things? I'm impressed.'

'My mind is cluttered with useless information about the city.'

159

'I don't think it's useless, and I don't believe you do either! Look how you found me this charming little place! I love it. I'll be able to stay in Venice for as long as I want now.'

The filtered quality of the light on a day like today gave a strange glow to the dilapidated stones of the sisters' building.

'I owe you some money,' Croy said. 'If you could wait a few minutes I'll get it for you.'

'Consider it a gift.'

'A gift! You are very generous. Are you sure?'

'I insist.'

'I'll make it up to you. You may have your pick of any of my paintings. They're all propped up against the walls of my room. We'll go and see.'

'That would be nice. But I don't want to show any favorites. I know how sensitive artists can be. Why don't you select one for me?'

'You're very clever. Agreed. But not right away, if you don't mind. Let me get to know you a little more.'

'My pleasure. And there should be a good opportunity for that. I've come to extend an invitation from a friend who's giving a party on the Sunday of the regatta. She's English, but she's been living here for a long time. She's the widow of an Italian. You'll receive a formal invitation from her soon.'

'How marvelous! The regatta!'

'You'll have an excellent view of most of the events from her palazzo on the Grand Canal.'

'A palazzo! This sounds better and better! My head was spinning from the heat and disappointment when I met you. Today it's from all my good luck! Or I should call it your kindness – yours and your friend's. What's her name?'

'Barbara da Capo-Zendrini.'

Croy frowned thoughtfully. It made her face look more sickly.

'Are you familiar with the name?' Urbino asked.

'Most unfamiliar! It will take me a while to learn that properly! I don't know much Italian. I hope that won't be a disadvantage at her party.'

'Almost everyone else who will be there speaks English. I advise you to allow enough time to get there, though. All the canals will be closed from about midday. The Ca' da Capo-Zendrini isn't far from the Palazzo Labia, if you know where that is.'

Croy shook her head.

'I'm sure she'll include a map with her invitation,' Urbino said, 'but I'll make a quick one for you now.'

'Why don't you make it in my sketchbook?'

She bent down and unzipped the top of her backpack. As she was extracting her sketchbook and a pencil, a small dark green bottle fell out on to the stones. The lavender label identified it as one of Perla Beato's products. Croy picked it up quickly and returned it to the backpack.

She found a blank page in the sketchbook. Urbino drew a simple map that showed how Croy could reach the land entrance of the Ca' da Capo-Zendrini and indicated where the palazzo was in relationship to Le Due Sorelle, the Grand Canal, and vaporetto stops. He returned the sketchbook and pencil to Croy.

'Thank you,' she said. 'I feel so well taken care of. I think I have enough energy to paint each of those other – how many? – three hundred and ninety-three bridges.'

Urbino doubted this. The more he looked at the woman, the more certain he was that she was ill.

'I just may stay here through the winter, who knows?'

A sudden gust of wind blew in from the lagoon. Croy clapped her hand down on the crown of her hat, exposing scratches on her upper arm. The skin around them was inflamed.

'What happened to your arm?'

'Oh, those.' Croy looked down at the scratches. 'I'm a cat lover, and there are so many around Venice. I made the mistake of petting the wrong one. The cat scratched at my hat, too, as you can see,' she added, self-consciously, although Urbino had said nothing about its condition and hadn't been scrutinizing it too closely. 'Then it fell into a puddle.'

'Well, you can always get a new hat if you want, but you should have the scratches looked at. Let me give you the name of a doctor who speaks English.'

'Oh, I don't think that's necessary. Don't worry. You're much too kind.'

After stopping for a glass of white wine near the Church of San Zaccaria at a café crowded with *carabinieri* from the nearby post, Urbino went to Clementina Foppa's paper shop. The *cartaio* was finishing with a customer at the counter. Her

162

attendant wasn't in sight.

Clementina gave him a smile that didn't reach her large brown eyes.

'It's nice to see you in better circumstances,' she said in her heavily accented English when the customer had left.

Urbino glanced over her shoulder at the board behind the counter. The obituary notice was no longer there.

'I looked for you after the service,' he said. 'I thought you might like to come to San Michele in the contessa's boat.'

'I needed to get back here.'

'It's a busy time of the year.'

'Not as busy as I need it to be.'

'Then you'll be happy to know that I'm buying some wrapping paper.' Urbino laughed and said, 'I'm a big spender today, you see.'

Clementina smiled, but once again her eyes remained sad, even cold.

'Every little bit helps,' she said.

Urbino went to the rack against the wall where marbled paper was displayed on rolls. He selected three sheets in different versions of the *fiamatto* pattern and five sheets that reproduced details of St. George and the dragon from Carpaccio's cycle of paintings at the Scuola di San Giorgio degli Schiavoni.

'You have gifts to wrap?' Clementina asked him when he brought the paper over to the counter.

'At the moment, no, but it seems that whenever I do, I don't have any paper.'

'Well, *I* never have that problem, you can be

sure.'

Her laugh sounded strained.

As she was rolling up the sheets of paper, Urbino asked her how she knew Albina Gonella.

'It was moving to see how many different people she touched,' he added.

'What else does life mean in the end? Not all this paper, and the stones outside, lovely though they are!' She waved her hand in the direction of the window, the Calle Lunga, and everything that lay beyond it. 'I knew her through my brother. He went to Florian's with Zoll. He struck up an acquaintance with her,' Clementina continued, switching into Italian as she put the wrapping paper in a cardboard tube with the name of the shop on it. 'One time Albina was a great help to him, or I should say to Zoll. He fell ill at Florian's and needed some herb he used to treat himself. He had run out of it. Albina went to get it at an *erboristeria*. Zoll had a lot of faith in herbs. Luca would have gone but Zoll insisted that he stay with him. They called a water taxi for Albina. She was taking a chance, abandoning her post like that.'

'Do you know what *erboristeria* it was? A friend has one in Dorsoduro.'

'That's the one. Erboristeria Perla. I know Perla Beato, too. She was at the funeral. Well, I suppose she's more of an acquaintance. Because we're both merchants although I don't think she'd like me to call her that.'

'You are an artisan,' Urbino said.

Once again Clementina gave him a sad, even brave little smile.

Two women, evidently tourists, entered the shop.

'Good morning,' she greeted them in English. 'If you have any questions, please don't hesitate to ask.' She turned back to Urbino and ran a hand through her feathered haircut.

'Luca asked me if I knew of a full-time job for Albina. He arranged for us to have coffee together. She was a nice woman, simple – and I mean that in the best sense. Sincere. I asked around to see if anyone needed help, but I had no luck. I have a woman who comes in and cleans up the shop every night, but I couldn't very well let her go and take on Albina, could I?'

Urbino assured her that no one would have expected it. He paid for the wrapping paper and left.

The Erboristeria Perla was a bright, canal-side shop in Dorsoduro between the Zattere and the church where Albina's funeral service had been held. It was in a pleasant area but like the area of Foppa's shop, it was one not well-frequented by tourists.

Everything about the Erboristeria Perla exuded health and good spirits, from the potpourri that scented the air to the verdant plants, the peach-colored walls, the moss-green carpet, all the well-displayed, attractively packaged products, and the marriage of nature sounds and acoustic music playing quietly in the background.

Two walls held wicker baskets of loose herbs and green glass bottles of capsule herbs. Signs and labels, handwritten on the shop's violet paper with its wheat sheaf logo, identified the baskets and bottles. Displayed throughout the large, light-filled space were incense, resins, candles, oils, soaps, salves, balms, honey, health food products, books, videos, music cassettes, posters, and mortars and pestles.

Two polished and poised attendants, who were dressed stylishly but subtly in the trademark violet color of the shop, were standing at strategic points. They greeted Urbino in quiet voices and with reassuring smiles.

From a room in the back Perla came toward him with her long-legged stride. She looked even more svelte in her shop than she looked elsewhere. Its ambiance suited her. She was dressed in a cream-colored cashmere dress with simple lines. Her blonde hair was pulled back in a chignon. The bruise on her left cheek had either completely faded or been more artfully concealed than it had been when he had seen her on the terrace of the Gritti Palace with Oriana Borelli.

'Urbino dear! It's been too long since you've been here!' she said brightly in English. 'Is this a social visit or a professional one?'

'A little of both.'

'Killing two birds with one stone.'

'Something like that.'

'So what do you need help with?'

On the way to the shop Urbino had realized it would be better if he appeared to have come for Perla's services, as he had done with Clementina, since his interest in sleuthing was well-known to the Beatos. It was a form of deception,

166

for a good end. Benevolent deception was the way he thought of it.

Perhaps to compensate for the deception he had decided to expose one of his embarrassments. The contessa was one of the few people who knew about it.

Several years ago he had developed gout in one of his big toes. The pain could be excruciating. The attacks were under control, the result of medication and not the mud and algae that a spa in Abano Terme had smeared all over him. Whenever he felt a twinge in his toe, he took some pills. For a person who enjoyed walking as much as he did and who could surprise even himself with the extent of his hypochondria, his condition was, though minor, an almost constant preoccupation. A severe attack could send him into a minor depression because of his fear that his mobility would soon be a pleasure of the past.

'From time to time, I get an inflammation in my big toe,' he began.

'You mean gout, Urbino dear!' Perla said cutting short any further evasiveness. 'Don't be shy to say it. It's quite common at a certain age. Do you know that it's associated with intelligence?'

'I doubt that. But if it's true, there have been many times when I wished I were a lot less intelligent!' He named the medication he took. 'But I thought there might be something homeopathic. I don't care for some of the side effects.'

'Of course you don't, you poor thing! Who does? And I know how doctors over-medicate!

Remember, I've been a nurse. Still *am* a nurse. You're in good hands here. Come with me.'

She led him over to ceiling-high shelves with green-painted wooden ladders beside them. The shelves were lined with green glass bottles. She selected some of the bottles, explaining their contents and how they would help him much better than what he was taking now. Before he knew it, he was dosed with five various herbs. She also gave him a little gift that she said would be beneficial for not only his toe but also his general well-being. It was a jar of chestnut tree honey.

'I'll write everything down for you,' Perla said.

One of the attendants collected the bottles of herbs and the jar of honey.

'Why don't I take that for you, too, signore?' the attendant said. He indicated the tube from Clementina Foppa's shop.

Urbino gave it to him.

'You were at Clementina's, I see,' Perla said. 'She has a lovely little shop, doesn't she? Thank God we're not in competition in any way. And she has to rely mainly on tourists for her trade.'

'Actually, it's Clementina who's indirectly responsible for the other bird I want to kill.' He couldn't resist saying this. He hoped that he did it with a straight face. 'Clementina mentioned that Albina Gonella came here once to pick up some herbs for a German man.'

'Yes, I remember. About three months ago. But I'm not free to talk about his medical condition if that's what concerns you. I'm sure you understand.'

'Of course. But I'm sorry to tell you that he died three weeks ago. He was ill beyond any reasonable help, unfortunately, as you probably feared,' he added, in case Perla thought he was casting an aspersion on her form of therapy.

Perla frowned and gave a small sigh.

'Died? Oh, dear. I was wondering why his Italian friend hadn't come by for more of the herbs. He was the one who usually came for it. The German only had enough for two months. I assumed he had gone back to Germany.'

'He died here in Venice.' Urbino paused. 'And by the way, his friend is dead, too.'

Intense astonishment touched her face.

'Dead? But he was so young. And he looked in the pink of health. I can usually tell if a person is ill.'

'I'm sure you can, but he wasn't ill. He was killed in a freak accident during the first big storm we had when he was struck on the head with a parapet stone. I know it sounds peculiar, but there you have it. And you know how violent the storm was. It happened only a short time after the German died.'

'The both of them dead! It's rather incredible.'

'And do you know that he was Clementina Foppa's brother?' Urbino added.

'Her brother? But I don't see any resemblance between the two of them at all.'

'They have different fathers. Actually Luca Benigni – that was his name – and Claudio look more like siblings. They're not, but I just mean that they resemble each other.'

Perla colored slightly.

'I suppose you're right. I'll have to give her my condolences.'

At the counter Perla wrote out a detailed description of the herbs and their properties on a sheet of violet-colored paper. When she finished and slipped it into the bag with the herbs, the honey, and the wrapping paper, she said, 'You have been filled with information today, Urbino. But that's your forte, isn't it? Why did you come here to tell me all this sad news? I mean in addition to coming for your gout?'

She put a bit of emphasis on the name of his ailment.

'I thought you'd like to know about it before Barbara's party. The German's stepson will be there. He's friends with Barbara's cousin.'

'This is like one of those connect the numbers games! Giulietta's doing them whenever she's not working one of her crossword puzzles. When you walked in, I had no idea I'd know so much before you went out again.'

Neither of them pursued the topic of the deaths of Zoll and Benigni, and for the next few minutes Urbino listened to Perla extol the virtues of his purchases. She had said many of the same things earlier, but he listened patiently.

He was about to thank her again and leave when the door from the *calle* opened. It was Romolo. He looked weary and troubled, but his face lightened when he saw Urbino.

'Isn't this a surprise! I hope it isn't a professional visit. But I don't think so. You're looking fit.'

'Romolo darling, you know very well that people don't come to me only when they're ill. They come to prevent themselves from *becoming* ill. Urbino *is* fit. He just needs a little help to remain in good condition. Isn't that true, Urbino?'

'Very true. By the way, Romolo, I hope that everything went well in Padua. I didn't have a chance to ask you at the funeral.'

'Padua?'

Perla became suddenly still.

'Yes, Padua, my dear.' She emitted a high, sharp laugh. 'You remember Padua? Rocco, your son? Your nasty tenant?'

Romolo gave his wife a look that was almost venomous, but it was so brief that Urbino wasn't even sure that he had seen it.

'Oh, Padua was fine,' he said. 'Rocco's doing very well, thank you. And I managed to accomplish a great deal. Who knows what would have happened if I had decided to stay here. Perla was right to insist that I go.'

He kissed his wife on the cheek.

'And as soon as Urbino leaves, my dear, I'm going to insist on something else. Gingko, sage, and spirulina for your memory! You're much too young to be having these lapses.'

# Seven

A ten-minute walk along three canals and over two bridges through heavy rain brought Urbino to the *locanda* where the contessa and Nick Hollander were lunching.

It was on a small, quiet canal with moored boats, most of which were covered with tarpaulin because of the weather. It had iron balconies with pots of flowers and iron-grilled lower windows. A four-sided lantern with the name of the establishment – lit on this dark summer afternoon – graced one side of the door. A tourist stood outside huddled under an umbrella, reading the menu displayed in one of the windows. The *locanda*, which had only seven simple rooms, was well known for its food, and it was always booked. Urbino hadn't even bothered to ask if a room might be free when he was searching for a place for Maisie Croy.

The owner, an attractive older woman, greeted Urbino warmly. He left his shopping bag and his umbrella in an alcove by the entrance. She led him to a small room to the left of the main one. It had a fireplace, which, though it wasn't working on this summer day, added a cozy note. The contessa and Nick Hollander sat at a table in the corner. On the walls around them, as in the rest

172

of the restaurant, were paintings – watercolors, charcoals, and oils of Venetian scenes along with portraits and modernist paintings suggestive of Picasso, Matisse, and Chagall. The *locanda* was one of those places that Maisie Croy had hoped her original hotel in Dorsoduro would be, for many of the paintings had been given in exchange for lodging and meals.

'You timed it perfectly!' the contessa said. 'We're ready for dessert.'

'Hello, Urbino.' Hollander looked fresh and rested. He was dressed in a gray suit with a dark blue open-necked shirt. 'Barbara and I were just talking about you.'

Urbino sat down.

'In Morocco they say that it means I'll have a long life. I hope so.'

'A long and healthy one, Urbino. Don't forget that,' the contessa said.

Hollander nodded.

'I told Barbara how helpful you were with the estate agent. Thanks so much.'

'You're welcome. Have you spoken with her yet?'

'Yes. She's coming to look at the apartment tomorrow morning. She's already familiar with it, she says. It seems to be well known. She was very encouraging.'

'I'd like to see the apartment, Nick,' the contessa said. 'And before you start to sell any of the things your stepfather collected or send them off to Germany. Urbino says there's a beautiful Longhi. And an Abraham-Louis Breguet! Who knows what other treasures there are! Surely you're having someone make an inventory and evaluation?'

'Fortunately, my stepfather left good records and accounts. He was very organized.'

'I have no doubt he was,' the contessa said. 'I'm sure you know what you're doing, Nick. If I want you to keep everything – all the things and the apartment itself – it's because I'm selfish, you see. You would have a pied-à-terre in Venice. You like boating so much, and well, Venice *is* on the sea.'

'Venice wouldn't work for me. Not the way it has for you and Urbino. Or the way it did for my stepfather, at least for as long as he could enjoy it.'

They fell into silence.

'I understand that it can only have sad associations for you now. But with time...' the contessa said gently. 'I've had my sorrows here, but they've only made me love it more.'

The waiter came over. All three of them ordered the *tiramisù*.

'I can tell how deeply you feel about your stepfather's death,' the contessa went on. 'Not from anything you've said, although we *have* had a nice talk,' she added, turning to Urbino. 'But I can see how vulnerable you are. You're fragile under it all, like the rest of us. We never know what's going to happen to ourselves or those we love, do we? Your stepfather should have had many more years to enjoy life. And his—'

She broke off abruptly, paused for a beat, and continued, 'And his – his spirit is such a good example to us all, isn't it? Look at the way

174

you're carrying on in that spirit, managing to enjoy yourself despite everything – well, I find that admirable! Don't you, Urbino?'

The contessa looked at him a little nervously. He wondered if she had come close to mentioning Albina's death, too, or might even not have caught herself in time as she just had about Benigni.

'I said more or less the same thing to him when we first met.'

'There, you see! But you do what you think is best with the apartment. In any case, you'll be welcome to stay with me whenever you're in town.'

'Thank you. I'm glad to have made two new friends, especially at this time.'

'Thanks to Sebastian,' the contessa said. 'That boy manages to do some good from time to time.'

Hollander used the contessa's reference to Sebastian to bring up the topic of Morocco and Urbino's travels through the country with him. Hollander, who was familiar with Morocco, showed an interest in Urbino's anecdotes and descriptions, and particularly his story about Habib and his painting.

'One of his paintings of Burano is in the other room,' Urbino said. 'Not as payment for services as some of the others are. Just a gift.'

'I'd like to see it before we leave.'

The waiter brought over their desserts.

Before they started eating their *tiramisù*, the contessa said, 'You didn't notice, Urbino. I'm hurt. And Habib would be, too, sweet, sensitive boy that he is.'

'What do you mean?'

The contessa tapped her chest gently in a motion that looked like a *mea culpa*.

She was wearing a necklace of cascading silver ovals. It was a gift from Habib to replace one that Urbino had bought her from Morocco. The original had been stolen from the Ca' da Capo-Zendrini under circumstances that had greatly troubled her. It was an incident that had played a puzzling role in a recent investigation that had centered on the burned-out San Polo palazzo Urbino had been standing in front of last week.

'It looks lovely on you,' Urbino said, 'as it always does.'

'This necklace is very precious to me, Nick. Not only in itself, but because of its associations.'

She began to explain what she meant. The explanation, which Urbino took up after a few minutes since most of the story was his to tell, carried them through dessert as well as drinks afterward.

An hour later Urbino and Hollander were in the library of the Palazzo Uccello, sipping wine. The contessa's motorboat had dropped the two men off on its way back to the Ca' da Capo-Zendrini. She was unable to join them. The first of her guests, a nephew by marriage, was arriving from Capri, and she was taking him up to Asolo for a few days.

Hollander was at the refectory table, looking

through the volumes of Urbino's *Venetian Lives* series that Urbino had taken down from the shelves at his request.

'Aren't you afraid that you're going to run out of lives?' Hollander asked. 'Not yours – or hers,' he added, indicating Serena who was settled on the sofa. 'But these. Browning. Ruskin. James. Proust. Mann. Byron. And what's this one? *Women of Venice*. Let me see.' He thumbed through it. 'Veronica Franco. Desdemona. George Sand. Peggy Guggenheim. My, my! I take back what I said. This may be an inexhaustible topic.'

'Or it may eventually exhaust me.'

Hollander got up and examined two small pastels displayed by the door. One was of a stern-looking man in eighteenth-century attire. The other was of a young woman, her hair in disarray, with one breast exposed.

'Rosalba Carriera,' Urbino explained. 'A Venetian painter.'

'She's one of the women of Venice you wrote about, isn't she? I saw her name in the book.'

'Yes. She was very popular, especially among the English. These aren't among her best, and they're slightly damaged if you look closely.'

'I'm not familiar with her. Maybe my stepfather was.'

'The Accademia has many of her portraits, and he might have seen the collection in Dresden. Fortunately they survived the fire bombing.'

'I prefer landscapes.'

'And seascapes, I'm sure. I have one in the parlor. It's by a contemporary Venetian painter.'

As they were about to leave the library to see the painting, Hollander said, 'And what are these?' He indicated a group of paintings on the other side of the door.

'They're by Habib.'

Before they had left the *locanda* Hollander had gone to the main dining room to see the young Moroccan's painting of a bright red flat-bottomed boat from Chioggia. The paintings he was looking at now, which were of doors from houses in Burano, were vivid, like the one of the boat.

'They're very good,' Hollander said. 'Your Moroccan friend has a lot of talent. My stepfather might have been a help to him. He was a patron for many young artists, though mainly in Germany.'

A few minutes later in the parlor Hollander was surveying the seascape. It was called 'Storm from the Adriatic'. It was a swirl of purples, grays, and reds. At its center were a torn white sail, a broken mast, and – upside down – one of the domes of the Basilica San Marco.

'I like it,' Hollander said. 'But it's disturbing.'

'The reality of Venice. It doesn't have much defense against the sea. You've seen how these storms rush in. They do a lot of damage. Not only to the buildings but also to people. Look what happened to Luca Benigni.'

Hollander continued to stare at the painting.

'Luca Benigni? What do you mean?'

'I thought you knew. He was killed during that first big storm we had, the one a few days after your stepfather died. Seems as if a loose parapet stone fell from a building and hit him on the head.'

Hollander stood there and stared back at Urbino. He seemed blank, amazed, and very shaken if one were to put that interpretation on his sudden paleness and a slight trembling in one eyelid.

'Good God! I didn't know that. What a strange way to die! I haven't seen him since the service. I thought he had gone out of town. Thank God it happened after my stepfather died.' Hollander lowered his gaze. 'The Mediterranean has the worst storms of all, you know.'

'Yes.' Urbino straightened the painting a fraction. 'And speaking of storms, someone was killed in the second one we had, someone Barbara and I knew. A woman who worked at Florian's.'

'This is all sounding more and more strange. I'm sorry to hear that. Two deaths in Venice from storms. I know that storms kill hundreds, even thousands of people at once, but it seems rather odd to me. Does it to you?'

'In a fashion. But I might not have been clear enough. Our friend, Albina, wasn't killed by the storm. She had a heart attack, it seems. She was outside in the midst of it.'

'It must have been frightening for her. It looked terrible enough from my room.'

Urbino made no response. After a few moments he asked Hollander if he would like another glass of wine. He declined. Hollander went over to a table and picked up an inlaid wooden box from Essaouira, then inspected a mirror from Marrakech in a painted and decorated wooden frame that was hanging on the wall above the table.

'The story of the theft of the Moroccan necklace was fascinating,' he said. 'And frightening. You and Barbara were in danger. It was clever how you figured things out. You have more than one talent.'

'Jack of all trades, you know,' Urbino responded. 'I confess to being a bit of a dilettante. I might as well admit to it, maybe be a little proud of it, since I'm criticized for it. Turn it into a virtue.'

'The more I know about you the more I realize that you would have had a lot in common with my stepfather. Pity you never met. I don't mean that *he* solved crimes, but he was a dilettante, too. And I see it as a distinct virtue. Tell me, are you working on one of your books now?'

'Goethe's experiences in Venice. But I've barely begun. Do you know Goethe?'

'I'm afraid not. But my stepfather collected editions of his works. They're in the house in Munich.' Hollander opened and closed the little wooden doors on the Moroccan mirror. 'And what about in the realm of detecting? Are you involved in anything there?'

'It's high season for tourism, but fortunately low season for crime. At least the kind I'm interested in.'

'Not bag-snatchings and muggings and cutthroat pricing?'

'No.'

'What does attract you?'

180

'It has to have something of a personal nature in it.'

'What do you mean?'

'I know it well enough when it comes along. Sometimes it sneaks up on me and sometimes it gives me a good, sharp bite.'

Hollander considered Urbino's response. He stared at the Moroccan mirror. Despite his humor, Hollander seemed uncomfortable with the topic of Urbino's sleuthing. This tended to be the response of most people, but in this instance Hollander had been the one to bring it up.

When he turned his face to Urbino, he smiled. 'You know what I'd like to see?' he said. 'If you don't mind, that is.'

'What?'

'Your gondola. It seems to have stopped raining, for a while at least. I'll help you take off the tarpaulin and put it back on.'

'Let's go down,' Urbino said.

As they were walking down the staircase, Urbino said, 'I'd take you out in it but Gildo isn't here and even if he were, I wouldn't impose on him. I've given him some time off. Not only because of the heat we've been having, but also because of the regatta. Maybe we can do it another time, after the regatta, and in better weather than this.'

Half an hour later, after seeing the gondola and examining the *felze* with a great deal of interest, this being the first time he had seen the small, detachable cabin outside of paintings and photographs, Hollander thanked Urbino and set out for the Gritti Palace on foot.

181

* * *

'So tell me, *caro*, did Nick enjoy himself after I left the two of you together?' the contessa asked Urbino over the telephone that evening from Asolo.

'He seemed to.'

Urbino described Hollander's visit. When he finished, he asked her what she thought of Hollander.

'I like him,' she responded without any hesitation. 'He's intelligent and interesting, and he has a good sense of humor. He reminds me of a cultivated sea captain.'

'I don't quite see that.'

'All that tanned skin and his bright blue eyes? And that bald head? All he needs are some side whiskers and a pipe. Well, maybe I got to know him better than you have so far. We had a nice talk over lunch. The more he told me about his stepfather the more I realized how unfortunate it is that we never had the opportunity to know him.'

'Hollander does talk about him a lot.'

'You somehow make that sound bad!'

'Do I?'

'Yes, you do. Don't you like him?'

Urbino decided to make a joke of it. 'I like him a lot better than I thought I would when I heard that he's Sebastian's friend.'

'Sebastian is a fine boy. That's not very nice of you.'

But Urbino could tell that the contessa was amused. She had her own criticisms of her young cousin.

182

'By the way,' Urbino said, 'did you mention anything to him about Albina?'

'Not a single word. I didn't even come close to a slip the way I did about Benigni. So you told him about them and he didn't know?'

'He gave every appearance of not knowing.'

'But you think he might have.'

The contessa sounded a little irritated.

'I have to keep an open mind, Barbara. Don't forget that although we don't know anything against him or anything that connects him to Albina, he inherited a veritable fortune. The apartment on the Grand Canal and everything in it, and from what he said, Zoll's house in Munich with Zoll's art collection.'

'All that's good reason for having killed Zoll. It has nothing to do with Albina.' The contessa drew in her breath sharply. 'But listen to me! Is this what you've brought me to? You—'

The contessa broke off, as if hesitant about voicing her thoughts.

'Listen, Barbara,' Urbino said in a placating tone, 'you might understand why I have to be open-minded and cautious – why *we* have to be cautious – after I tell you what I learned today before I joined the two of you for lunch.'

He gave an account of his conversations with Clementina and Perla.

'But I don't understand exactly what all this has to do with Nick,' the contessa said when he finished.

'Maybe nothing, but maybe something. And maybe a lot, at that. Of course, we already knew that he had a connection with Benigni, but we didn't know he had one, so to speak, with Albina.'

'So to speak? What does that mean?'

'It means that since Albina knew Zoll and Benigni, he could have known Albina – through them. But by saying that I get a little ahead of myself.'

'You are *too* far ahead of *me!*'

'Surely you see it, Barbara? When I said that I was suspicious about Albina's death and when we agreed that three deaths so quickly together were unusual, we had no idea that there was any relationship between the three of them.'

The contessa took this in without any immediate response. Then she said, 'But why are you so focused only on Nick Hollander?'

'I'm not.'

'Because there's the little *cartaio*,' the contessa pointed out. 'Benigni was her brother – her half-brother. And she knew Zoll and Albina.'

'Exactly.' Urbino paused. 'And Perla. She knew all three. She was providing Zoll with herbs.'

'And from Perla we can move to Romolo, I suppose?'

Urbino seemed to detect a slight ironic tone in the contessa's words.

'Yes.' He decided to take her words at face value. 'Following a certain line of logic we can, and should. To get back to Hollander, there's something I'd like you to do.'

'I'm afraid to ask what it is.'

'I'd like information on Hollander Tours. How they're doing financially. What kind of reputa-

184

tion they have. Who might be involved with the firm besides Hollander and his mother. It wouldn't be hard for your solicitor in London to find out information like that, would it? And if anyone knew he was looking for information, there would be no way to link it directly with you or me.'

'I could do that. Is it important?'

'It could be. We can neglect nothing that might bring us closer to the truth. And I think I'll get Rebecca's help with something else. She has contacts in Munich. She worked with a colleague on a project there. Several lawyers were involved. Maybe she can find out about Zoll's will. And meanwhile there are other angles to look into. No, I'm not focusing only on Hollander, but at the moment he suggests some of the most obvious angles. Because of the money, though I'm not saying that Zoll was murdered.'

'I'll ring Bascomb tomorrow,' the contessa said. 'But we shouldn't expect him to get back to me right away. It's the end of August. Most of his office is on holiday. It might not be until after the regatta that we hear from him. In the meantime, why don't you try to get these notions out of your head? Unless you think that there's some reason for urgency?'

'You know the answer to that. In situations like these, there always is. Or at least we must assume there is. Give my regards to Ausonio.'

Ausonio was the conte's nephew from Capri.

After his conversation with the contessa, Urbino called Rebecca Mondador. It didn't prove hard to enlist her help, and he didn't have to tell her more than he wanted or needed to. She was happy enough that her suspicions about his involvement in another case were confirmed and that she could be of assistance again.

That night Urbino took another corpse tour of the city, but this one was different from the one he had indulged in last week.

All the corpses on this night's tour were recent.

The rain had come to an abrupt stop before midnight, but now, as Urbino walked to Dorsoduro, there were dark, rolling clouds overhead. The city was the way he liked it. Empty, silent, serene. Urbino and the few other lone souls were like night guards making their rounds of the corridors of a vast museum after the crowds had departed. A sense of camaraderie passed between them as they met each other in the night.

Some of the *calli* were flooded, but tonight, so as not to impede him on his walk, Urbino had put on a pair of high boots he had bought last winter on a visit to relatives in Inveraray. And in his pocket was a flashlight.

His first stop on his tour was a dank *sottoportico* between the Grand Canal and the Campo Santa Margherita. The odor of decaying garbage and cat urine was faint but unmistakable. Pools of water were like black glass.

He played his flashlight over the uneven stones. A cigarette butt was wedged against one wall of the *sottoportico* where the pavement was slightly higher. There was no way of knowing whether it had escaped the cleaning that Giulietta had given the area yesterday or had been

186

deposited afterward. The cigarette had not completely disintegrated, and still revealed traces of blood-red lipstick.

This was where Albina had died. Since she hadn't collected her keys from Da Valdo, she must have died on her way to the café – unless she had decided to return before getting there or been forced to do so by the storm or something else – or someone.

Information about the physical disposition of the body on the stones might have helped him to determine whether Albina had been on her way to her apartment or from it when she had died. This was the kind of information only the police would have. On some of his previous cases, Urbino had established contact with the Questura, and received the begrudging help of the commissario. But he didn't think that the circumstances of this case would encourage Commissario Gemelli to open an investigation or give Urbino any information. And his relationship with the man had always been strained, at best, even when Urbino had helped him solve crimes for which Gemelli took most of the credit.

Urbino stared down at the stones. Had Albina been rushing? She had been tired that night, so he doubted that her pace had been any quicker alone than it had been with him. No one seemed to have seen her. But Urbino believed that she had encountered at least one person, and in far less pleasant circumstances than Urbino had been encountering people tonight.

Some person, either a stranger or an acquaintance, possibly even a friend, had been responsible for her death.

Urbino had an instinct about these things, and something wasn't right. The fact that someone had broken into the Gonella apartment only reinforced his suspicions. Some person, for some reason, had been after Albina, and had caused her death, had benefited from it. This person was now happy she was dead, but not just happy. Surely also anxious and worried about being exposed.

Albina might very well have died from a heart attack – although he wasn't convinced of even this – but a heart attack could be provoked, either intentionally or not. Fright, a struggle, a fatigued woman trying to run away from danger – any of these could have brought about a crisis in a person who had a heart condition. And he shouldn't forget about the possibility that some substance, under the guise of a medication or, unbeknownst to her, put in her food or drink, could have caused the attack.

With one last look at where Albina had spent her last moments, Urbino left the *sottoportico*.

He walked down the dark, silent *calli* and through the deserted Campo Santa Margherita and the Campo Barnabà to another spot in Dorsoduro. It was at the far end of the quarter, in the area between the Palazzo Guggenheim and the Salute. He walked down half its length until he stood beneath a building that was in the process of being renovated. The lower windows were boarded over. A temporary metal door had been installed at the entrance. All the shutters

188

had been removed. No construction scrim had been placed around the building.

He leaned back and looked up toward the roof. He could make out an empty space about three feet wide in a corner of the top story. The sky was visible through it. Transferring his gaze to the pavement, he saw a small pile of bricks placed neatly on the ground and against the side of the building.

This was the *calle* that Clementina Foppa had mentioned, the one where her half-brother had been killed. Surely the storm would not have been able to do any damage to Benigni if the parapet stone had been secured properly. He examined the pavement again but couldn't see any evidence of the stone, which must have broken into pieces. The fragments must have been cleared away.

The young man's family would be entitled to compensation if there had been any neglect and it could be proved. Once again Urbino regretted that he didn't have access to information that was in the possession of the police. They surely would have looked into the matter because of the circumstances and its implications for compensation to the victim's relatives.

Who would get the money if money were forthcoming? Clementina? Their mother? Benigni's father? Were Benigni's mother and father still alive? Urbino knew little about Benigni and nothing about his family.

But no money would be forthcoming – no money *should* be forthcoming – if Benigni hadn't died as the result of an accident. What this could mean, of course, was that the person or persons who would benefit might not be happy if his death was determined not to have been caused by negligence.

That Urbino was entertaining this latter possibility was not because he was a person who found it difficult to accept fateful accidents. Not at all. He had often been in the wrong place at the wrong time. In fact, his parents had died in an automobile accident precisely because of that. An unexpected visit had delayed their departure from the house. Yes, accidents did happen, and sometimes they were the most bizarre ones imaginable like what they said had happened to Luca Benigni.

But Urbino found it difficult to accept that two people who knew each other, albeit not well, had died within such a short time of each other in the manner in which everyone seemed to believe they had.

Albina Gonella because her weak heart had failed her at that particular moment on that particular night.

And Luca Benigni because a large falling building stone had smashed his head.

These two deaths in themselves would have provoked his curiosity. But it was the third death – or rather the *first* one – that was making him look beyond appearances for some kind of criminal cause.

It was this first death that brought him to the final stop on his corpse tour this evening. It was a building a mere five minutes' walk from the one where Benigni had met his death.

It was on the main *calle* that continued toward the Salute. One of the palaces along its length had a little gated courtyard verdant with plants. But he passed the courtyard, turned off the *calle*, and walked down the much narrower passageway to the Grand Canal and stood on the wooden *traghetto* landing. On the other side of the water was the Gritti Palace Hotel.

There, alone, beside the dark mirror of water, Urbino surprised himself by breaking out in his untrained tenor:

> *Tantum ergo sacramentum*
> *Veneremur cernui*
> *Et antiquum documentum*
> *Novo cedat ritui*
> *Praestet fides supplementum*
> *Sensuum defectui*

These Latin words from a Vesper hymn that were part of the Roman Catholic ritual of Benediction, with their simple, haunting melody, would spring unbidden to Urbino's lips during odd moments, especially when he was lonely, nervous, or preoccupied.

With the notes fading around him, Urbino turned to look up at the second story of the building to his left. This was Zoll's apartment – or now Nick Hollander's apartment. Beyond its dark windows the first death had taken place. Urbino and the contessa had seen the German a short time before he died, and he had looked gravely ill. There was no question of that. If he had died the next day, neither of them would have been surprised. Death had been planted in his gaunt, bloodless face.

But Urbino told himself that he should be consistent in his logic – or was it his illogic? If it was possible that a woman could die because of the weakness of her heart but could also be, in some sense, the victim of foul play, it was equally possible for a man to be murdered even if he had only a few days, hours, or minutes of natural life left – especially a man who had a disease and was taking medication. Zoll had been dying of leukemia, but this didn't mean that he had died *from* leukemia.

Urbino needed to consider this possibility and look into it, if only to eliminate it. As he had said to the contessa, they should not neglect anything that would bring them closer to the truth.

Urbino's eyes moved away from Zoll's apartment to the Gritti Palace across the water. Lights were showing from two of the windows on the second floor. Hollander had said his suite looked out on the Grand Canal. Perhaps he was standing behind one of the lit windows at this moment, gazing toward the apartment he was determined to sell. The possibility made Urbino move backward into the shadows as he had drawn away from the library window when Maisie Croy had examined the Palazzo Uccello.

Hollander was the most obvious link between Zoll and Luca Benigni. And he apparently had been a major beneficiary of his stepfather's will. Urbino hoped that Rebecca would be able to clarify this area more.

But what might Hollander's link to Albina

Gonella be? For Urbino could not shake the conviction that Albina's death was connected to Luca's.

As he was considering this, standing there next to the Grand Canal and near the building Zoll had died in, some other names surfaced. Among them were Clementina Foppa and Perla Beato. Both had known all three of the recently dead.

Yes, there was a great deal to consider.

Urbino walked out of the *calle* and turned in the direction of the Salute. He would take the vaporetto back to Cannaregio from there. He was afraid that he wasn't going to be able to do what the contessa wanted him to do. There seemed to be no way he could get what she had called his 'notions' about Albina out of his head.

In fact, his head was now filled with many more notions of a similar nature that were both directly and indirectly related to the original one.

He entertained them for the trip up the Grand Canal, sitting in his preferred place in the stern of the boat. He watched the scene unroll on both sides as his notions unfolded themselves darkly in his mind.

# Part Four

## Benevolent Deceptions

# Eight

Three pieces of a puzzle. Albina Gonella, Luca Benigni, and Konrad Zoll. How did they fit? Might they fit at all? Could the puzzle be one he was imagining? Was he seeing things he wanted to see and not what was actually there?

These were some of the questions that were Urbino's almost constant companions in the hours and days subsequent to his corpse tour.

For a few days he confined himself to the Palazzo Uccello, turning over the pieces of the puzzle and examining them.

He spent a lot of time up on the *altana*. After the rainy days sunny weather had returned but without the debilitating humidity and storms that had cursed the city earlier in the month. He always brought his Goethe with him, but despite the wisdom and the beauty of the German's impressions, he couldn't remain focused on them for long without drifting off into his own impressions and speculations. He would stare out across the roofs and chimneys at the stretch of the lagoon in one direction or the deep gash in the buildings that was the Grand Canal in the other direction. Natalia came up to the *altana*, not to put out the laundry or to water the plants, but to try to coax Urbino down into the more

197

sociable quarters of the house. But he assured her he was fine where he was. She left each time, shaking her head at the strangeness of the American.

Then, one morning, a week before the regatta, when the weather was all too obviously returning to its earlier, insufferable pattern, he set out from the Palazzo Uccello to try to answer some of the questions that had been swirling in his head during all those hours on the *altana*.

The path he pursued in the following days was as improvised as it was calculated, a combination that often led him to unforeseen, remarkable destinations.

He warned himself, however, that sometimes they were also unwelcome and even dangerous ones.

'A glass of Cynar, Signor Urbino?' Giulietta asked Urbino as she preceded him into the living room.

It seemed that he would have to endure more of the distasteful drink. But he was surprised when Giulietta brought only one glass in from the kitchen, went to a sideboard, and poured him a generous portion. The situation became clear after she seated herself next to him on the sofa. A half-filled glass of the liqueur stood on the little table next to her beside one of her crossword puzzle books, several sharp pencils, and an open packet of cigarettes. Urbino hadn't noticed cigarettes in the apartment on his previous visits. Was it possible that she had taken up the habit – or returned to it – as a consequence of Albina's death and the break-in?

'Everyone in the house feels as safe now as the Contessa Barbara in her palazzo,' she said. 'As for me, I'm not waking up every two minutes during the night and listening for every strange sound.'

'That's good to hear. But it still must be difficult to be alone now that Albina is gone.'

'Yes. I miss her.'

Giulietta's voice quavered. She had hardly any make-up on, none of the bright red rouge and lipstick she had worn when he had visited her last.

'Of course you do. All those years.'

Urbino picked up the Cynar and took a little sip.

'I've been thinking of something that might make you feel better. It should make us all feel better, you, me, the contessa, all of her friends.'

'What's that?'

It was one of the things that Urbino had run through his mind on the *altana*.

'You know I'm a writer, Giulietta,' he began.

'Yes. I saw your books in the window of a store near the piazza, but they were in English.'

'I've decided to write a little book. About Albina. And I'll write it in Italian.'

Giulietta took a sip of her Cynar.

'A book about Albina?'

'Yes.'

The book would be a convenient excuse for the questions he planned to ask her and others about Albina. Most of the people acquainted with him knew about his sleuthing, and any questions

199

from him following a death risked being placed in this category. But they were also aware of his biographies, and by drawing attention to this other interest of his, he might be able to throw them off the track or slightly disorient them, enough to gain an advantage. But aside from being a camouflage, the book would also be a nice tribute to the woman. He would have it published at his own expense.

Jesuits had put their stamp on Urbino at an impressionable age. Their habit of sophistical argumentation and explanation was much too expedient to abandon, especially in his detecting work. His plan to write something about Albina was a good example, but he needed Giulietta's approval to make the truthful deception as smooth and effective as possible.

'But Albina wasn't famous,' Giulietta protested. 'She didn't do anything important.'

'That's true. She had a simple life, but simple lives can be the most beautiful. They can be very interesting in their own way. Most of the saints were simple people.'

Urbino feared that he might have gone too far. Giulietta didn't strike him as a pious woman. Even if she had been, it was doubtful whether she would have been sympathetic to any comparison between her sister and a saint or, in fact, any comparison that placed Giulietta in a lesser light. Urbino tried to repair whatever damage he might have done.

'What I mean is that everyone is important, even in apparently little ways. Think of the good things you've done for others and for your sister that have made their lives better. Just the other day you went out and cleaned up the area under the *sottoportico* where Albina died. You did it for her, didn't you?' Giulietta gave him a somewhat distracted nod in response. 'That's the kind of thing I'm talking about.'

Giulietta straightened her shoulders and cleared her throat.

'Well, I suppose that would be nice of you, to write something about Albina.' But there wasn't much enthusiasm in her words. She drained her Cynar. 'How can I help you?'

'I'd like to know as much about her as you'd care to share with me. You spent your whole lives together. I won't be able to put most of it in the book but the book will only be the better for knowing as much about her as possible.'

Giulietta poured herself another glass of Cynar and stared down at the viscous brown liquid. She seemed to be assessing what he had said.

'I'll tell you whatever you want to know,' she said as she looked up. 'My memory is good. Albina used to ask me about things that had happened in the past. I remembered our first house better than she did, even though I'm five years younger. We lived in Castello, behind the Church of San Francesco di Paola.'

This was the quarter where the Le Due Sorelle was located. Giulietta went on to describe the apartment in detail, and even – it seemed – every doll the two sisters had ever had. Nursing his Cynar, Urbino soon settled back for a narrative of Albina's life in which Giulietta played a central role.

It was a familiar tale: two daughters brought up in a strict family, sheltered, uneducated beyond secondary school, unmarried, without any close relatives after the deaths in quick succession of their parents. They had moved to the smaller apartment in Dorsoduro twenty years before, where it would appear they had lived together in a shifting alliance of intimacy and distance, affection and coolness. Neither had ventured far from Venice. They had once made a trip together to Rome, and on another occasion to distant cousins in Treviso. Giulietta had once spent a week alone in Vienna with an Austrian woman, a regular visitor to Venice whom she had met through her dressmaking business which at one time seemed to have been much more flourishing than it was now.

Contrary to what was usually the case, Giulietta's account became less detailed as it moved to more recent events. He listened, he nodded, he sifted what she was saying for anything relevant. Nothing particular struck him.

'I noticed that Clementina Foppa was at the funeral Mass,' he said when Giulietta had finished. 'Did Albina know her well?'

'I don't think she ever mentioned the name. Which one was she?'

Urbino described the *cartaio*. Giulietta shook her head.

'I don't remember her.'

'She told me something very nice about Albina,' Urbino continued. 'She helped a German man who was sick. She went all the way from Florian's to Perla Beato's *erboristeria* to get herbs for him. Like the ones she brought you.'

'I'm not sick! She should just take them back!'

'I didn't mean that you were sick, Giulietta, but this German was. Unfortunately, he died about a week before Albina did. Clementina Foppa's brother was the German's friend. That's how she met your sister.'

'Was he at the funeral?'

'I'm afraid not. He's dead, too.'

Urbino explained the circumstances of Benigni's death.

'I remember some of the neighbors talking about it,' Giulietta said. 'The young die all the time.'

From the tone of her voice this reality seemed to give her some satisfaction.

'Did Albina mention it?'

'No.'

Giulietta stared at him. With some effort, Urbino downed a large portion of his Cynar and stood up.

'I should be leaving, Giulietta. I've taken up enough of your time.'

'But you didn't write anything down.'

'Like you, I have a good memory. By the way, would you mind identifying Albina's keys? I mean each individual one.'

Giulietta's eyes shot to a sideboard near the door where the keys lay in a ceramic plate.

'I know you told me to put them in her room with her other things,' Giulietta said. 'I forgot. But I suppose it makes no difference. What do the keys have to do with your book?'

'They don't have anything to do with it. It's because the apartment was broken into.'

'Yes. Don't forget that my apartment was broken into.'

It was almost as if she said it to remind him of the break-in.

She got up and brought over the keys. She had no trouble identifying them.

'This one is for the old lock on the door downstairs.' She pinched the largest key and held it up. 'And this one is for the old apartment door. And the small one – the one that's bent a little – this one opens her jewelry box.'

'Was it broken into?'

Giulietta nodded.

'But everything was still in it. Sentimental things. No real gold and diamonds or things like that.'

'But yet she kept the box locked.'

'Sentimental things can have value. Usually greater value than a diamond. A diamond can be replaced.'

'Of course. But maybe she put something valuable in the box lately.'

'We weren't the kind of sisters who told each other everything. And I didn't snoop.'

Urbino, a snooper himself – for what else was he doing now? – somehow doubted that Giulietta had made it easy for her sister to keep whatever secrets she had had over the years. But Giulietta had confided no secrets about Albina as far as he could determine. Was this for her sister's sake or for her own? The same question could be asked about her assiduous cleaning of the *sottoportico*.

Albina might have put something in her jewelry box for safekeeping. She could have been going back for her keys to prevent someone from opening the jewelry box if the keys fell into the wrong hands.

But did this make much sense? Someone *had* broken into the box. No key had been needed. But people didn't always think logically. And Albina might have been worried about someone who could open her jewelry box stealthily, with a key, not about someone who would go to the extreme of breaking into it.

If something had been taken – something that Albina had wanted to keep safe and that Giulietta was unaware of, or so she said – it was probably the motivation for not only the break-in but also Albina's death.

Urbino thanked Giulietta and left.

Fifteen minutes later Urbino was going over what he had learned from Giulietta as he entered the Campo San Barnabà on his way to the vaporetto stop. A group of sunburnt backpackers was gathered in front of the church. They had put down their loads and were trying to eat their *gelati* before the brightly colored ice cream melted in the heat.

A tourist stopped Urbino to ask directions to the Ca' Rezzonico. While he was explaining the route the man should take, a young woman walking toward him through the Sottoportico del Casin drew his attention. She looked familiar but the shadows of the passageway obscured a clear view. When she emerged, he identified her as Clementina Foppa. The *cartaio* seated herself at an outdoor table in the café across from the church.

'Isn't this a pleasant surprise!' she exclaimed when Urbino went up to her table. 'Why don't you join me? Oh, let me take that away.'

She freed the chair across from her of a small paper bag with the name of her shop on it. Urbino glimpsed the edge of a book-sized object wrapped in marbled paper. Clementina placed the bag on the ground by her feet.

'Thank you.' Urbino sat down. 'How are you?'

'Well enough, in this heat.'

Her pale face, with its bright red lipstick, was beaded with perspiration. She took a lace handkerchief from the pocket of her dark gray dress and patted her face. Urbino noted again her unusually muscular arms.

When the waiter came, they both ordered *limonate*. Their table provided a good view of the small square, with its church, its canal, and the bridge that led to the Fondamenta Rezzonico. The square was busy with shoppers, children, strollers, and tourists. Most of the latter spent no time to enjoy the charms of the spot, however, but surged on toward the Piazza San Marco.

Clementina said that the Campo San Barnabà was her favorite square.

'Do you live near here?' Urbino asked.

'No. On the Giudecca near the Fondamenta di San Giacomo.'

It was a working-class quarter near the Church

of the Redeemer.

'I like the Giudecca, but don't get there often enough. What is it about this square that you like so much?'

'The vegetable and fruit barge, for one thing.' She looked in its direction and then gazed up at the campanile. It had a conical spire, the only one of its kind in the city. 'The spire, too. But most of all because the square is small and compact. I like small things. Maybe because I'm small myself.'

'Petite.'

'A nicer way of putting it,' she said, giving him an appreciative smile. 'And San Barnabà has an interesting history. Many of the impoverished nobility used to live here. My mother would tell us stories about how poor her noble family had become over the centuries.'

The waiter brought their *limonate*. They sipped them in silence as they looked out into the square. When a dog came up to their table and started to nose at Clementina's bag, she picked it up, drew another chair over to their table, and put the bag on the chair.

'It's a gift for Albina Gonella's sister,' she said. 'I don't know her but I thought she might appreciate a visit. I'm stealing a little time away from my shop. She lives near here.'

Urbino found it a little unusual that Clementina was making a visit of charity to someone she didn't know. But why shouldn't she want to reach out to someone else who had just suffered a loss? Surely it was a natural, commendable instinct. And she had gone to Albina's funeral. It

207

could be a way of remembering her own dead.

'Yes, near the Campo Santa Margherita,' Urbino said. 'I was just there myself. But I confess I wasn't thoughtful enough to bring a gift.'

Clementina flushed.

'It's nothing much. Just a book for photographs. After my father died, my mother and I found comfort in organizing photographs of him. It brought back so many good memories. Luca and I did the same thing after she died.' She paused and bit her lip. 'And now I'm doing the same thing with photographs of Luca. But it's – it's not going so well, I'm afraid.'

Her face went awry in a childish manner, as she struggled to hold back tears. She gave in and started to weep. She took out her lace handkerchief and wiped her eyes.

'Excuse me,' she said. 'But it's hard. I pretend it isn't sometimes. I have to go on, the shop and all. But Luca was the only person I had. The only one who meant anything to me. We had different fathers, yes, but he was my brother in all ways.'

'I'm really very sorry. I know how difficult these things are from my own experience. There's always comfort in sharing grief. What about Luca's father?'

'He died a few years ago after he moved to California. So Luca and I only had each other – except for a few distant cousins of his in Sicily.'

Tears welled in her eyes again.

Not only did Clementina's tears stir Urbino's sympathies but they also made it difficult to ask her any questions that might disturb her further.

He sat looking at her as she dried her eyes. She

returned the handkerchief to her pocket, and took out a pack of cigarettes. They were the same brand as the one on the table beside Giulietta's sofa.

'I hope you don't mind?' she said.

'Not at all.'

She lit a cigarette with a small gold lighter and inhaled deeply, blowing the smoke over her shoulder. Her eyes glistened with tears.

'It's strange, isn't it?' she said. 'The way a person can break down with almost a complete stranger. It's somehow easier. It surprises me though. There it is, right under the surface ready to come out.'

'It hasn't been long.'

'I don't think it'll ever be any different. I've never got over my mother's death. Now with Luca gone, what it's done is to reopen that wound. It never healed. But listen to me! I'm sorry about all this. I really am.'

'Believe me, I understand. And it's never good to keep these things in. It's good to talk about our dead, no matter how painful.'

Urbino was being both sincere and calculating, and where one shaded into the other wasn't clear even to him. But if he didn't think it would be appropriate to ask Clementina questions, this didn't mean that he couldn't encourage her to talk.

The *cartaio* stubbed out her cigarette. She had hardly smoked it. Her bright red lipstick had left its mark on the tip.

'You're right,' she said. 'It does help to talk. I don't think people realize that until they have a loss. Everyone thinks they shouldn't mention the dead, that you don't want to talk. When Zoll died, poor Luca came over and cried like a baby. Knowing that it was going to happen didn't make it easier for him. All he wanted to do was talk about Zoll, tell me the things they had done, little things. He'd probably still be doing it now if ... if he hadn't died himself.'

She took a deep breath. Urbino thought she was going to cry again. But she took out another cigarette and lit it.

'My brother was a very devoted boy, Signor Macintyre. Would you believe that he gave up his studies in March at Ca' Foscari to take care of Zoll? He was very bright. He could have done a lot with his life.'

'What was he studying?'

'Art history. That's how he met Zoll. They both loved art. They struck up an acquaintance at the Accademia Gallery. That was two and a half years ago.'

She stubbed out her cigarette, this one even less smoked than the previous one. She drank some of her *limonate*, looking at Urbino in what seemed to be a calculating manner.

'I think you will understand this,' she said after she put down the glass. 'Understand and not judge him. Luca was gay. It was never a problem for me, or for our mother. His father didn't know. Luca didn't think he would understand. Zoll was the first man that Luca had a serious relationship with. He told me everything – well, almost everything. He loved Zoll. He would have done anything for him. And Zoll felt the same way. Or he certainly seemed to from what I could see. I was happy for Luca.'

There were so many questions that Urbino wanted to ask, but so far Clementina had made questions unnecessary. Perhaps she wasn't finished yet.

She gave Urbino a faint smile.

'Maybe you think that Luca was after money. He wasn't. He wasn't manipulating Zoll. I'm not saying that Zoll wasn't generous, but it's not as if he made him a beneficiary in his will.'

'Are you sure of that?'

'Well, that's what Luca told me a few weeks before he died. Zoll had a son that he left almost everything to.'

'A stepson.'

'I thought it was a son.'

'He's in Venice now. Have you met him?'

Clementina looked at her wristwatch.

'Met him? What reason would I have to meet him? Excuse me. I should get to Giulietta's apartment. My assistant is looking after the shop. She's trustworthy enough, but you know how it is.'

She seemed eager to leave now. Perhaps she had said more than she wanted, but if she had, it hadn't been because Urbino had been asking her a lot of questions. She had seemed more than willing to confide in him, at least on her own terms.

The vaporetto to San Marco was packed with tourists, some of them already drunk at this hour. Urbino stood next to the railing, not even thinking about trying to make his way to the stern.

An elderly Venetian couple stood beside him, complaining that they couldn't find a seat. Urbino offered to arrange two bags so that they might sit on them, being sure to use the Venetian dialect, but the husband declined.

'We're getting off at the Accademia,' he said.

Urbino chatted with them about the upcoming regatta until they reached their stop, which was the next one.

For the rest of the ride down the Grand Canal, Urbino tried to block out all the noise and confusion around him by looking at the buildings along the banks, but he projected his gaze at the upper stories and roofs of the buildings. In this way he was able to remove himself further from all the activity surrounding him, getting a view of one *altana* after another, chimneys, tiles, and high-perched balconies. He stared for long moments at the Gothic balcony of Zoll's apartment and the windows of the Gritti Hotel across from it before refreshing his eyes with the white dome of the Salute.

He ran over in his mind what Clementina had told him about Luca. He regretted that he had not felt comfortable asking her more questions. Their conversation had left him with the feeling that he had been, in some sense, manipulated. But in what direction and for what motivation he didn't have the vaguest idea.

Either he had just had the benefit, with little effort on his part, of some frank confidences or some of the most calculated, even fabricated, of revelations.

Urbino managed to find a small, unoccupied table at Florian's, but it was not in the Chinese Salon. It was in the Liberty Salon beyond it, with its arched vault ceiling, gleaming wood wainscoting, and hand-painted mirrors. He ordered red wine and a selection of cheeses. When the waiter brought them on a silver tray – bigger than the marble top of the table – Urbino detained him for a few minutes. The waiter, whose name was Marcello, worked on the same daytime shift that Claudio did.

He confirmed that Zoll had frequented the café over the past year, but usually in the morning. They preferred the Liberty Salon to any of the other rooms.

'And they always ordered the same thing. A bottle of mineral water for the German with a slice of lemon and either Prosecco or Corvo for his young friend.'

Marcello told him that he had been working the day Zoll had fallen ill and Albina had gone to Perla's shop. He shook his head regretfully when Urbino informed him that Zoll was dead.

'I could see that the poor man was sick. He could hardly walk sometimes. His friend had to help him.'

'His friend is dead, too. Maybe you heard about it. He was killed when something fell on him during the first of the two big storms we had.'

Marcello raised his eyebrows in evident surprise.

'No, I didn't know. Life is strange, signore.'

'It is indeed. Did either of them prefer any of the waiters more than the others?'

'They were kind with us all. The Italian was the one who usually paid. From his own pocket, and always with a generous tip. But it must have come from the German. One of the customers took a photograph of the three of us – me, the German, and his friend. Around the Feast of the Redeemer. I've been waiting for them to return to show it to them. I have it with me all the time.'

'May I see it?'

From the pocket of his white jacket, he withdrew the photograph.

It showed Zoll and Benigni in the Liberty Salon. Marcello stood behind the handsome young man, who had a bright smile on his dark face. Benigni had his arm around Zoll's shoulder. The German was smiling and looking not at the camera but at his companion.

'Would you mind if I borrowed this for a few days? I'd like to show it to the German's stepson. He's in town to settle some affairs. It will make him feel good to see his stepfather enjoying himself so soon before he died.'

When Urbino finished his wine and cheese, he went upstairs to the foyer between the restrooms. The same woman who had been there the other day was sitting at the little table with the plate of coins. He asked her questions similar to the ones he had asked Marcello. She said that she had never noticed that Zoll and Benigni had favored one of the staff more than another.

As Urbino was edging his way out into the arcade through the press of people, his name was

214

called behind him. It was the manager.

'When you were here the other day I forgot to mention that Albina left an envelope with me for Claudio. It has the name of the Cassa di Risparmio di Venezia on it.' This was a local savings bank. 'No address or anything else. I telephoned him a few times but couldn't get him. You'll probably see him before I do. Would you tell him about it? Albina left it the last day she was here, the day before she died.'

On his walk back to the Palazzo Uccello, Urbino stopped for a coffee at Da Valdo's. He showed the photograph of Zoll and Benigni to Valdo, who said that he didn't recognize either of them.

The waiter gave him a different response.

'The older man, no,' he said, 'but I remember the younger one very well.'

'Was he a regular?'

'He came once that I know of. Alone. An Italian. A Venetian, I think, though he didn't speak in dialect. It was the night of the first of those big storms, right before it swept over us. Rushed inside and sat in the back. And left in a hurry, too, almost without paying for his Prosecco. As if he had suddenly remembered something. Or maybe he noticed the storm was coming and wanted to get home before it hit.'

'Was Albina Gonella here at the time?'

'Oh, no, signore, it was at least an hour before she usually came.'

'No, Signor Urbino, I haven't seen him since yesterday,' Gildo said when Urbino asked him

215

about Claudio. The gondolier was shining the gondola by the water entrance. 'He said it's a good idea for us to rest a while. He's staying home. He isn't the way he usually is. It's because of Albina.'

Gildo's good-looking face was shadowed by concern.

'Are you sure you wouldn't like to go out today?' he asked. 'It will calm me. It's not as hard as it seems, you know.'

'You're wrong, Gildo. It's much harder than you make it seem. You make it seem almost effortless, but I know better than that.'

'But sometimes I get more energy by using energy.'

Urbino smiled.

'An interesting theory. But if we go out, it won't be during the heat of the day.'

Urbino went to the library. He lay on the sofa, stroking Serena, who fell asleep on his lap. He soon joined her in a fitful nap. An hour later, he got up, took a shower, and had a cup of espresso.

He took the San Marcuola *traghetto* to Santa Croce. From there it was a quick walk into San Polo, where he had agreed to do an errand for Natalia before seeking out Claudio near San Tomà.

The shops had reopened after the siesta. Urbino stopped to talk to some of the shop owners and residents before delivering the small box of cookies Natalia had baked that morning. They were for an elderly woman friend who lived near the Campo San Polo.

He stopped for a glass of white wine at a café

in the square, gazing at the isolated campanile and the small fountain where pigeons and other birds were bathing and drinking. He imagined the bull runnings, parading soldiers, masked balls, and religious sermons that had once animated the large, open space. One of the palaces to his right had been the scene of the Baron Corvo's disgrace, when his hosts had evicted him in the middle of winter for having used their friends and acquaintances in his writing.

Maisie Croy had been impressed that Urbino knew how many bridges there were in Venice. As he had joked, his mind was full of useless information, and more of it started to surface about the square. But he pushed aside these odd bits and pieces to think about Claudio and the envelope that Albina had left for him at Florian's.

Did the envelope contain money? It would seem to be a likely possibility since the envelope came from a savings bank. But why would Albina be giving Claudio money, either in cash or in the form of a check?

Urbino realized how little he knew about Claudio. He had been considering the waiter as a kind of stable element in the picture, fixed mainly by his apparent devotion to Albina. Urbino's contacts with him had been limited to his services at Florian's, two private recitals that Romolo had arranged, and his friendship with Gildo. Lately he had seen more of him than usual because of the upcoming races. From what he and the contessa knew, Claudio was alone in the city, but had a widowed mother and younger sister living in Rovigo.

Claudio impressed him as a sensitive, refined man whose ambitions extended beyond Florian's. Urbino couldn't believe that he would be content to remain there as a professional waiter for the rest of his life. But Florian's was a good place from which not only to view the world that passed through its doors and under its arcade, but also to contrive a move into that different world. At least two waiters that Urbino and the contessa had known over the years had profited from being placed there. One had married an older American woman and sometimes returned with her during carnival. The other had been given the management of a coffee house in Berlin.

Claudio might think that his fine singing voice – or his good looks – would eventually free him from waiting tables, even though working at Florian's was considered a pinnacle for most waiters in the city.

These thoughts about Claudio began to be intruded upon, without any perceivable connection at the moment, by a piece of history about the Campo San Polo. The square had been the scene of a bonfire of vanities similar to Savonarola's forty years later in Florence. It had consumed elegant gowns, make-up, ribbons and bows, masses of hair extensions, and cages of pet birds. Because Urbino was of a somewhat ascetic temperament despite the evident luxuries and pleasures of his life, he always felt ill at ease, as he did now, when contemplating the story of the bonfire. Surely, in a different time and a different place, he might have had some of his beloved objects put on the flames.

Or, more frightening, he himself might have thrown the objects of others into them.

Because these thoughts tugged at his mind with such persistence as he finished his wine, he couldn't help but feel that they had some relevance to his thoughts about Claudio – or if not to those about Claudio specifically, then to his inquiry into the circumstances of Albina Gonella's death.

What this relevance might be, if any, eluded him. But when he left the café, he felt a sense of greater unease than he had felt when he had sat down.

# Nine

Claudio's apartment was above a vacant shop in a narrow *calle*. He was the only occupant of the brick-exposed building that was in the process of extensive renovation. The other tenants had been forced to move, but Claudio had insisted on staying despite the inconveniences and even dangers. From what Urbino understood, he was no longer paying rent. This very well could be Claudio's main motivation for staying, since he seemed to spend a lot of his money on clothes and opera tickets at La Fenice and La Scala, often staying in Milan for a few days.

The doorway leading from the *calle* was warped, flaking, and broken. One set of hinges was rusted off. Urbino was often amazed at how insecure many buildings in the city were. The Gonella sisters and the other tenants of their building had lived with a damaged street door, and Claudio was doing the same although his situation was different since he should have already left the premises. Living rent-free had its price.

Urbino pushed open the door with little trouble and started up the dark staircase. Claudio lived on the second floor. Two of the marble steps near the second-floor landing were damaged. Chunks of marble had split off.

The sound of workmen's shouts came from the floor above.

'Signor Urbino,' Claudio said in surprise when he opened the door to Urbino's knock. His face was sad and fatigued.

Claudio's living room was crowded with objects, but not because it was particularly small. It was actually large, with a high ceiling and two wide windows at one end. But Claudio had brought into it all the furniture from his bedroom – two armoires, a large triple pier glass, and a disassembled bed whose mattress leaned against the back of the sofa. A pillow and rumpled sheet on the sofa indicated that Claudio was using it as his bed. On the far side of the living room was a doorway, but the door that should have been attached to it was placed against the wall a few feet away.

Beyond the doorway the late afternoon light pouring through the unshuttered windows revealed brick walls stripped of most of their plaster and a twisted brass chandelier hanging from exposed wiring.

The most unusual feature of the bedroom was its floor. Except for a small area immediately in front of the door and along the wall to its left the floor was non-existent. Only a few wooden beams and boards remained, and these were sagging in some cases and splintered in others. Very little of the layer of mortar that had once covered the wood remained. Large flat pieces of stone leaned against the left wall. One stone had broken into smaller pieces the size of bricks.

'My God, Claudio, this is a dangerous situation.' Urbino went over to the bedroom doorway. Twelve feet below was the stone floor of the *pianoterreno*. 'You need some kind of barrier. Let me help you move the door across the bottom, at least. We can put it on its side.'

'Don't trouble yourself. I'm careful. Two of the workmen said they would nail some boards across tomorrow.'

Claudio's voice didn't have its usual resonance. It was slightly weak, even hoarse.

'Be sure they do it,' Urbino insisted. 'Do you want me to speak to them?'

'No. I'll take care of it. Please sit down. Would you like something to drink?'

'No, thank you. I'm fine.'

When Urbino and Claudio were seated across from each other, Urbino mentioned the envelope that Albina had left for him at Florian's.

Claudio seemed puzzled, even surprised

'Do you know about it?'

'No. And my phone hasn't been working for the past ten days because of the construction. An envelope? An envelope from the Cassa di Risparmio? Oh,' he said after a few moments. 'It must be money. Yes, yes, that's what it is,' he said more emphatically. 'I gave her fifty euros a week before she died. She was running short. But I didn't want it back. I told her that.'

'But why did she leave it at Florian's?'

'She knew if she tried to hand it to me, I would have refused to take it. Well, I'm not going to take it back. I'll buy flowers for her grave and have a Mass said at the Carmini.'

'He did? I'm sorry to hear about it, but why are you asking me about him?'

Urbino gave him the same reason as he had given to his colleague earlier, that Zoll's stepson was in town and would appreciate knowing about his stepfather's life in Venice. 'I didn't speak with them much,' Claudio said, 'only when they came to my station. They usually went to the Liberty Salon. You can tell his stepson that he made a good impression on all of us. They were both kind. And now they're both dead.'

'So you know that his friend died?'

'Luca Benigni. I saw his death notice. I forget where. I thought of how lonely the German must be. Who died first?'

'The German.'

Claudio's eye drifted toward the stripped bedroom and the wall with the pieces of stone.

'Better than the other way,' he observed.

Urbino agreed that it was.

He found it strange that Claudio hadn't asked him how Benigni had died, but perhaps he already knew. He might have asked someone about it when he read the death notice. Where had he seen it? Clementina Foppa lived on the Giudecca. Most likely she would have placed the notices there, possibly also at Ca' Foscari where Luca had been a student.

As Urbino went down the dark staircase a few minutes later, he paid attention to his footing and looked out for the broken steps. On his way to the *traghetto* that would return him to Cannaregio, he became more convinced with almost

'That would be nice. When will you go by to get it?'

'Not before the regatta. It would make me sadder than I am. And I don't want to go to Florian's and see everyone there. I need to concentrate on doing a good job in the race.'

'I could get it for you. I pass that way a lot.'

'I'll get it myself.' Claudio said this in a clipped voice, but then added more gently, 'Are you sure you wouldn't like something to drink?'

'Maybe just a glass of water, if you don't mind.'

While Claudio was in the kitchen, Urbino made a visual survey of the room. Beneath all the confusion, he perceived an order of sorts.

No clothes were strewn about. The dark green drapes on the two windows were pulled to each side and tied neatly with a gold-colored cord. On a side table stood a small cylinder of marbled paper in the popular red *fiammato* pattern of the notebook he had bought for the contessa at Clementina's *legatoria*. It held pens, pencils, a letter opener, scissors, and a pair of sunglasses. On the wall beside the entrance to the hallway was a collection of photographs in inexpensive, uniform wooden frames. From a distance Urbino made out a woman in a wedding dress standing beside a man. Urbino assumed they were Claudio's parents. Another photograph was a group shot of Claudio and his colleagues in front of the entrance to Florian's.

An old bookcase between the room's two windows held three large boating trophies on its top shelf. On the other shelves were books, mainly paperback editions, arranged neatly. Urbino wished he could get up and examine the titles. Books could provide a great deal of information about their reader. *Regate e Regatanti* lay on the end table by the sofa.

Claudio returned with two glasses of water. When Claudio was sitting down again, Urbino said, 'I thought you'd like to know that I'm writing a little book about Albina. It will have anecdotes about her life from her sister and her friends. I'd like you to contribute. Giulietta already has. So if you have anything special you'd like to share about her, this could be a good way to do it.'

'There are many things I could tell you. But if you don't mind, can we do it after the regatta?'

Urbino was disappointed but he said that would be fine.

'And when you're talking to other people who knew Albina,' Urbino said, 'would you mind telling them about my book and encouraging them to see me? I'm not going to sell the book. I'll give copies to all of you once it's finished and published.'

Urbino took a sip of water.

'If I could find some people who might have met her from the time I walked her home until the French couple found her body, it would be a big help. I had just left her with Giulietta when I bumped into you. I was with the three women, the ones who needed to get to the train station?'

'I remember.'

'You were going in the direction of Santa Margherita, it seemed. Did you see her?'

224

'No.'

Claudio held the glass in his two hands, looked down at it.

'Did you see anyone you know on your w people who also knew Albina? They might seen her. She was going back to Da Valdo f something she had forgotten. That's wher had her heart attack.'

'Poor Albina! A lot of people were wa around. Maybe some of them knew her an her. I don't know about that. I went th Campo Santa Margherita, yes, but I turned from the Canalazzo. I went to the Zattere. to walk there at night. I walked along it hour, by myself, and then came back here home before the storm came. I knew it v the way and didn't want to be caught in it

Urbino nodded. He noted to himself th was more information than he had ask Claudio got up and went to one of the w and looked out.

'Well,' Urbino said, 'I hope I can find so who saw her during that time. It would b forting, aside from whatever it might co to my little book.' He finished his wa stood up. 'By the way, about somethi entirely. How well did you get to know t man man, the one who came with his friend to the Liberty Salon? He was a re the morning for more than a year. I don if you know it, but the German died re

Claudio turned from the window. pression was tight with strain but he did surprised.

225

each *calle* he went down and each bridge he passed over that Claudio was hiding something.

Half an hour later as Urbino was taking the *traghetto* back across the Grand Canal to San Marcuola, he went over what Claudio had told him.

According to Claudio, his walk the night Albina had died had taken him away from where the French couple had found her body near the Grand Canal. He had strolled down the wide promenade of the Zattcre along the Giudecca Canal. It was just the kind of thing that Venetians did in the evening, especially in the summer. Urbino favored the walk himself.

It was possible that Claudio hadn't been on the Zattere that night or had been there for only a short time, and had then gone somewhere else. He could have sought out Albina or have met her along the way.

But Urbino was at a loss to imagine what might have happened next in either case. And might Claudio have known about the envelope then? Could he have wanted to get it from Albina, not knowing that she had already left it at Florian's? He had seemed surprised to learn that she had left something for him. But if he had wanted to get the envelope from Albina that night, wouldn't he be eager to collect it now that he knew where it was? If so, Urbino doubted that it would be for the fifty euros that Claudio said was in the envelope. Nor could he be sure that Claudio wouldn't take the first opportunity to go to Florian's and collect it.

227

If Claudio had met Albina the night she died and it had been a friendly meeting, he would have mentioned it, wouldn't he have? And if it hadn't been friendly, then what might have been the reason for the conflict between them? Urbino kept coming back to the envelope, or rather its contents.

To all appearances the relationship between Claudio and Albina had been one of mutual love and respect. And Claudio seemed deeply affected by her death. It was possible, of course, that he could be both deeply affected by it and feel in some sense responsible for it.

After all, wasn't this close to the way Urbino felt himself? Wasn't he still reproaching himself for what he had done – and not done – when he was with her before she died?

But Claudio hadn't been the only person Urbino had seen that night in Dorsoduro who knew Albina.

Earlier, he had met Romolo and Perla Beato on the Accademia Bridge. They had spoken for a few minutes and then they had rushed off so that Romolo could catch the vaporetto for Santa Lucia to get the Padua train. Perla had then set off in the general direction of their apartment in Dorsoduro.

But it was also the direction of the Campo Santa Margherita, near where Albina had lived and died – and the Zattere where Claudio had said he was taking a walk.

Urbino's boat reached the San Marcuola landing. The air was cooler than it had been earlier in the day. A gentle breeze blew from the lagoon.

'That would be nice. When will you go by to get it?'

'Not before the regatta. It would make me sadder than I am. And I don't want to go to Florian's and see everyone there. I need to concentrate on doing a good job in the race.'

'I could get it for you. I pass that way a lot.'

'I'll get it myself.' Claudio said this in a clipped voice, but then added more gently, 'Are you sure you wouldn't like something to drink?'

'Maybe just a glass of water, if you don't mind.'

While Claudio was in the kitchen, Urbino made a visual survey of the room. Beneath all the confusion, he perceived an order of sorts.

No clothes were strewn about. The dark green drapes on the two windows were pulled to each side and tied neatly with a gold-colored cord. On a side table stood a small cylinder of marbled paper in the popular red *fiammato* pattern of the notebook he had bought for the contessa at Clementina's *legatoria*. It held pens, pencils, a letter opener, scissors, and a pair of sunglasses. On the wall beside the entrance to the hallway was a collection of photographs in inexpensive, uniform wooden frames. From a distance Urbino made out a woman in a wedding dress standing beside a man. Urbino assumed they were Claudio's parents. Another photograph was a group shot of Claudio and his colleagues in front of the entrance to Florian's.

An old bookcase between the room's two windows held three large boating trophies on its top shelf. On the other shelves were books, mainly paperback editions, arranged neatly. Urbino wished he could get up and examine the titles. Books could provide a great deal of information about their reader. *Regate e Regatanti* lay on the end table by the sofa.

Claudio returned with two glasses of water. When Claudio was sitting down again, Urbino said, 'I thought you'd like to know that I'm writing a little book about Albina. It will have anecdotes about her life from her sister and her friends. I'd like you to contribute. Giulietta already has. So if you have anything special you'd like to share about her, this could be a good way to do it.'

'There are many things I could tell you. But if you don't mind, can we do it after the regatta?'

Urbino was disappointed but he said that would be fine.

'And when you're talking to other people who knew Albina,' Urbino said, 'would you mind telling them about my book and encouraging them to see me? I'm not going to sell the book. I'll give copies to all of you once it's finished and published.'

Urbino took a sip of water.

'If I could find some people who might have met her from the time I walked her home until the French couple found her body, it would be a big help. I had just left her with Giulietta when I bumped into you. I was with the three women, the ones who needed to get to the train station?'

'I remember.'

'You were going in the direction of Santa Margherita, it seemed. Did you see her?'

224

'No.'

Claudio held the glass in his two hands and looked down at it.

'Did you see anyone you know on your walk, people who also knew Albina? They might have seen her. She was going back to Da Valdo to get something she had forgotten. That's when she had her heart attack.'

'Poor Albina! A lot of people were walking around. Maybe some of them knew her and saw her. I don't know about that. I went through Campo Santa Margherita, yes, but I turned away from the Canalazzo. I went to the Zattere. I like to walk there at night. I walked along it for an hour, by myself, and then came back here. I was home before the storm came. I knew it was on the way and didn't want to be caught in it.'

Urbino nodded. He noted to himself than this was more information than he had asked for. Claudio got up and went to one of the windows and looked out.

'Well,' Urbino said, 'I hope I can find someone who saw her during that time. It would be comforting, aside from whatever it might contribute to my little book.' He finished his water and stood up. 'By the way, about something else entirely. How well did you get to know the German man, the one who came with his Italian friend to the Liberty Salon? He was a regular in the morning for more than a year. I don't know if you know it, but the German died recently.'

Claudio turned from the window. His expression was tight with strain but he didn't look surprised.

225

'He did? I'm sorry to hear about it, but why are you asking me about him?'

Urbino gave him the same reason as he had given to his colleague earlier, that Zoll's stepson was in town and would appreciate knowing about his stepfather's life in Venice. 'I didn't speak with them much,' Claudio said, 'only when they came to my station. They usually went to the Liberty Salon. You can tell his stepson that he made a good impression on all of us. They were both kind. And now they're both dead.'

'So you know that his friend died?'

'Luca Benigni. I saw his death notice. I forget where. I thought of how lonely the German must be. Who died first?'

'The German.'

Claudio's eye drifted toward the stripped bedroom and the wall with the pieces of stone.

'Better than the other way,' he observed.

Urbino agreed that it was.

He found it strange that Claudio hadn't asked him how Benigni had died, but perhaps he already knew. He might have asked someone about it when he read the death notice. Where had he seen it? Clementina Foppa lived on the Giudecca. Most likely she would have placed the notices there, possibly also at Ca' Foscari where Luca had been a student.

As Urbino went down the dark staircase a few minutes later, he paid attention to his footing and looked out for the broken steps. On his way to the *traghetto* that would return him to Cannaregio, he became more convinced with almost

226

He breathed the air deep into his lungs as he walked across the *campo*. When he reached the *rio terrà* behind the church, he stopped and took the photograph of Benigni, Zoll, and Marcello from his pocket. He studied Benigni's face closely.

Yes, he said to himself. There *was* a definite resemblance to Claudio. Possibly Claudio himself hadn't noticed it. Most people could be oblivious to their resemblance to others unless the other person was famous or someone pointed out the resemblance.

All the way to the Palazzo Uccello, Urbino considered various scenarios that could have developed as a result of this resemblance if someone had mistaken one man for the other.

One of them, Luca Benigni, was dead. Did this mean that the other, Claudio Balbi, was in danger? Or did it mean that he was safe, now that Benigni might have died in his place?

'I know you too well, *caro*,' the contessa said over the telephone a few hours later. 'You aren't waiting until after the regatta. You're pursuing your notions about Albina.' She paused. 'To be honest, I think I like you even better for not doing what I said.'

'You make it too easy for me to be disobedient. And I've been very much so. All day today. And it's been a very full day, perhaps even a fruitful one.'

He gave an account of what he had learned from the time he had visited Giulietta, finishing with his conversation with Claudio. He confided

229

some of his speculations.

'Before Clementina Foppa told me her brother was gay, I wondered about what Hollander thought about the relationship between Benigni and his stepfather,' Urbino said. 'Now it's even more of an issue – that is, if he knew.'

'I'm sure he did. Didn't you suspect as much about Zoll and Luca Benigni?'

'Yes.'

'It's probably what broke up Zoll's marriage.'

'Yes, but not his relationship with Luca. The marriage was over before Zoll came to Venice. But I suppose Nick could have resented Luca.'

'Not necessarily Luca,' the contessa corrected, 'but his stepfather, because of the divorce, or rather the circumstances that led to it.'

'I know you criticized me for being suspicious that Hollander always says good things about Zoll but it could be a way of concealing his resentment.'

The two friends then passed on to the resemblance between Claudio and Luca.

'Yes, I suppose they do resemble each other,' the contessa said, 'though I didn't get a good look at the poor young man that one time. They're certainly the same physical type.'

'I think you'll see the resemblance more when I show you the photograph.'

'Are you suggesting that someone mistook Benigni for Claudio? Then Claudio might be in danger.'

'He could be in danger, yes. But it's also possible someone could have mistaken him for Benigni.'

'Who might this someone be?' she said.

'I'm trying to work that out. And there's another possibility. Someone might have been intentionally taking advantage of the resemblance.'

'Where might that lead us?'

'I'm not sure where any of this will lead us.'

'Maybe it would help if we knew what's in the envelope Albina left for him,' the contessa suggested.

'Of course it would, if only to eliminate possibilities.'

'Do you really feel that Claudio is hiding something?'

'Yes, but whether it has anything to do with Albina's death is something else entirely.'

One of Urbino's hardest tasks, whether in his sleuthing or his biographies, was trying to uncover the secrets that existed in everyone's lives and deciding which of them were significant and which ones he should reveal, which ones he should leave alone.

'Before I forget, Barbara, would you do me a favor and invite Giulietta Gonella and Clementina Foppa to your regatta party? It would give me the opportunity to talk to them again in pleasant circumstances. And having them all under the same roof would give me an opportunity to observe them. I know it's late to ask someone but you should be able to find a way around it.'

'You have greater faith in my social skills than I do. And I don't even know Clementina Foppa. It will seem strange.'

'Why not mention how impressed you are with her work? Tell her how the notebook was a gift for you.'

'Aren't you devious! All right, I'll ring her, and Giulietta, too. But they've both had a death in the family. They might decline.'

'I doubt that.'

'You have everyone figured out. Is that how it is?'

'Hardly. That's one reason why I'm planning to talk with Oriana.'

'Oriana?'

'Well, she knew Albina, and she knows Claudio – and Perla and Romolo Beato. And if anyone would notice a resemblance between two good-looking men, it would be Oriana.'

'You're right there. But did she know Benigni?'

'It's another thing I'd like to find out.'

'So you're thinking of rounding out an already busy day by making a trip to the Giudecca?'

'Not tonight. Tomorrow. Actually, I was wondering if you'd like to go out in the gondola tonight? The weather's turned cooler. About eight thirty or nine? We could talk these things through a bit. You know how that helps. It's a lovely evening.'

'I thought Gildo needed to rest.'

'He keeps insisting that going out in the gondola would be good for him.'

'And you can't deny the poor boy the pleasure of being of service to you! You've found the perfect victim. It sounds romantic, *caro*, but I need to stay in tonight. Why don't you ring Nick

Hollander? He said how envious he was of your gondola. Unless you'd rather float along by yourself and drift from one thought to another, as you like to do so much – *too* much,' she corrected.

'Maybe I'll see if he's free. And speaking of Hollander, have you heard anything from Bascomb about Hollander's tour company?'

'I doubt if we're going to hear anything until September.'

'There's something else I'd like you to do involving Hollander, if you don't mind.'

'What?' the contessa asked, after hesitating a few moments.

'I know there isn't much time between now and the regatta, and how busy you are with the preparations,' he began. 'And you have to entertain Ausonio...'

'You're building up to something that I don't think I'm going to like.'

'I'd like you to arrange an outing to Torcello with Hollander. The three of us. In your motorboat. For Tuesday morning, if possible.' Tuesday was the day after tomorrow. 'And be sure that you include Ausonio. Hollander was in the Capri Regatta last year. They can talk about Capri. Do your absolute best to persuade him. Will you do that?'

The contessa didn't respond right away. When she did, her tone was coolly disapproving.

'You are trying to get me to be deceptive in some way. No, don't tell me how. But I can sense it.' She paused. 'If I say I'll do it, it's only because I know it must be important. Yes, I'll

233

ring him. We'll have an outing. I'll even pack a picnic lunch. How's that for cooperation?'

There are few things more enjoyable than a gondola ride on a mild summer evening, especially when it's your own private one and you don't have to worry about the cost of a fifty-minute glide. Although Urbino might have preferred different company, he couldn't have found anyone more appreciative than Nick Hollander was proving to be.

'It's not the same city seeing it from a gondola,' Hollander said as Gildo's warning *'Hoi!'* echoed from the buildings around them and the boat turned into the Canalazzo.

Hollander was dressed in a beige linen suit and a white shirt that showed off his tan. He didn't look as fresh and rested as he had looked at the restaurant and the Palazzo Uccello. He was a little haggard, and the lines seemed more prominent on his weather-beaten face. 'The view from the water is always a different view, but Venice is a special case. The first time I saw it was from the water. I took a boat from Piraeus. Enchanting.'

It was a little past nine o'clock. The cloudless sky above them was a deep, dark purple and sprinkled with stars.

Urbino had said he would bring the gondola to the Gritti Palace, but Hollander had insisted on coming to the Palazzo Uccello on foot.

'It will make up for the idleness,' he had said. He had brought a chilled bottle of champagne in an ice-filled carrying case and two champagne glasses as well as a chilled bottle of mineral water for Gildo.

At Urbino's request, Gildo had removed the *felze*. To be enclosed together in the small cabin would have been more intimate than Urbino – and Hollander, perhaps – would have liked. It would also have put an unnecessary barrier between themselves and the scene they were enjoying now.

For the first part of their slow advance through the waters of the Grand Canal, there were no serenading flotillas of gondolas anywhere in sight, but only lone ones like their own, and even these had only two occupants taking advantage of the romantic hour. The boats zigzagging the Canalazzo from one stop to another only added to the charm of the scene, their wakes giving Gildo little trouble in his maneuvering and providing his passengers with only a slightly more exaggerated version of that rocking motion that is one of the delights of riding in a gondola.

An occasional motorboat might make the maneuvering a little more difficult and the rocking more energetic, as was happening now as they passed beneath the façade of the contessa's palazzo, but still the champagne in their glasses was in no danger of spilling out.

Urbino pointed out the Ca' da Capo-Zendrini to Hollander.

'It's even grander than it looks in the photos Sebastian showed me,' Hollander said. 'Such marvelous detail. Look at that frieze of lions.'

'All of these palaces were designed to be seen from the water. They show their best side to the

Grand Canal. The land entrances are rather uninspired. You might have noticed the same thing with my building.'

'By the way, why is your place called a palazzo, but Barbara's isn't? Many big buildings in Venice are called "Ca", I've noticed.'

'It's an abbreviation for "casa", house. A Venetian usage.'

'I never thought the Venetians would indulge in understatement,' Hollander said, 'but it's appropriate for Barbara's palazzo, being British as she is. She's looking after a fellow Brit quite well. The outing to Torcello on Tuesday is a great idea. And it'll be nice to meet her nephew.'

'So you'll be going with us?'

'Yes. I'd go even if I had already seen Torcello.'

'You'll love it. "The Mother of Venice". I'll enjoy showing you the mosaics in the basilica. And if we're lucky we might be able to go to the top of the campanile. There's a great view of the lagoon.'

Urbino was about to say more but he held himself back. He didn't want to risk making Hollander suspicious once the outing materialized.

The gondola slid through the dark waters toward the Rialto Bridge, Gildo's oar making a gentle, soothing plash on those occasions when the sounds around it didn't overwhelm and absorb it. Soon after they drifted past the Ca' da Capo-Zendrini, Urbino was tempted to draw attention to the ornate Ca' d' Oro, with the marble tracery of its façade emphasized tonight by the illumination within the deep recesses of its loggia, but he kept his silence. He didn't intrude on Hollander's thoughts as his companion looked out at the scene.

Hollander occasionally asked him a question about one of the buildings, canals, or bridges. What soon developed was a pleasant rhythm of long periods of silent observation and much shorter ones of explanation of the passing scene. And in this manner they reached the Rialto Bridge, draped in red banners and lined with tourists.

By this time the water had become thick with gondolas. Seven passed them in a row.

'*Ciao, Venezia! Ciao Venezia! Ciao! Ciao! Ciao!*' The tourists clapped and chanted the refrain along with the singer, a stout man in his fifties, and to the accompaniment of an accordionist.

People waved to Urbino and Hollander from the parapet of the bridge. They entered beneath the high structure where the sound of the gondola's passage was softly echoed against the stone. When they emerged, they took in the scene of the animated diners in the arbor restaurants and the people strolling along the quays and crowding the vaporetto stops. Up above the crowded pavements, the painted shutters of the wide windows had been thrown open, and gave them glimpses of high ceilings, ornate Murano chandeliers, and rich interiors in which occasional figures and moving shadows could be seen.

Hollander had a rare and admirable quality, at

least from Urbino's point of view. He could remain silent and still, and not make the other person feel uncomfortable, and he seemed in no way uncomfortable himself. After leaving the Rialto behind, there was a long interval of silence that corresponded to the stretch from the white marbled Palazzo Grimani on one bank to the Palazzo Balbi, with its two obelisks, on the other.

'This is where the finishing line of the regatta will be,' Urbino pointed out. 'Between the Palazzo Balbi and the Ca' Foscari. A floating stand for the judges is set up. It's called the *machina*. This is where Napoleon watched a regatta. He stood on the balcony of the Palazzo Balbi.'

'So we'll be following an imperial tradition on Sunday.'

Urbino smiled.

'And it's interesting also that Balbi is the last name of Gildo's rowing partner – Claudio Balbi,' Urbino said. 'He's a waiter at Florian's. Barbara and I think that he resembles your stepfather's friend Luca Benigni. You might have been struck by the resemblance if you've ever seen him at Florian's.'

'They say that each of us has a double. No, I don't believe I've even noticed him. If I had, maybe I wouldn't have seen the same resemblance. Here, have some more.'

Hollander poured champagne into Urbino's glass.

'Thank you,' Urbino said. 'It's very good. My stomach has been bothering me,' he added, putting another element in place for their trip to Torcello. 'The champagne has settled it a little.'

'That's good. This Balbi, the waiter, is he related to the Balbis of the Palazzo Balbi?'

'I doubt it – or if he is, it's very distant.'

When they went past the Ca' Foscari, Urbino drew attention to its Venetian Gothic façade.

'It's the seat of the university,' he said. 'Benigni's sister told me that he was a student here.'

'Interesting,' Hollander said as he looked at the building. But since he said nothing more, it was unclear whether he was referring to Urbino's comment or the frieze of *putti* with the Foscari coat of arms.

After a few minutes Urbino broke the silence.

'I expect Gildo and Claudio to make a good showing in the race. They're both fine rowers.'

Hollander shifted his attention to the poop, where Gildo seemed to be moving them without difficulty down the waterway.

'He's certainly doing this in fine form,' Hollander observed. 'So what changed your mind about giving him a rest?'

'*He* changed my mind, in a fashion. He said it would be better for him to spend some time rowing the gondola before the regatta.'

'And who were you to argue? Who are *we* to argue, I should say. This is really splendid. I enjoy taking everything in like this. It's so peaceful. It encourages meditation.'

Urbino interpreted Hollander's comment as a polite suggestion that they have less conversation. Urbino had more than made up for his own earlier quietness by saying a lot, perhaps even too much. For the rest of their ride down the Grand Canal, he only spoke when Hollander asked him a question. These questions were few, and always about the scene before them. The silence between them seemed particularly pointed as they passed beneath the dark Gothic windows of Zoll's apartment. Across the water, the terrace of the Gritti Palace, filled with patrons, was brightly lit.

When they were going past the Salute, Urbino suggested that they have a nightcap at Harry's Bar. Hollander agreed, somewhat reluctantly, it seemed.

But the place was crowded on this summer night, with four tables occupied with noisy groups from the film festival.

Their time together at Harry's was an anti-climax to their gondola ride down the Grand Canal. Hollander did most of the talking, and told Urbino about two prospective buyers for Zoll's apartment, one an American couple, the other a Milanese businessman.

The men parted in the *calle* outside Harry's, with the expectation of seeing each other on the morning of their outing to Torcello.

# Ten

At ten the next morning Urbino decided to drop by and see Romolo Beato at his studio. It was only a few steps from the Zattere near the Church of the Gesuati. In front of the entrance to his building a black-clothed figure had prostrated itself on the pavement, a large, black kerchief concealing the face, a dirty hand extended upward for a coin. It was difficult to determine whether it was a man or a woman. They were appearing with more and more frequency throughout the city. Urbino dropped some coins in the hand before ascending the staircase. He received no acknowledgement. Many people found the figures frightening because of their anonymity and the way they remained in a suppliant position for hours in the same place, never, it seemed, raising their head. But Urbino was certain that they somehow observed everything that was going on around them.

Romolo's studio, which was on the third floor, was simple, clean, and uncluttered, as befitted the man himself – or at least the man beneath all the changes Perla had made in his lifestyle and attire during their five years of marriage.

When Beato had graduated from the Conservatory, he had enjoyed modest success in Naples and Rome as a tenor soloist. He had also performed in Barcelona and Düsseldorf in touring ensembles. But for the past twenty years, except for occasional local performances, most of them non-professional, he had devoted himself to vocal teaching and coaching, and he was one of the best.

Romolo had just finished with a student and had ten minutes before his next one.

'Urbino, how nice! Have you come to improve your tenor?'

The portly Romolo was dressed in a flattering peach-colored shirt and gray trousers. His thick white hair had been recently cut.

'Maybe someday. There are so many things I'd like to improve and develop, or learn for the first time. Botany, Chinese, carpentry – I've got a long list.'

'So little time, yes, but don't become discouraged. You're still young. Sit down.'

They seated themselves on a small sofa that provided a view through its tall windows of the line of buildings and churches on the Giudecca.

'Would you like some water?'

He indicated a pitcher and glasses on a table by one of the windows.

'No, thank you.'

'Are you sure? Perla adds a herb or tincture or something to it that's supposed to make it more soothing to the throat. Let's say that it doesn't do any damage. Not that I know of, anyway.'

Romolo was looking at him with a slightly puzzled expression on his round, open face, evidently curious about the reason for this

242

unexpected visit.

'I've come about Claudio.'

Romolo visibly flushed and glanced away from Urbino momentarily toward the window.

'Claudio? Is something the matter?'

'That's what I thought you might help me with. I saw him yesterday. He wasn't looking well. He's brooding about Albina. I'd feel remiss if I didn't ask you if you had noticed anything during his lessons. The voice reveals a lot.'

'Even more than you think.'

'When I saw you before you went to Padua, you said he was progressing well. That was the night Albina died.'

'The only time I've seen him recently was at the funeral. Of course he wasn't in control of his voice, but there was a tremendous amount of emotional pull in it. He's always had a problem of using his air correctly, and we've been working on his approach to the high notes. He's a little afraid of them. He had a lesson scheduled two days after the funeral, but he never came.'

'I'm worried that he might be wearing himself out between his grief over Albina and his practice for the regatta.'

'Grieving can be a problem, but as far as physical exercise is concerned, it's the best thing for him – or for his voice. *Vox sano in corpore sano*. If your body isn't healthy and strong, your voice won't be either.'

'It's lucky for your students, then, that they have Perla.'

'What do you mean by that?'

A shadow of annoyance crossed Romolo's

face.

Urbino gestured toward the pitcher and glasses.

'Her special tinctures and herbs.'

'Oh, I see! Ha, ha! Yes, Perla and I are a good team.'

The door from the hallway opened and a stout young man entered.

'I'll be with you in a few minutes, Antonio.'

The student went over to the pitcher and poured himself a glass of water.

'I'll leave you to your student, Romolo. Keep up the good work.'

'You, too.'

Urbino wondered what work of his Romolo had in mind. It seemed that this would be an excellent opening to mention his book about Albina, partly as a way of showing Romolo that he interpreted his comment as referring to his biographies and not his sleuthing. Romolo listened with interest and observed that it was a good idea and an excellent way of remembering the dead woman. He said that he had a few things that he'd be happy to pass on to Urbino.

'Let's get together after the regatta,' he said, 'at our place.'

He promised that he would tell Perla about Urbino's project.

But Urbino had the opportunity to do this himself a few minutes later when he met Perla on the landing below Beato's studio. She was carrying one of her shop's small bags.

'Getting your tenor strengthened?' she said

with a smile. She looked cool in a lime green dress. Her blonde hair was loose around her shoulders.

'Romolo said the same thing.'

'That's what happens after you've been married for a while. You start to think and say the same things.'

'There are a lot of things worse than that.'

'Well, we haven't reached the familiarity breeds contempt stage. We'll skip that one completely, if you don't mind. So tell me, is it guilt that brings you here to Romolo's studio?'

'Guilt?'

'You're the kind of fair-minded person who would be consumed with it. You pay my shop a long overdue visit, and now you've done the same with Romolo's studio. That's very considerate of you – and very clever.'

'You've caught me. But I came for a good reason. It's for Claudio's sake.'

Perla flinched almost imperceptibly.

'Claudio? Is he here?'

She looked up in the direction of the closed door of Romolo's studio.

'No, but I wanted to ask Romolo how he thought Claudio was coping with things. Albina's death, I mean. What I was hoping to hear was that he was keeping to his lessons. I know how important his singing is to him, and if he can focus on that, I think it would be a big help.'

'He has the regatta to take his mind off things.'

'True, but that has its own share of worry.'

'Well, I hope Romolo was able to put your

mind at ease.'

'Not really.'

What might have been alarm, quickly controlled, widened Perla's brown eyes.

'Oh, no, it's not his fault,' Urbino said. 'It's just that he said he hasn't seen Claudio since before Albina died. It seems he canceled his last lesson and apparently hasn't rescheduled.'

'Let's hope he's fine.'

'Have you seen him recently?'

'Me? No, not since the funeral, and I don't go to Florian's as much as I used to.'

'He's been taking some time off from Florian's recently.'

'How good for him. But excuse me. I have to get moving. I want to drop this off.'

She indicated the package.

'Something to make the water more beneficial for the singers?'

'So Romolo told you? Yes, that's what it is.'

Before Perla could dash up the stairs, Urbino mentioned the book on Albina and how Romolo had said that the three of them would get together after the regatta.

'We'll have a whole evening of remembering her,' Perla said. *'Ciao!'*

As Urbino approached Ca' Foscari, the main seat of the university, after leaving Romolo's studio, he kept his eye alert for any of Benigni's obituary notices. He didn't see any.

He passed through the Gothic doorway into the courtyard with its covered wellhead and stone staircase, and went into the building's *androne.*

The palazzo's large ground-floor hall that extended to the water entrance, where the Grand Canal sparkled in the sunlight on the other side of high glass doors, had been renovated from its original Gothic style. It was now a serviceable, soulless space. He searched a bulletin board, but he didn't find Benigni's death notice.

He went to the window of the *portineria*, with its computers and video cameras, and asked what floor the Department of Art History was on.

He was told that it had moved to another location closer to the Zattere. The man took out a small map and pointed out the palazzo, which was next to the Church of the Ognissanti.

Fifteen minutes later Urbino was in the entrance hall of the building examining a wall plastered with posters and notices. He must have looked a little disoriented, for a middle-aged woman with straight white hair in a blunt cut came up to him. She was carrying a pile of art books.

'Excuse me, signore, may I help you?'

He explained that he had come on behalf of the sister of one of the art students.

'Luca Benigni. He died recently. She – we – want to be sure that his colleagues and teachers know about it. I thought there was a notice here, but I haven't found it, not so far.'

'Oh, yes, Luca.' Her voice rang with a depth of feeling. 'There was a notice on the board, with his photograph. There was another one in the neighborhood somewhere. The one here must have been removed.'

'You knew Luca?'

'He took my lecture course on Giotto. Why not tell his sister to put up another obituary in a few weeks? The returning students will have a chance to see it. And please give her my condolences. He was a nice boy and quite intelligent. He did an excellent project about the Scrovegni Chapel.' The Scrovegni Chapel, which had a beautiful and historically significant fresco cycle by Giotto, was in Padua. 'I didn't see much of him during the last academic year, though.'

'He was taking some time off. He had a friend who was ill.'

She nodded.

'Signor Zoll from Munich. He contributed books on Islamic art to our library and came to some of my lectures. I heard that he's very ill. He paid us a visit in April. He didn't look well. Do you know how he's doing?'

Urbino told her that Zoll had died at the beginning of the month, about a week before Luca.

'I'm very sorry to hear that, but I can't say that I'm surprised.' She gave Urbino her card. 'As soon as we get another obituary, I'll see to it personally that it stays up long enough to give people a good chance to see it. And I'll put up something about Signor Zoll. He was very well liked. Please give my condolences to his relatives.'

After leaving the building, Urbino walked around the neighborhood, first in one direction, then another, looking for the other death announcement that the professor had seen. This quarter was on one of the routes between the Zattere and Claudio's apartment near San Tomà. It was a likely area for him to have seen the notice.

Urbino eventually gave up his search. He saw a lot of graffiti, but no obituaries for anyone. The second storm had battered the city after Clementina had put up Luca's. In all likelihood, it had blown away or, as had happened at the Department of Art History, it had been removed.

'How did your ride with Hollander go?' the contessa asked Urbino that afternoon at the Ca' da Capo-Zendrini. They were in the *salotto blu*, a small, comfortable room whose furniture, art, and bibelots reflected the contessa's sensibility. She had returned to Venice with Ausonio a few hours earlier to prepare for the Torcello outing tomorrow.

'It was a nice evening. He's looking forward to the Torcello trip and meeting Ausonio. Where is Ausonio? I'd like to say hello.'

Urbino started to move from the mantelpiece.

'You'll have to wait until tomorrow. He's in the conservatory. Once he gets involved in there, you have to drag him out physically. He'll have a long list of what we're doing wrong with the plants.'

Ausonio was a fanatical amateur botanist, someone Urbino admired, given the fact that he wished he knew more about botany himself. The contessa had one of the best private conservatories in the city. A horticulturalist from Padua made regular visits. She had kept it more or less the way it had been before she had married the conte. Whenever Ausonio visited, he was full of criticisms and recommendations.

'I hope things go smoothly tomorrow,' she said, straightening a cushion beside her on the sofa.

'Even at this time of year Torcello will be rather quiet. Not like Venice anyway, or even Murano and Burano. Don't worry.'

'I *am* worrying! And it's not about Torcello. It's about you! The more I think about this trip, the more I feel that you're making me complicitous before the fact or something like that.'

She made a sound of exasperation and diverted her gaze from Urbino to the Veronese over the fireplace above his head. It showed a golden-haired, bare-backed Venus dividing her attention between two handsome bearded swains beneath a lush tree. It was one of the Conte Alvise's wedding gifts to his new wife. The contessa always found comfort in contemplating it, mainly, Urbino assumed, for its pleasant associations. In any case, although he liked Veronese, the painting wasn't quite to Urbino's taste. It struck a note of discord in the intimate room and seemed a peculiar choice of subject for a wedding gift.

'Yes, complicitous,' the contessa repeated when she looked back at Urbino. 'I don't know how or why. I don't want to know.'

'Ignorance is usually not a defense,' Urbino joked.

'I can see I'm not going to get anywhere with
250

you. Go home, and whatever you might be thinking of, think again, and don't do it!' She rose from the sofa. 'Pasquale will bring Ausonio and me to your place at eight thirty tomorrow morning.'

'Perfect.'

'You'll be there, won't you?' the contessa asked pointedly.

'I'll be waiting for you at the water entrance, most eagerly.'

As he had promised, Urbino was at the Palazzo Uccello's water entrance when the contessa's motorboat drew up the next morning. The contessa and Ausonio were sitting in the cabin.

'You're dressed for the day,' the contessa said when he seated himself beside her.

She was evidently relieved to see him in his boater and blazer. The heat of the day, as well as the desire to avoid playing his part too obviously, had made him decide against flannels and a red bow-tie, however.

'The same could be said about you, Barbara,' Urbino responded, taking in her flowing fawn and cream dress and the large-brimmed hat slightly angled on her head.

Urbino and Ausonio renewed their acquaintance. Ausonio was a tall, thin man in his late thirties whose fair hair was receding at the temples. He spoke excellent English. Urbino apologized for not having paid him a visit recently.

When they were approaching the Rialto Bridge, Urbino gave a small sigh and said, 'My stomach has been acting up for the past few days.'

The contessa looked at him sharply.

'It has? You didn't mention it yesterday.'

'You know how I am, Barbara. I don't like to complain.'

She raised her eyebrows slightly at this.

'To be honest, Urbino,' Ausonio said, 'you look a little peaked. Have you been sleeping well?'

Urbino, caught between gratitude to Ausonio for unknowingly helping him out in this way and irritation at a comment he didn't think was true, gave them both a weak smile.

'It kept me up last night. And it's been getting worse since I got up.'

'You have to take care of yourself,' Ausonio said. 'You look very pale.'

'Do I?'

The alarm in Urbino's voice was not feigned.

'Indeed, you do. Doesn't he, Barbara?'

'Urbino has always been pale.'

The contessa spoke with hardly any inflection.

Urbino said nothing more about the topic until they arrived at the Gritti Palace. Hollander waved from the terrace and a few minutes later he was getting into the boat. The contessa introduced him to Ausonio.

Once again Ausonio was a help to Urbino.

'I hope you're feeling more fit than Urbino,' he said to Hollander. 'He's under the weather. Just look at the poor fellow.'

By this point Urbino was beginning to think that he did indeed look as bad as he was saying he felt.

'What is it?' Hollander said.

'My stomach. I thought I'd feel better once I got out of the house.'

'I'm sorry to hear that.' Hollander examined Urbino's face more closely, something that Urbino always found discomfiting.

'You'll all have to excuse me,' Urbino said, 'but I won't be good company for a trip all the way to Torcello.' He arose from his seat. 'I'm going to have to go back home. I'm sorry, Barbara.'

The contessa wore an impassive expression.

'What a disappointment for you. For us all. Pasquale will take you back. It won't delay us.'

'No, please. That will make me feel guilty.'

'We certainly don't want that,' the contessa observed.

'I'll have a Fernet Branca here at the Gritti,' Urbino went on, 'and rest for a while. Fernet Branca soothes my stomach. Then I'll call a taxi.'

He stepped out on the hotel's landing platform.

'Enjoy yourselves,' he said to them in a quiet voice. 'I'll be fine.'

'I hope so,' the contessa said as Pasquale started to maneuver the boat away from the landing. 'Now that I look at you more closely, I agree with Ausonio. You look very poorly. Quite haggard.'

And, in this manner, the contessa managed to both retaliate against Urbino for his deception of her and collaborate in his own deception of Hollander.

Urbino did have a Fernet Branca on the Gritti terrace, as he had told the others that he would do. He also stayed there for a short while looking out at the Grand Canal. But he didn't call a water taxi when he left the hotel.

Instead he took the *traghetto* across the water to keep the appointment he had set up with the estate agent handling the resale of Zoll's apartment.

She was a tall, middle-aged woman who spoke excellent English. She was waiting for him in the *calle* outside the courtyard of the building.

When they were going up the stone staircase, Urbino said, 'As I mentioned on the phone, I would appreciate it if you didn't say anything to your client about it. I'm here on behalf of someone who prefers to keep her interest in the apartment unknown unless she decides to buy. She knows Mr. Hollander and, well, it could be embarrassing.'

'I understand completely, signore. In any case, it isn't our policy to let clients know every time someone is looking at a property. It can get their hopes up unreasonably. But your friend could have come herself. We wouldn't have revealed her identity any more than we will yours.'

'She might come at a later date, but she's busy at the moment. I know what she's looking for, and can save her time.'

When they entered the apartment, Urbino examined some of the details of the foyer while the woman went into the salon and drew aside the drapes and opened the doors to the balcony.

Fortunately, she was the type who left the client alone after mentioning a few things about the disposition of the rooms, the renovations, and the furniture and items that would be sold with the apartment. Or perhaps she realized, from what he had already said, that Urbino was the type of client who wanted to be left to himself. Whichever it was, she said that he was free to look around and then she went out on the balcony.

Urbino wasn't looking for anything in particular. He had no intention of opening the doors of all the armoires and cabinets in the bedrooms or raising the lids of the eighteenth-century chests across from the balcony. Neither did he have the time to do it.

But he had faith in his powers of observation, and perhaps even more faith in the law that the world revealed itself in plain sight and not in hidden corners.

The apartment had been thoroughly cleaned since he had been there with Hollander. This might have been significant if cleaning a property were not something invariably done before it was shown.

The urn with Zoll's ashes was no longer on the mantelpiece, and the breviary, the carriage clock, and the Pietro Longhi painting had been removed. Hollander must have taken these items, as well as some others that Urbino wasn't aware of, back to the Gritti Palace where the hotel would have put them in a secure place.

There was some disorder in the apartment that hadn't been there before. It wasn't a matter of a commode with marquetry of different woods that was no longer precisely aligned with the small tapestry above it or a carved mahogany armchair that was now cater-cornered in the salon instead of being directly against the wall.

It was less obvious things than these. The books in the darkwood case in the salon, which he had previously noted had been arranged neatly, gave evidence of having been disturbed. All of the books were still upright, but some of them were pushed to the back of the bookcase, while others occupied their original position closer to the front. Also, some of them had been turned upside down so that they were not uniform with the others and their titles could not be easily read.

In addition, the escritoire in the large bedroom no longer impressed him with its neatness that had betokened an organized owner. Instead, the pieces of stationery, letters, postcards, and colored index cards, which he wished he had the time and opportunity to examine, were haphazardly scrambled among the various pigeonholes. Previously they had been placed in much more orderly fashion. He risked pulling out a few items. For his efforts he found a thank-you note, in French, from someone named Sabine, for a dinner Zoll had given at the Danieli last Christmas, and a postcard that showed the leaning campanile of Santo Stefano, with nothing written on it. There was also a crossword puzzle in German, ripped from a newspaper, and completed in pencil.

One of Urbino's favorite Poe tales was 'The

Purloined Letter', with its philosophy of the best place to hide something being in plain sight. One of his cases had resolved itself along these lines, and he regretted he couldn't put it to the test again by examining all the items in Zoll's escritoire, but he restrained himself.

The misplaced books and the disarray of the escritoire suggested that someone had been searching the apartment. The most likely person was, of course, Hollander, but Urbino warned himself against moving from an assumption to a fact.

The apartment had been cleaned. Workers could often not resist taking something, and usually what they took was something small that wouldn't be easily or quickly missed. It was also possible that in the process of cleaning and temporarily moving pieces of furniture, books had fallen or been removed, and the items in the pigeonholes of the escritoire had cascaded out only to be stuffed back in somewhat haphazardly.

Once again, as inevitably happened in his investigations, Urbino was faced with several possible explanations for something that might – or might not be – of great significance. As he was considering these possible explanations on his way out to the balcony where the agent was standing at the balustrade looking out at the Grand Canal, his eye became caught by something.

It was a collection of watercolors hanging on the salon wall to one side of the foyer. He had noted them before, but something drew him back to examine them again.

Six medium-sized watercolors were arranged in three horizontal rows to form a pattern of an inverted pyramid. They were rather amateurish in their renditions of Venetian scenes but they had a certain charm. The fact that an art connoisseur like Zoll had presumably bought and arranged these less than accomplished watercolors revealed a sentimental side to the man.

But it wasn't what the watercolors seemed to say about Zoll that struck Urbino. He was far less interested in them as a group, no matter how nicely arranged they were, than he was in one particular watercolor.

It was of a bridge in Dorsoduro, the Ponte Pugni that went over the canal between the Campo Santa Margherita and the Campo San Barnabà. One of the approximately 400 bridges in the city.

The name signed in the lower right-hand corner was a demure but unmistakable 'Maisie Croy', the ailing woman who seemed to have such an unusual ability to turn up in the most unexpected of places.

Twenty minutes later Urbino stared down at an inscription carved into the seat of a small white marble stool at the Peggy Guggenheim Museum:

*Savor Kindness*
*Cruelty Is Always*
*A Possibility Later*

It was a good philosophy, except that he found

258

it a bit too optimistic. In his experience, cruelty between people was often more of a probability than a possibility. For the next hour he wandered through the rooms of the palazzo and out on to the water terrace, contemplating the 'Truism' of the language artist Jenny Holzer.

Kindness and cruelty. Love and hate. So different and yet so related. The first could easily develop into the second, and sometimes the two could even flourish together like two agitated flowers on the same plant.

On some surface level the startling images and forms he encountered throughout the Guggenheim – a naked bride, a tumescent man astride his horse, a woman with her throat cut, and androgynous figures flaunting breasts and penises – made an impression on him. How could they not, despite his familiarity with them from many previous visits? But his thoughts were far away from all these specimens of modern art although, in truth, not far away from the building in which they were displayed.

For the Palazzo Guggenheim was in Dorsoduro, and Dorsoduro was where all the disturbing events beginning with Zoll's death had taken place.

As Urbino sat at the stone balustrade beside the shimmering waters of the Grand Canal, he looked toward the Gritti Palace and Zoll's palazzo apartment a short distance to his right. His imagination populated them and the surrounding area with images as disturbing as the ones safely framed in wood and firmly cast in bronze and iron at the Guggenheim. And the advice he had encountered when first entering the Guggenheim was a silent, but powerful accompaniment to the images he conjured up.

*Savor kindness, cruelty is always a possibility later.*

# Eleven

'I take back what I said on the Gritti terrace a few weeks ago, Urbino dear,' Oriana said the next morning in her living room on the Giudecca. 'You're a very predictable man sometimes. At least to the women you let into your life. Don't you realize that by now?'

She was wearing a kimono in bright lacquer red with black dragons on it. She hadn't yet applied any of her dark mascara and bright red lipstick.

But on her face were her trademark large sunglasses. They were something between a prop and an affectation, but on this morning, they were also something of a necessity. Bright sunlight streamed into the spartan living room from which almost every objcct vaguely nonutilitarian had been banished. The sunlight reflected off the glass cubes of tables, the chrome tubing, and unadorned white walls.

Little of the décor in the Ca' Borelli living room was to Urbino's taste, but nonetheless he always felt uplifted when he was in it. For beyond its ceiling-high windows was a picture postcard view across the Bacino to the shining domes of the Basilica, the brick Campanile, the rose-colored Doges' Palace, and the sweep of the

261

Riva degli Schiavoni.

'Predictable?' Urbino said as he seated himself carefully in one of the slingshot chairs.

'Yes. And as soon as I saw it was you who was ringing my bell at this ungodly hour, I knew why.'

'You did?'

Urbino shifted himself in the chair. He tried in vain to find a comfortable position.

'I know you've come for information.' She lit up another cigarette and inhaled deeply. 'You only come to see me for two reasons. For suggestions for Barbara's birthday presents and for information. Since her birthday is a long way off, it's information you want. Let me get some coffee for us and you can start.'

As she was going to the kitchen, she stopped and turned around. 'But you're looking a little pale, Urbino. Some anisette in your espresso is just what you need. Barbara telephoned last night and told me you felt too ill to go to Torcello. They had a good time, despite it, she said. See how easy it is not to be missed?'

When they were sipping their coffee a few minutes later, Urbino said, 'It's about Perla Beato that I'm here.'

Oriana nodded as if this, too, had been predictable.

'I need to know if it's for one of your cases or for your own curiosity,' Oriana said with a direct look.

'I'm not interested in gossip for gossip's sake.'

'You can't pull the wool over my eyes! You thrive on gossip. But I'll grant that you're not

262

mean-spirited. So I assume, then, that you're looking into something.'

'Yes, but don't tell anyone, please.'

Oriana threw her head back in an exaggerated laugh.

'This is quite amusing. You're asking me to be discreet while at the same time expecting me to be indiscreet. Urbino, I love you! So what is it about Perla that I might know – and might agree to tell you if I do?'

'Perla's a lovely woman,' Urbino began, 'and very successful with her business. She does a lot of good with it, I'm sure. And she was – *is* – a nurse. She's always sociable and animated, and—'

'Let's cut to the chase,' Oriana interrupted. 'You want to know if she's having any problems with Romolo.'

'Something like that.'

'Before I might tell you anything – if there's anything to tell – you have to promise *me* something. Whatever I tell you will go no further. I wouldn't want to cause her or Romolo or anyone else any embarrassment and discomfort.'

'And neither would I. I'm not the kind of person who would do that unless it was necessary. I mean for the sake of someone who was in a difficult situation. Or if something seriously illegal were involved. So, yes, I promise.'

'You've provided yourself with more than enough wiggle room.' Oriana sipped her coffee. 'Well, Perla doesn't seem to be having any problems with Romolo that I can see. But that doesn't mean that he's not having his problems

263

with *her*. Perla's only thirty-four.'

'And Romolo's almost twice her age.'

'With a son not much younger.'

'You're not suggesting...?'

'Of course not, darling! Rocco is gay, anyway, though Romolo has yet to see it. No, it's someone else.'

'Maybe you'll feel better about telling me if I ask about one particular person. If it isn't this person, then you don't have to tell me anything more than you already have.'

'That seems reasonable.'

Urbino thought he detected some disappointment in her tone.

'Claudio Balbi,' he said.

'Bingo!'

'How long has it been going on?'

'Two, three months. Perla is absolutely infatuated, and what woman wouldn't be? He's a fine specimen and very uncomplicated.'

'You implied that Romolo suspects something.'

'I'm not sure *if* he knows and *what* he knows. The two of them don't have the kind of relationship that Filippo and I do.'

She said this as if the Borelli arrangement of mutual infidelity and tolerance were the ideal. It seemed to work well enough for Oriana and Filippo, although they had had their share of separations and near divorces. But there was something more honest in their way of handling their affairs, however, than sneaking behind a partner's back as Perla was doing.

'If I had to bet money,' Urbino said, 'I'd say

264

that Romolo suspects, maybe more than only suspects, to judge by one or two of the things he's said. How do you think he'd react if he found out that Perla was having an affair?'

'It certainly wouldn't be the way Filippo does, and I've told Perla just as much. Even aside from the kind of relationship that we have, Filippo is more easy-going.'

'I'm sure you noticed the bruise on her face.'

'A basket of herbs fell on her when she was moving it at the shop, or so she said. I didn't pursue the topic. Romolo has a temper, a pretty bad one, although he seems as cool as anything. I don't know what he'd do if he found out about Rocco, though half his male students are gay. One time he practically bit Perla's head off when she said that he should give in and get glasses, that she was tired of him squinting.'

'Romolo has bad eyesight?'

'I wouldn't call it bad, but he has a hard time making out some things at a distance, and even things up close.'

'How does Claudio feel about Perla?'

'I don't know, but I can guess. And there's what Perla tells me. He enjoys being with an experienced, attractive woman who doesn't expect much in return but his attentions. He's not looking for marriage, he's not looking for children – he's not even looking for Missoni sweaters and Ferragamo shoes. But don't get me wrong. I'm sure a little extra money from the *erboristeria* and maybe even Romolo's property finds its way into his hands. But the boy isn't mercenary.'

'How can you be sure of that?'

Oriana stubbed out her cigarette.

'I have a sixth sense for these things. I have to.'

Urbino drained his espresso. He took out the photograph of Zoll, Luca Benigni, and the waiter from Florian's.

'Look at this photograph. Do you recognize anyone in it?'

She got up and took the photograph to the large window. She examined it without removing her sunglasses.

'It was taken in Florian's,' she said. 'That's one of the waiters. I've never seen the older man before. Who is he?'

Urbino explained.

'Well, I'm not surprised he died. He looks very ill. I've seen the man he's sitting with a few times, though. And now that I think of it, he was with an older man once. He's good-looking. And it's funny. One time when I saw him across the piazza I thought he was Claudio. You can see the resemblance a little in this photo, don't you think?'

After leaving Oriana, Urbino decided to stretch his legs and stimulate his thinking by walking down the long Giudecca embankment.

Before beginning his ramble, he looked across the Bacino to where the Doges' Palace, the columns of the piazzetta, and the domes of the Basilica shimmered. After the storms and the rains, the intense heat and humidity, the city was being blessed with cool, gentle breezes and billowy clouds. The sound of all the boats between him and the Molo, as it drifted across to him, blended together into its own kind of water music. And what would have been, up close, an animated mass of people in varying degrees of exhaustion and appreciation, was only a slowly moving impressionistic blur along the Molo and the Riva degli Schiavoni.

Reluctantly, Urbino abandoned the view. Soon, he was passing the large dome and squat bell towers of the Church of Santa Maria della Presentazione, also known as Le Zitelle, the Spinsters. It was almost inevitable, given his preoccupation these days with Albina's death, that his thoughts would drift not to the pious, unmarried women who had given the church its nickname, but to the two spinsters on the other side of the Giudecca Canal in Dorsoduro – Albina and her sister. Had either of them ever had any marriage proposals? Had they had their share of broken hearts? Or was he guilty of trying to impose a familiar, conventional pattern on their spinsterhood? Giulietta's account had been absent of any references to men, except for their father. The bond between the two sisters must have deepened as the years had gone by and neither would, or could, have abandoned the other, even if the opportunity had come.

After exchanging greetings with two elderly women sitting on benches and becoming caught up in a crowd of young people in front of the Ostello di Venezia, he crossed a bridge and reached the Church of the Redeemer.

Five weeks ago the church had been at the

center of the Feast of the Redeemer. In commemoration of the deliverance of the city from the plague in the sixteenth century, a temporary floating bridge was built over the Giudecca Canal between the Zattere and where Urbino was now standing, to provide access to the church for the Patriarch of Venice, civil and ecclesiastical figures, and crowds of merrymakers. The feast was filled with traditions of mulberries and mandarin oranges, displays of fireworks, and bathing in the Adriatic at sunrise.

Like the regatta and carnival, the feast drew the attention of many foreigners. Urbino and the contessa had seen Zoll and Benigni in the piazza only a few days after the celebration. Hollander had said how enthusiastic his stepfather had been about all things Venetian. But perhaps he had avoided this particular celebration since it would have reminded him that he was not going to be delivered from his own form of the plague.

Urbino spent several minutes in the church's cool, chaste interior. As he had told Clementina Foppa, his visits to the Giudecca were not as frequent as he would have liked, but his mind was too preoccupied this morning to properly appreciate the church and its exquisite Veronese. He accepted the offer of a Franciscan friar, however, to see the monks' pharmacy. There, the aromas of herbs in the garden and the exhibit of old alchemical instruments encouraged thoughts about Perla's *erboristeria*, and from these he passed on to ones about her affair with Claudio. In another age in Venice someone like Perla, with her esoteric knowledge of herbs and potions, might have risked being accused of witchcraft and Claudio cited as one of the victims of her malevolent charms.

After leaving the monks' pharmacy, Urbino turned off the embankment to explore the *calli* and cul-de-sacs of the working-class neighborhood behind the church. This was where Clementina lived. He kept his eye out for any of Luca's death notices.

He stopped a few residents, and mentioned the young man. They praised him and his sister, and expressed regret at his death. They confirmed Urbino's suspicions about the death notices. They had been blown away by the last big storm.

Back on the main embankment Urbino soon came to an iron bridge that spanned the island's widest canal. Wooden, flower-bedecked terraces, fishing boats – mainly *burchielli* – and nets drying in the sunshine made a pretty picture, one that Maisie Croy would surely be tempted to render.

As he proceeded farther along, the view of San Marco and the Molo became gradually lost to view behind him. What took its place across the Giudecca Canal was the broad Zattere, the dome of the Salute, and a tower that leaned prominently against the blue sky with its cushions of clouds. The tower kept forcing itself on his attention. It was the campanile of the Church of Santo Stefano, near Caffé Da Valdo.

Urbino stopped for a Campari soda and stared at the campanile. He couldn't shake the feeling that it was signaling something to him about itself or, more likely, about Da Valdo, where

Albina had spent the last hours of her life.

After walking along the embankment for several more minutes, he sat on a bench on the grassy verge of the Fondamenta San Biagio. A sleek, white cruise ship was moored at the Maritime Station across the water. Small palm trees, close to the ground, rustled in the warm, gentle wind. Behind him were modern brick buildings. Mainly residential, they had long ago displaced the villas and gardens for which the island, especially this part, had been famous since the time of Michelangelo, who had come to the island in search of solitude.

A great deal had changed over the centuries on the Giudecca, more than in most of the rest of Venice.

You had to exercise your imagination to reconstruct it all. This was an activity that Urbino excelled at. As he sat on the bench, however, he didn't exercise his imagination on the Giudecca that once had been – or, in fact, on the Giudecca at all.

Instead, he tried to imagine scenes from less than a month ago. These included Albina's movements during the last hour of her life, the dark, flooded *sottoportico* where she had died, and Luca Benigni's murder in another part of Dorsoduro.

For Urbino was even more certain than before that Luca and Albina had died from foul play. In the one case, Luca's, it had appeared to be an accident – had been arranged to seem like one. In the other, a woman's weak heart would seem to have played into the dark plans of someone

270

who not only hadn't cared whether she lived or died, but had wanted her dead. Needed her dead. And in both deaths the storms had played a major role. They had helped conceal the crimes, had provided violent distractions, and had even seemed, in the case of Luca Benigni, to be the cause of death.

Albina's fate and Luca's fate had been linked. And filaments, like those of a spider's web, connected them with some of the same people, who were themselves, in turn, connected with each other. Konrad Zoll, Claudio Balbi, Nick Hollander, Clementina Foppa, Giulietta Gonella, and Romolo and Perla Beato. And to this group, ever since his visit to Zoll's apartment yesterday morning, Urbino had to add the name of Maisie Croy.

Urbino left the Fondamenta San Biagio and went back in the direction he had come from, stopping at the Sant' Euphemia boat landing. The vaporetto was approaching. In a few minutes he would be on the Zattere, where Claudio had said he was taking a walk on the night of Albina's death. Urbino now believed that he had not gone to the Zattere but had arranged to be with Perla at the Beato residence, while they believed themselves to be safe with Romolo in Padua.

Urbino doubted if Claudio was the first of Perla's affairs. And he also had little doubt that his days as her lover were numbered.

And what might Romolo do if he found out about Claudio before the affair was over? What might he already have done? Oriana had empha-

271

sized that he wasn't cut from the same cloth as Filippo. Romolo's vision wasn't the best, and Luca had resembled his wife's lover even to the keen-sighted.

Two passengers got off when the vaporetto docked, and only Urbino boarded. From his position in the stern, he gazed back at the Giudecca, where so many questions had formed themselves as he had taken his walk. And now another one emerged.

Could someone, capitalizing on the resemblance between Claudio and Luca, have eliminated Zoll's companion, somehow sealing Albina's fate?

And what about Zoll himself? Even with his mortal disease, he could have been murdered. This was something Urbino had considered before, and it now returned with more force. The most likely suspect was Hollander, who had inherited a great deal of money and property. But if he were going to inherit it anyway, why risk everything by killing Zoll when he was going to die soon? And where did Luca Benigni and Albina fit into this particular scenario?

And if Zoll had been killed, who had been in the best position, other than Hollander, to do it? Benigni, certainly.

And what about Maisie Croy? What had her relationship been to Zoll? Had she told Urbino the truth when she had said the scratches on her arm had been caused by a cat? How had her watercolor of the Ponte dei Pugni come into Zoll's possession?

And if Zoll had been killed, how had it been

272

done? An overdose of medication, a withholding of medication, the gradual or sudden administration of a poison of some kind?

Urbino got almost as much satisfaction from figuring out the why and the how of things as he did in ultimately identifying the perpetrator of a crime. There had been some occasions when he had been certain of the guilt of someone, but it had meant nothing to him until he had been able to reconstruct the sequence of events that had brought the person to commit the inevitable, murderous act.

With most of the questions he was asking himself, he could go only a short distance, as would have happened if he had left the Giudecca embankment and gone down some of the narrow island's alleys that dead-ended on the lagoon. He would have been obliged to retrace his steps as he often had to do when he became lost in the contessa's garden maze.

With all his questions about the deaths of Luca Benigni, Albina, and Zoll, he found himself blocked as he tried to move forward. But he believed he would eventually find a free and clear direction forward. He just hoped it would be soon.

In the hours after Urbino's walk on the Giudecca several things transpired which seemed to answer some questions but only at the expense of posing other more troubling ones.

Urbino dropped by the *legatoria* near San Marco that he usually patronized. After buying a collection of pencils covered in marbled paper, he asked the *cartaio*, a heavy-set, whiskered man, a few well-considered questions about the marbling process.

'Yes, Signor Urbino,' the man said. 'Those of us who deal with the paper before it is marbled have to be careful. We use a solution of alum on the paper. It's to allow color to be drawn into it. The alum is toxic. But many shops get the paper already treated. Many don't even do their own marbling.'

Urbino thanked the *cartaio* and left. On his way to the Marciana Library across from the Doges' Palace, Urbino went over what Clementina had said during her demonstration of the marbling process. He didn't recall her mentioning alum, but this didn't mean that she didn't have the chemical in her shop or didn't have easy access to it.

Could she have managed to administer alum to Zoll? Had her brother been involved? What would have been their motivation? The obvious one would seem to be financial gain, as it would have been for Hollander. One of the classic motives. Zoll's death might have meant money for Luca, and money for Luca might have meant money for his half-sister, struggling with her newly established business. It was Hollander, however, who had inherited Zoll's fortune.

But it was certainly possible that Luca might have got something, too, depending on when the will had been made. He had known Zoll for over two years, and Zoll's knowledge of his own imminent death could have resulted in his drawing up a new will. Even a small sum could have been a temptation for Luca. And perhaps money for Luca would have meant more money for Clementina when Luca died, although she had said that he hadn't been a beneficiary in Zoll's will.

Urbino wondered when Zoll's last will had been made out. Before or after he had met Luca? Urbino was counting on Rebecca to shed some light on this through her contacts in Munich.

At the Marciana, however, where Urbino did some research in the large reading room, he was pulled in directions that had little if anything to do with Clementina. It was all because of watercolors. Very clearly spelled out in the books was a warning against cadmiums and cobalts, which, like alum, were toxic. Watercolorists were advised against wetting the brush with their mouth to avoid ingesting the poisonous substances.

What would happen if one or both of the chemicals were administered in large doses?

But what motivation would Maisie Croy have had? There was nothing linking her to Zoll, Luca, or Albina – nothing concrete except for her watercolor of the bridge that had somehow come into Zoll's hands and on to the wall of his Grand Canal apartment.

Two women, Foppa and Croy, and both of them with access to poisons through the normal line of their work.

Poison, it was said, was a woman's preferred method of murder. Urbino believed this to be true, but not because women were by nature more devious than men. Women, as food-preparers and care-givers, however, were in an excellent position to administer poisons.

Yes, food-preparers and care-givers. Had Foppa or Croy been able to get close enough to Zoll to slip him some poison in his food or medicine? Or maybe Luca, who was perfectly placed to do it? And once Zoll had been poisoned, how and why had Luca and Albina been murdered?

But there was another person, and also a woman, who was in an even better position to poison someone. And she too had access to poisons in the natural line of her work. Urbino was dead certain that Perla Beato's *erboristeria* contained substances which, in large dosages or when combined together, could be lethal. And Perla had been a nurse – or rather, as she herself had said to Urbino when he had visited her *erboristeria*, she still *was* one.

The evening brought further complications as well as clarifications.

First the contessa called. She had received a preliminary report from Bascomb about Hollander Tours.

'From what he's learned, it's in financial trouble. He said that on the surface everything looks to be flourishing; but they're not too far from collapsing. I'm surprised.'

'You shouldn't be. Even an old established firm, one like Bascomb's itself, can look prosperous but have a rotten foundation. Look at some of the palaces here. Their piles are rotten.'

'Poor Nick. He's putting on a brave front. I know what you're thinking. He needed money

276

and he killed his stepfather for it. But he was going to die anyway, and from what Bascomb says Hollander Tours could easily keep floating for at least another year without any capital. And Zoll had a natural death sentence.'

'I agree with you. I don't think Hollander killed Zoll.'

Half an hour later Urbino got another piece of information that did nothing to shake his belief that Hollander hadn't killed his stepfather even though it gave him one of the strongest of motives.

Rebecca's contacts in Munich had informed her that Konrad Zoll had drawn up a perfectly legal will six months earlier when he had learned that he had only a short time to live.

There were several bequests – one to the Egyptian Museum in Berlin – but the bulk of his large fortune he left to Hollander.

'I've been regretting that I told you those things about Perla,' Oriana said that evening when Urbino phoned her. 'And now you want more information.'

'I wouldn't ask unless it was extremely important. And whatever you could tell me is probably a matter of public record anyway. I could unearth it, but it would take time.'

Urbino heard Oriana take a long drag on her cigarette.

'Well, Perla never swore me to secrecy, and as you say, you could find out easily enough. Yes, she did have a problem as a nurse. At the Ospedale Civile.' This was the municipal hospital in the Campo Zanipolo. It was in the quarter from which Urbino had seen Romolo rushing when Urbino had been in the bookshop near Santa Maria Formosa. 'Three of her patients died during her night shift within a period of a few months. They hadn't been seriously ill. She was suspended while an investigation was made. But she was cleared of any suspicion of negligence. She still is a nurse and could practice if she wanted to. But it soured her about the profession. It was one of the main reasons she studied homeopathic medicine.'

A few nights later Urbino was jolted from a deep sleep by the ringing of his bedside telephone. He looked at the clock. One fifteen.

*'Pronto!'*

He sat up.

'Signor Urbino?'

He recognized the voice immediately.

'Giulietta? What's the matter? Has someone broken in again?'

'No, no! May God protect me! If he breaks in again, I might be as dead as Albina!'

Giulietta was close to shouting.

'You know who broke in?'

'No! I wish I did. We could protect ourselves then. All of us!'

'The doors are secure now. It's your nerves.'

But Urbino sensed it was more than this.

'Why are you saying this, Giulietta?'

'I wouldn't have to explain anything if I hadn't lied to you. It's on my conscience. I'm afraid I'll pay a high price. Yes, lied. It was because I was scared, but now I'm more scared. I can't sleep a wink.'

'Lied about what?'

A deep sigh came over the wire.

'About nothing being stolen. Something *was* stolen!'

Urbino was fully awake now.

'Something of Albina's?' Urbino prompted when Giulietta fell silent.

'Nothing of Albina's, no. Something of mine! A pistol.'

'A pistol?'

'Yes!' she cried. 'I've had it for years.'

'But what were you doing with a pistol, Giulietta?'

'Nothing! And I never did anything with it, I swear. But I had it.'

'Where did you get it? From Albina?'

'Albina? That mouse? She wanted me to get rid of it. Remember I told you about my trip to Vienna with a friend? I got it there.'

'Why?'

'It was such a pretty little thing, with a mother-of-pearl handle. A lady's pistol, my friend said. Her father collected guns. They were in a big cabinet. So many of them.'

'Your friend gave it to you?'

'I'm ashamed to admit it, Signor Urbino.' Giulietta lowered her voice. 'I stole it, you see. I want to tell you the truth now. Maybe it will protect me. It was in a box. Dark wood, all carved, with mother-of-pearl on it, too.'

'Why did you take it?'

'My friend had so many. And it was so pretty.

Albina and I lived alone. I thought that it would protect us if something bad happened, but now it's the exact opposite!'

'Did it have bullets with it?'

'Of course!' Giulietta said, raising her voice again. 'Could it have done any good without bullets?'

'But that was dangerous, Giulietta, having it in the house.'

'It was never dangerous when it was in the house. Only now that it's out of it! The bullets weren't *in* the pistol! They were in the box. But everything's gone: the box, the pistol, the bullets! And if the person shoots someone with it, I will be to blame.'

'Did you ever tell anyone about it?'

'Only Albina.'

'Do you think she might have mentioned it to anyone? Now that I think of it, she might have been about to tell me the night she died. She said that you could protect the two of you. It must have been the pistol she was thinking about.'

'She talked too much, not like me. Maybe she did tell someone.'

'And your friend? The one from Vienna? Did she notice it was gone?'

'If she did, she's never mentioned it.'

'You have to tell the police about this, Giulietta. They need to know.'

'Would you tell them for me, Signor Urbino, please?'

'You must do it yourself. First thing in the morning, and in person. You can't wait any longer. The day after tomorrow is the regatta. I

280

mean the day after today,' he corrected himself, it now being the early hours of Saturday. 'Everything is going to be busy and confused on Sunday.'

Urbino gave her the name of Corrado Scarpa, the contessa's police contact.

'I hope you don't think I'm a bad woman. I know I stole and I lied.'

'I understand these things. And I'm sure the police will. Everything will be all right.'

Urbino hoped that Giulietta was more reassured by his words than he was.

# Part Five

## The Finishing Line

# Twelve

'It's as if we put in an order, paid a top price, and got even more than we expected – or deserve,' the contessa said to Urbino on regatta afternoon.

They stood on the loggia of her palazzo waiting for her party to begin and looking out at the sweep of the Grand Canal.

Fleecy white clouds drifted in slow procession against a French blue sky, driven by a pine-scented breeze from the Dolomites. Little diamond points speckled the waters of Grand Canal, undisturbed by its usual traffic on this day of the celebration.

People crowded any free space that bordered or overlooked it. Banners supporting teams for the races were draped from the windows and the balconies of the buildings. It was much worse around the area of the finishing line by Ca' Foscari, which would provide a clear view of not only all the races but the water parade as well.

'You look handsome, *caro*.' The contessa ran her hands down the front of his dark blue linen jacket and straightened his tie. Her bracelet of three gold strands with the intertwined letters *B* and *A* reflected the sunshine.

'And you're a vision as usual,' Urbino responded.

The contessa was wearing a pleated silk Fortuny dress in a shade of sea green and weighted with corded pearls of Murano blown glass. Around her neck was a gold chain with an oval pendant of Titian's portrait of Caterina Cornaro at the Uffizi. The contessa had commissioned a painter to make the miniature copy so that she could wear it today. She had swept her blonde hair up and back like Cornaro's coiffure in the portrait.

'Let's hope my little gathering goes smoothly and Gildo and Claudio do well.'

'They already have. To have got this far is a major achievement.'

Voices and laughter spilled out onto the loggia. A few moments later Vitale, the contessa's major-domo, came through one of the high wide doors and nodded to her.

'It's begun, *caro*,' she said.

She planted a quick kiss on his cheek and went into the *salone da ballo*.

Draperies of red, white, blue, and green adorned the *salone da ballo*. These were the colors of the ribbons that would be awarded to the winning teams at the end of the competition. Through an artful arrangement, these decorations didn't clash with the Murano chandeliers, gilded moldings, and stuccoed ceiling of the room. Nor did they seem out of place with the sixteenth-century tapestry of Susanna and the Elders that dominated one wall.

A long buffet table covered with a dark blue cloth offered delicacies of various kinds, including the more mundane tradition of the regatta, *brodo* and boiled meat. The foods were placed in a series of large and small bowls, chafing dishes, and plates in the shape of some of the boats that would appear in the water parade and races – *caorline*, *gondolini*, *mascarete*, *desdotone*, *pupparini*, *bissone*. The centerpiece was a three-foot replica of the *Bucintoro*, the doge's ceremonial barge. Its elaborately carved dark wood and gilded figurines, with a lion of St. Mark on the prow, set off the mounds of caviar piled in its hull.

Beneath the tapestry stood a platform with a five-piece orchestra. The soprano Annamaria Terisio and the tenor Michele Altieri, who frequently performed at the contessa's gatherings, had just sung, to considerable approval, a series of arias and duets from Donizetti's *Caterina Cornaro*.

The orchestra was now playing popular tunes. Guests swept across the floor. Oriana and Nick Hollander were proving to be excellent dancing partners, especially in the absence of Filippo who, to Oriana's delight, had another engagement. Clementina Foppa was in the arms of a middle-aged man with a goatee and glasses who had come with Romolo's son, Rocco.

After dancing with the contessa until an elderly Da Capo-Zendrini nephew cut in, Urbino went to sit with Giulietta. It was the first opportunity to ask her if she had gone to the police the day before.

'I did. I feel much better, Signor Urbino.' She looked much better, too. She wore a linen dress in a shade of violet that suited her. Make-up, applied in a restrained manner, had erased most traces of fatigue and worry. Her fingernails had been manicured, and the two broken nails were less noticeable. 'Signor Scarpa was kind.' She looked out on the dance floor. 'Aren't you going to ask me to dance?'

'Gladly!'

They took their place at the edge of the other couples. Giulietta proved to be both graceful and energetic through not only the rest of this number but the next one as well.

When they finished, he got two glasses of champagne from a waiter passing through the room. Giulietta had apparently overtaxed herself for she asked to sit down. Urbino was going to seat himself next to her when Clementina Foppa joined them. She declined his offer of champagne and took the empty armchair next to Giulietta. The *cartaio* had a dour expression on her small face. The two women fell into a conversation about their respective dresses. Urbino excused himself when Clementina started explaining where she had found the material for her dress, whose blue, gold, and scarlet swirls resembled marbled paper and whose sleeves were cut very high to the shoulder, exposing her muscular arms in a somewhat unattractive manner.

Urbino went over to Maisie Croy who was standing alone by the buffet table. Her red hair, although carefully arranged, couldn't completely conceal a bald spot near the crown. She wore a striped cotton dress in blue and white.

'Are you enjoying yourself, Miss Croy?'

'Very much. Barbara is wonderful. And if I eat any more of this delicious food, I won't be fit enough to carry my kit.'

Croy held a plate heaped high with delicacies. Although each time Urbino saw Croy, she seemed to look more ill, evidently she still had a good appetite. He looked down at the scratches on her arm. They were fainter now.

'Maybe a little dancing before the water parade will help. I'm at your service.'

'That's kind of you, but I'm a terrible dancer.'

'I'm sure that's not true. How is the painting going?'

'It's nice to be painting scenes away from Dorsoduro these days. And Barbara said I could set up my easel on the loggia after the regatta.'

A few minutes later Hollander and Perla joined Urbino and Croy. Somehow Hollander had performed the difficult task of disengaging himself from Oriana, at least for now, unless it was Perla who had managed it. By the doors to the loggia Romolo was having a conversation with the man in the goatee who had come with his son.

'Nick says he knows boats like the back of his hand,' Perla said. 'I've brought him to the table to see if he's just pulling my leg. You wouldn't do that, Nick, would you?'

Urbino introduced Croy. Perla gave her a superficial smile and a quick look that took in her hair. Hollander shook Croy's hand.

'I believe I've seen you painting around Venice,' he said.

'Guilty as accused.' Then she added, *'Ich mag*

*Ihren Ring, Herr Hollander.*' She turned to Perla and Urbino, 'Excuse me. That's rude, but I couldn't resist. I used to teach German.'

Urbino looked at the ring on Hollander's finger. It was a dinner ring with the words *'Freiheit'* and *'Liebe'* in relief in silver against an onyx background.

'I'm afraid I don't understand German, Miss Croy,' Hollander said.

The watercolorist stiffened

'I'm sorry. I assumed you did, since you were wearing the ring. I said that I like it. "Freedom" and "Love", it says. Lovely words. Especially together.'

'Yes. It belonged to my stepfather. He was German.'

Urbino explained that Hollander's stepfather had died recently in Venice. Croy murmured condolences. Urbino watched her closely. Fear seemed to glitter in her eyes.

'It was among his things,' Hollander said. 'He wore it often. I thought it would be a way of bringing him here. He would have loved all this.'

He indicated the sumptuous ballroom, the orchestra – which was now playing music from *La Traviata* – and the loggia, bathed in sunshine and reflected light from the Grand Canal.

'I'm sorry to have stirred up sad thoughts,' Croy said.

'Nick is a strong man,' Perla said. 'I wish I could have helped your stepfather more with my herbs and preparations. I have a shop of herbs and homeopathic cures in Dorsoduro,

Miss Croy,' Perla explained to the red-haired woman. '*Erboristeria Perla.*'

'I've been there.'

'It must have been when I was out or I would remember. I hope you found what you needed and that it's helping you.' But before the embarrassed Croy might respond, Perla said, 'So, Nick, are you ready for my little test?'

'Test? What do you mean?'

Perla indicated the buffet table.

'The boats. You said you know so much about them. I thought I'd ask you to identify as many as you could.'

Hollander looked at the boat-shaped receptacles on the table.

'I'm afraid I'm going to disappoint you — or please you, depending on what you're expecting. All I can identify is the gondola, the *gondolino*, and the *Bucintoro*. But I'm sure Urbino can help us with the others.'

'I know what they are, silly,' Perla said. 'I just want to see if *you* do. Oh, Romolo, darling,' she said when her husband joined them. 'Our new friend is an impostor.' She put her arm around Romolo's waist and pecked his cheek. 'Nick pretends to know more about boats than he does. I don't think that's very nice.'

'So maybe, my dear, you prefer when someone pretends to know less about something than he actually does?' Romolo responded.

Perla gave a high, nervous laugh.

'That's very clever, signore,' Croy said. 'I'm Maisie Croy.'

'Romolo Beato.'

'You have a nice singing voice, Signor Beato,' Croy said.

Romolo and Perla stared at Croy.

'How do you know that?' Perla asked.

'I wandered into the garden after the concert. I heard you singing a little with the tenor, Signor Beato. I was some distance away but I could hear how lovely it was, and without any music. I didn't want to disturb you. You should give us a concert yourself.'

'You have good ears as well as good eyes, Miss Croy,' Hollander said.

'I hope I wasn't intruding.'

Croy's apology seemed directed almost as much to Hollander as it was to Romolo.

'Intruding?' Romolo said. 'In no way. Thank you for the compliment. But my poor old voice is a whisper compared to Michele Altieri's – and many others', even one of my own students. He has excellent power. He—'

'Romolo is a voice teacher,' Perla said, cutting her husband short. 'His voice is divine. Don't believe a single syllable of what he says. He sells himself short.'

'My wife flatters me. She likes me to think I am better than I am. I will tell you who has a divine voice, and he isn't a professional. He's in the regatta. The student I was just talking about. Claudio Balbi. He's rowing in the *gondolini* race with Urbino's gondolier.'

'How interesting!' Croy exclaimed. 'I'll be looking for him.'

'As we all will be,' Romolo responded. 'We wish him the best, him and Gildo. Excuse us.'

He took Perla's arm. 'I'd like to introduce my wife to Altieri. But I warn you, my dear, don't say what a great singer I am!'

He guided Perla away with an unnecessarily firm grasp on her elbow.

A few moments later the contessa and Oriana joined Urbino, Hollander, and Croy. Oriana followed the Beato couple with her eyes until they were engaged in conversation with Altieri.

'You promised me another dance, Nick,' Oriana said. 'If we don't do it soon, we won't do it at all. We have to go up to the *altana* to see the water parade.'

The contessa's palazzo, although some distance from where the parade would terminate at Ca' Foscari, provided an adequate view of the finishing line from its *altana*.

'Nick might not be in the mood to do a lot of dancing,' the contessa said. 'Remember that he's going through a bereavement.'

'But he came today,' Oriana insisted. 'I don't think he's the kind of man who needs to go through the forms to prove the depth of his feelings.'

'I thank the both of you for looking after me.' Hollander smiled at the contessa. 'But I'll pass on another dance, Oriana. I'm a little tired.'

Hollander had made the best of a somewhat delicate situation, caught as he was between the contessa and Oriana. If he had ended up sacrificing a promise to Oriana in order to please his hostess, Urbino could find no fault with it. It was exactly what he should have done.

'We all have our bereavements,' the contessa

293

said, 'but we go on in the midst of them. And they can last a long time.'

She glanced at her bracelet. The sharp-eyed Croy noticed.

'I was talking with one of your guests,' Croy said. 'The woman sitting on the sofa with the young lady. Her name is Giulietta. She said that she had recently lost her sister. And the young woman with her mentioned that she herself had lost a brother. You're right, Barbara. So many of us have our bereavements.'

'And you yourself, Maisie?'

'I've had my share,' the watercolorist said quietly. 'I think your bracelet is a memento of your husband, Barbara. Am I right?'

'He gave it to me on our last anniversary. How did you know?'

'I heard someone talking about the Conte Alvise. *"A"* for Alvise.'

The contessa nodded.

Urbino stopped a passing waiter. Soon the five of them were enjoying more champagne.

'Barbara has Giulietta's dead sister to thank for still having her bracelet,' Oriana said.

'What do you mean?' Croy asked.

'Her sister found it at Florian's where she worked. She gave it to a waiter. Claudio Balbi. He returned it to Barbara. He's in the *gondolini* race.'

'Yes, I just heard about him. Lucky for you, Barbara!' Croy exclaimed. 'And what an honest woman she was.'

Half an hour later Urbino was part of a small

group being lectured to by Rocco Beato's friend, the man in the goatee. Emilio Ruzzini was an engineer for the city. He was an enthusiast for the controversial movable dikes at the three openings in the Lagoon where the Adriatic entered Venice. They were many years from completion.

Ruzzini, who had large, expressive eyes, sat on a long green leather sofa by the windows to the loggia. Seated beside him were Ausonio and two middle-aged Neapolitan women, relatives of the Conte Alvise. Urbino and Rocco stood a few feet away. They were familiar with what Ruzzini was saying, but they listened politely.

'The project is called MOSE,' Ruzzini said. 'Do you understand? Moses. It stands for Modulo Sperimentale Elettomeccanico. Because of Moses and the flood. Whenever the tide level rises beyond a hundred and ten centimeters, the seventy-eight mobile dikes will be filled with air. They float to the surface.' He made a rising motion with a hand. 'The openings are closed. *Ecco*: No more will Venezia be under water.'

'Is it necessary to go to such an extreme?' Ausonio asked.

'It should have been done decades ago!' Ruzzini said with exasperation. 'The government supports it. Every *acqua alta* destroys the city little by little. We've had fifty major floods in the last ten years and we sank more than twenty centimeters in the twentieth century. Twenty centimeters. So much! Even a great building like this one is in danger.' He looked around the large festive room. 'The city has no defenses against

295

the sea. It never had.'

'Emilio likes nothing better than to talk about MOSE,' Rocco said quietly to Urbino. He was tall and thin with straight brown hair that he wore long. In his loose brown suit and black shirt without a tie he looked very much the professor. 'You don't know how many times I've had to listen to this. Sometimes I punish him by giving him a lecture on Giotto.'

But he looked at his friend affectionately.

'Would he be upset if I brought up the cost and the probable ecological damage?' Urbino asked.

'Don't you dare! I'll suffer for it all the way back to Padua. Why don't I take you away from temptation? Let's go over there.' He indicated the wall opposite them, above which hung the coat of arms of the Ca' da Capo-Zendrini family. 'And on the way, let's get one of these.' He took a glass of champagne from one of the waiters.

'I've had enough for a while, thank you.'

Urbino and Rocco went beneath the coat of arms with its blue and scarlet shield, three doves, and two lions of St. Mark. Not far away Clementina and Giulietta were still sitting on the sofa. They seemed out of place. Perhaps it hadn't been a good idea for him to suggest to the contessa that she invite them, and especially so late. But he could keep them under observation and this was a great advantage.

When Giulietta saw Urbino, she waved and gave a bright smile. Clementina was staring in the direction of Maisie Croy, who was examining one of the Da Capo-Zendrini family portraits with two sisters from the Convent of Santa

Crispina.

'I haven't had champagne this good since my father sold one of his buildings,' Rocco said. 'Perla threw a big party.'

'I hope your father straightened out his problem with the tenant in Padua when he came to see you.'

They both looked over at Romolo and Perla who were alone beside the entrance. Perla kept throwing glances at Oriana and Hollander, who were standing out on the loggia with the contessa, looking over the balustrade at the Grand Canal.

'Came to see me?' Rocco said. He looked genuinely surprised. 'When?'

'A few weeks ago.'

'You must be mistaken. I don't get to see my father as often as I like. You would think we lived in different countries. I haven't seen him since the beginning of the summer. I was the one who took care of that tenant.'

'I must have misunderstood.' Urbino paused. 'By the way, did you ever meet a young Italian man in Padua? Luca Benigni. He was a student of art history at Ca' Foscari. He worked on a project on Giotto.'

'Luca Benigni? No, the name's not familiar to me. But I come in contact with so many students. I might have met him and not remember. Why do you ask?'

'Oh, I hear he did an excellent project on the Scrovegni Chapel, and I thought your paths might have crossed because of your own work on Giotto.'

'Well, I am at the Scrovegni Chapel a lot, but I don't recall any Luca Benigni, either there or at my own university.'

Distant music sounded from the Grand Canal. The contessa came into the *salone da ballo*.

'The water parade is arriving at Ca' Foscari!' she called out.

Most of the guests went up to the contessa's large *altana*. Those who were unwilling or unable to make the climb retired to a small room overlooking the garden where the contessa had installed a large-screen television for the direct transmission of the water cortège and the subsequent races.

The *altana* had a blue-and-white striped canopy today as a protection against the sun. On top of the canopy a crimson pennant with the golden lion of San Marco waved in the breeze. Banks of deep purple petunias and ivy adorned the wooden structure. From this perch above the Grand Canal, the contessa and her guests took in the spectacle of the water cortège in the distance.

But one of the best views of the parade on this afternoon was not from the contessa's gaily decorated *altana*. It was from the second-floor balcony of the Grand Canal palazzo apartment behind whose windows Konrad Zoll had died a month before. All the balconies of the other palaces were crowded, as was the terrace of the Gritti Palace. Boats, filled with onlookers and merchants selling slices of melon, were clustered five and six deep along the banks of the Canalazzo.

But Zoll's balcony was deserted, the shutters closed.

The lively, colorful procession along the Grand Canal wasn't for Zoll's eyes or those of his equally dead companion Luca Benigni.

Accompanied by music, in which drums and trumpets predominated, the procession drifted past the empty balcony.

First came the massive, opulent *Bucintoro*, the *Serenissima*, with its gleam of gold, velvet, silk, and jewels – or rather good approximations of them, at least from a distance. Liveried rowers were stationed along the richly decorated, carved bows. Scarlet-clad trumpeters raised their instruments to the walls of the palaces. Uniformed and helmeted guardsmen held lances.

Behind the *Bucintoro* came the black *sandoli* of the *vigili urbani* and a swarm of gondolas rowed by costumed gondoliers. Most of the gondolas carried officials of the Venice municipality, but some of them – and these the ones that received the most attention – floated men and women in sixteenth-century brocade who enacted the roles of the doge, the dogaressa, Caterina Cornaro, ambassadors, and ministers. With the dignity of the historical personages, they waved and smiled to the people. As the doge passed, many of the Venetian spectators bowed in a traditional gesture of respect for the Venetian Republic that once had been.

Eight-oared *bissone* – with plumes, allegorical carvings, and gilded chairs – and six-oared *balotine*, adorned with the omnipresent Lion of San Marco, had their part in the scene. A colorful

299

piece of cloth trailed from the stern of each *bissona*, symbolizing the connection between Venice and the element that defined the fragile city and – as Ruzzini had said – could end up destroying it.

The most recognizable Venetian boat of all, the gondola, was prominent on the watery boulevard throughout the procession, from start to finish. But these were not black and funereal as they were on normal days, but brightly decorated in the colors and banners of the city's rowing associations. Brawny, striped-shirted oarsmen moved them down the green waters and called out to the spectators.

The entire cortège was a vision of gilded poops, statue-adorned sterns, flapping doges' banners and standards, ceremonial umbrellas, bright canopies, brocaded garments, and colored cockades and feathers.

It all formed a picturesque, floating tableau vivant beneath the Tiepolo sky. Thousands of eyes appreciated it, but none from Zoll's balcony.

For some of the spectators gathered on the contessa's *altana*, there was melancholy mixed with their enjoyment, for they observed all this pomp from a distance and heard not the full-bodied notes of the music but something fainter, dying on the air.

From time to time Urbino, standing in a corner of the *altana* beside the contessa, looked around at the other guests, and on some occasions even studied them more than he did the distant

300

procession. One could understand a lot about a person by observing them when they themselves were preoccupied by observing someone or something else.

Of all those he could see on the crowded *altana* from where he was standing, Croy seemed the most enthralled, Nick Hollander the most abstracted, and Romolo the angriest. Romolo glared down at the water parade when he wasn't glowering at Hollander a few feet away next to Oriana.

Perla, who was wedged a little uncomfortably between Romolo and Ausonio, was going through all the motions of enjoying the spectacle. But it was evident to Urbino that she wasn't at ease.

Ruzzini had managed to gather around him a small group of guests again. They were giving him whatever attention they could spare from the procession. But this time Rocco Beato's friend wasn't holding forth about floods and Moses, but about the parade itself. From time to time some of his descriptions and explanations reached Urbino above the music, the cheers, and the conversation of the other guests.

Urbino soon realized that he was being observed himself. But it was by no less a benevolent person than the contessa. She caught his eye, and touched his hand.

She leaned closer and whispered, 'Those who look on see more of the game than gamesters see.'

After the water parade, most of the guests
301

returned to the *salone da ballo* for more food and refreshments. Although the first of the races, that of the young people's *pupparini*, would be starting shortly, it would turn at the Ca' Farsetti by the Rialto Bridge and not pass by the Ca' da Capo-Zendrini as the others would.

Although all four races began at the Castello public gardens, where a rope, the *spagheto*, was stretched across the starting line, and proceeded across the Bacino of St. Mark and into the mouth of the Grand Canal where they moved up the waterway, they took different routes.

All races, however, had their finishing line at the same place. This was the spot Urbino had pointed out to Hollander during their gondola ride. It was between the Ca' Foscari and the Ca' Balbi at the *volta* or great curve of the Grand Canal. There the *machina*, an elaborately carved and brightly gilded platform with a canopied stage, represented the finishing line. The floating platform, which held dignitaries and VIPs, had four flags attached to it which the first four teams had to grab for their victory. Ceremonies for the winners were held on it.

Terisio and Altieri soon were offering more arias and duets from *Caterina Cornaro*. Guests were in an even more convivial mood than earlier, having imbibed large quantities of champagne and been stirred by the historical cortège. Some wandered to the room with the television set to see the *pupparini* race. But the contessa intended to shut the television and close the room during the *gondolini* competition so that she and her guests wouldn't know of the placement of the competitors until they reached the Ca' da Capo-Zendrini.

Urbino spent part of the time trying to sort out a disagreement between Vitale, the major-domo, and Pasquale, the contessa's boatman and chauffeur, that had developed when two guests had decided to leave before the races. This had taken Urbino down to Pasquale's post on the ground floor.

As he was returning to the *salone da ballo*, he passed the contessa's morning room, one of her favorite spots in the house. It was a cozy room that contained some of her most treasured things. The door was partly open. Muffled footsteps sounded within.

'Barbara?'

He pushed the door open all the way and stepped in.

Maisie Croy was the only occupant. She looked disconcerted.

'I was looking for the toilet. And then I saw these. I couldn't resist.'

She indicated a group of watercolors on the wall beside her. They were English landscapes, impressionistic renditions of the Venetian lagoon and the Dolomites, and two small paintings of the Ca' da Capo-Zendrini and the Palazzo Uccello. They had been done by some of the contessa's friends who, like Croy, sought out the city as a subject for their skills.

'Yes, they're lovely. Let me show you where the toilet is.'

He closed the door to the morning room behind them. After pointing out the correct door to

Croy, he returned to the *salone da ballo*. Terisio and Altieri had finished their concert, and once again, some of the guests were dancing, less gracefully than they had earlier.

He went over to Giulietta, who had returned to the sofa that she had favored most of the afternoon. Clementina was still with her.

'Signor Urbino,' Giulietta said, getting up. It was almost as if she wanted to get away from Clementina. 'Let's dance again. Please.'

'Perhaps you would like to dance afterward?' Urbino said to Clementina.

'No, thank you. I prefer to watch,' she responded in a low voice.

Her eyes looked watery with tears.

After a few minutes of dancing, Urbino brought Giulietta back to the sofa. Her face had suddenly become flushed and then gone pale, and he had felt her becoming slightly limp in his arms. He looked around for Clementina, but didn't see her anywhere. He called over Perla, who was walking toward the loggia with Hollander.

'I can take care of her, if you want,' Perla said. 'But the woman talking to Rocco is a doctor. Nick, would you go get her?'

Supporting Giulietta between them, Urbino and the doctor – a middle-aged English woman who only reluctantly relinquished her champagne glass – brought her to a small chamber near the ballroom. They made her comfortable on the sofa and drew the drapes, but they left the windows open so that a slight current of air could come into the room.

'She'll be fine,' the doctor said. 'She became overheated. And the champagne didn't help. I'll stay with her for a while. But perhaps someone can relieve me when the women's race begins. I don't want to miss it.'

When Urbino informed the contessa about what had happened, she went to check on Giulietta. She returned and said that she was sleeping.

'I feel a little guilty,' Urbino said. 'We were dancing a little too fast perhaps.'

'She's in good hands.'

Despite the contessa's reassurances, Urbino remained concerned, and he checked on Giulietta ten minutes later. He found not only that she was soundly sleeping as the contessa had said, but also that the doctor, in a dereliction of her duties and in confirmation of the flowing fountains of champagne, had dropped off to sleep in one of the armchairs.

When he returned to the *salone da ballo*, he stood watching the scene. Many of the guests were drifting out to the loggia again. After a few minutes of observation, he made a brief tour of the room and the loggia, exchanging quick greetings and smiles. He didn't stop for any conversation. When he failed to see Clementina Foppa, he asked the contessa if she might have left.

'I don't think so. I'm sure she would have said goodbye if she had.'

Soon the *mascarete* race would pass the house before turning at the buoy at San Stae. Before relieving the doctor, Urbino went down the corridor and looked into some of the rooms, including the morning room. He didn't find Clementina – or anyone else – in any of them. He then went down the broad staircase to the garden.

He walked through a courtyard of Venetian brick and past statues of chained Turks in Istrian stone. A few steps brought him up to a pebbled path lined with clipped boxwood, laurel hedges, and stone mythological figures. It led toward a pergola with a Roman bath. The pergola, covered in Virginia creeper and English ivy, was the contessa's and Urbino's favorite spot in the garden.

The heavy scent of cigarette smoke struck his nostrils. Urbino continued to the pergola. Foppa was in the process of grinding a cigarette beneath her shoe. She started.

'Oh, I didn't hear anyone coming.' She looked down at the crushed cigarette.

'I didn't know what to do with it. There's nowhere to throw it. How is Giulietta?'

'Sleeping. She should be fine. By the way, I met one of your brother's professors the other day. She had good things to say about him. She'd like you to give the Department of Art History another copy of his death notice. She'll post it at the beginning of the new academic year.'

Clementina thanked him with a faint smile.

'I'll see that she gets one. I should get back upstairs for the race. Are you coming?'

'I'll have to miss the *mascarete*. But go ahead.'

She seemed about to say something else, then

thought better of it and left.

Urbino stood in the pergola until Foppa had time to leave the garden. He stared down at the cigarette stub with Foppa's bright red lipstick staining it. He went upstairs to relieve the doctor and sit with Giulietta.

# Thirteen

Urbino, sitting beside the sleeping Giulietta in the darkened room, had to be contented with cheers, shouts, and applause that lasted only a few minutes and that corresponded to the appearance of the women's racing boats in the Grand Canal. He kept track of the enthusiastic responses.

There was one for the women's *mascarete* as they approached the *paleto*, and another for the returning boats on their way back to the floating *machina* at the Ca' Foscari finishing line.

He hoped that Silvia, the contessa's maid, would relieve him before the next race began, but another forty minutes elapsed. He feared she had forgotten.

The next surges of sound were in response to the *caorline*, powered by their six oarsmen, as they went past the Ca' da Capo-Zendrini to turn around the *paleto* near the train station and then raced past again to Ca' Foscari.

Giulietta stirred several times in response to the sounds from outside, but she didn't awaken. At one point he heard her mumble, 'The pistol, the pistol.'

Urbino occupied himself by reviewing some of what he knew and suspected about the deaths of

Zoll, Benigni, and Albina. He tried to make various connections in his mind. Many of them were plausible until he reached a wall he couldn't get beyond and had to retrace his steps.

He had his suspects, and they were all under the roof of the Ca' da Capo-Zendrini. He looked down at Giulietta lying asleep on the sofa beside him as he ran though all the motives – revenge, greed, jealousy, thwarted love, as well as combinations of these – and attempted to assign them to the various players, one of whom he believed was a much darker player than the others.

The trouble was that he could think of a motive for each one of them, but motive was nothing if there hadn't also been opportunity. And even with both and with knowing both, he still needed to understand the filament of relations between the deaths of the mortally-ill Zoll, his companion Luca Benigni, and a woman who had played a secondary role in both their lives.

But *had* the role been secondary? Wasn't this precisely what he needed to understand?

When Silvia slipped into the room ten minutes after the *caorline* had gone by the Ca' da Capo-Zendrini, Urbino felt as if he would be able to see things more clearly if he had one more piece of information – or, more probably, if he only understood the significance of a piece already in his possession.

But perhaps this was just a comforting illusion.

He joined most of the other guests on the loggia where they were waiting for the most popular race of all, the one of the *gondolini*.

\* \* \*

For Urbino, standing beside the contessa, the *gondolini* race was a rush of color, sound, and thoughts. The eight light boats sped past the Ca' da Capo-Zendrini. Each was painted a different color: white, celestial blue, red, rose, brown, orange, canary yellow, and the green of Gildo and Claudio's *gondolino*.

Because the contessa had shut off the television, none of the guests had any idea of the placement of the competitors. If any did know – mobile telephones being an anachronistic, but inevitable element in the spectacle these days – they were wise enough to remain silent.

Urbino's eyes immediately sought out Gildo and Claudio's *gondolino*. It was seventh, and it seemed it would soon overtake the canary yellow one in sixth place. This was an excellent position for them, considering that returning champions dominated a race that was known as the race of the rowing champions. The two brothers who had taken the red ribbon the previous year were in front. Usually, the winners were evident as early as when the boats passed under the Accademia Bridge, for the leading positions seldom changed. But there was a shifting of position among the other boats.

The two young men were dressed, like the other rowers, in white pants and blue-and-white striped T-shirts, but their belts and bandannas were in the color of their boat. The other gondoliers had similarly distinguished themselves in their own colors.

Claudio stood at the prow, gripping the oar that was held in place by the *forcola*. Gildo, his reddish-blond curls catching the sunlight, was in the middle of the slim craft, manipulating the oar in its lock on the other side of the *gondolino*. They rowed with force and grace. Neither of them looked up at the Ca' da Capo-Zendrini.

Along with the other spectators on each side of the Grand Canal, the contessa's guests waved, clapped, shouted. Although there must have been supporters of the other teams among the contessa's guests, no one cried out encouragement for anyone but Gildo and Claudio.

Perla, standing next to Romolo, called out the names of both rowers, revealing none of the preference she must have felt. Romolo was straining forward, his eyes squinted in order to give him a clearer image of the competitors. He didn't seem to take his intense look off the boat in which his wife's lover – his student – was performing so well.

When the *gondolini* had moved out of sight on their way to the *paleto* beyond the train station, most of the guests stayed out on the loggia, for the boats would soon be passing below them again as they raced to Ca' Foscari.

'I'm so proud of them,' the contessa said. 'They're doing marvelously! Oh, here's Silvia.' Concern crossed her face. 'I hope Giulietta's all right.'

Fortunately, according to Silvia, Giulietta was not only all right but she also insisted on seeing what remained of the races. Urbino found her sitting up on the sofa. Some of her color had returned. Urbino gently guided her out to the loggia, with Silvia on her other side.

'At least I want to see Claudio go by once,' she said. 'For Albina's sake.'

Giulietta got her wish a few minutes later, when the *gondolini* went past again toward the finishing line.

Gildo and Claudio were now in sixth place. As the two rowers went by this time, Claudio looked up at the loggia and gave a smile. It seemed directed at no one in particular. Perla, Giulietta, and even, surprisingly, Clementina, who had momentarily discarded her morose air, waved.

One would have expected Hollander, with his keen interest in boating, to be more caught up in the moment. But he took his eyes away from the swift scene in the Grand Canal and gave his attention to Giulietta. When he found Urbino staring at him, he looked back down at the boats.

Urbino's thoughts and speculations were racing as swiftly as the *gondolini* which were soon spots of receding color moving toward Ca' Foscari.

After the contessa and her guests learned that Gildo and Claudio had placed an amazing fifth, just missing the green ribbon, the party began to break up. Although the contessa said that everyone was welcome to stay as long as they liked – and in some cases, like Giulietta's, even overnight or longer – she understood that most of them were eager to enjoy the activity in the streets that followed the regatta. The Beatos, Hollander, and Maisie Croy had left in quick succession fifteen minutes ago. Clementina had set out on her own a few minutes after Croy had

312

made her exit, with effusive expressions of gratitude.

'You may go, too, *caro*,' the contessa said when she found Urbino alone on the loggia, staring down at the Grand Canal, thick now with water traffic, horns, shouts, and laughter. 'I think other duties may be beckoning.'

'Let's say there are some things on my mind that I need to look into.'

'Be careful,' she said, touching him on the sleeve of his jacket. 'Remember how easy it is to lose what you have.'

The sparkle of her restored bracelet gave an accent to her words.

Although a constant stream of people moved toward the train station now that the regatta was officially over, another larger and much more energetic one surged in the opposite direction toward the Piazza San Marco. It carried Urbino along in its noise and activity.

This stream flowed down the broad and narrow streets and pooled into the squares, where music played and people sang and danced, but the stream always kept moving toward the piazza with mounting noise and liveliness the closer it got to that destination.

Trapped in the middle of a crowd moving down the Salizzada San Lio between the Rialto and the Piazza San Marco, Urbino caught sight of a woman standing in front of a café farther along the street. The people around him obscured a view of her dress, but her hair was metallic red. The way the setting sun was striking her face not only erased her features but also momentarily transformed her head into a death's skull.

Could it be Maisie Croy?

As Urbino watched, a waiter emerged from inside the café and shook his head firmly at the red-haired woman.

By the time Urbino reached the café, the woman was no longer there. Chairs were upturned on the tables inside. The café was in the process of closing.

When he reached the Piazza San Marco, Urbino managed to find some free space beneath the clock tower and took in the scene.

Crimson and gold banners were draped from the windows above the arcades. Italian and Venetian flags flapped in the wind. A congestion of boats filled the Bacino. People milled around by the water between the twin columns and in front of the Doges' Palace, whose upper story glowed pink in the dusk. As for the Piazza San Marco itself, the mosque-like Basilica and the brick Campanile presided over a scene that hadn't seen such crowds and merriment since carnival. A large proportion of the great square's occupants were Venetians. It was as if in the midst of high season and in honor of the serene republic that the regatta celebrated, they were proudly reclaiming the large public space for themselves after months of silent relinquishment.

An old man was playing an accordion with energy and spirit and singing an old Venetian tune in dialect. Children leaped and danced

314

around him, while their parents socialized and looked for friends and family in the throng. Two figures, draped in red, green, white, and blue and wearing white half masks, cavorted on stilts. Drifting slowly up into the darkening sky above the piazza was a cluster of balloons.

Spanish tourists sat down a few feet from Urbino to share a bottle of wine. Companions soon joined them.

A stout, middle-aged woman was singing and dancing by herself near the Caffé Quadri, spinning, weaving, and moving her arms around wildly.

A well-dressed woman standing next to Urbino stared at her.

'People are crazy,' she said in English.

'Or happy,' he couldn't help correcting her before crossing the square to Florian's. As Urbino had expected, Florian's was jammed. The line waiting to get in kept being dispersed by the flow of people under the arcade. Fortunately, he had no intention of sitting in any of the rooms or at any of the tables placed under the arcade or in the square.

The attendant at the door let Urbino inside.

He went to the bar area. He was congratulated as if it had been he and not Claudio and Gildo who had made such a great showing a few hours before.

'He came here after the race,' the baristà said. 'The clients were excited when they found out he had been in the regatta.' He shrugged. 'But he had a quick drink, accepted our congratulations, and left.'

315

'Did he say where he was going?'

'Believe it or not, he was going home! Going home after running in the *gondolini*!'

'Has anyone else come looking for him?'

'A woman. She has an *erboristeria* in Dorso-duro. She missed him by a few minutes. Rushed right out again.'

Urbino snatched a few words with the busy manager. Claudio had picked up the envelope Albina had left for him.


Urbino went out under the arcade. The long, wide corridor was a sea of slowly moving merrymakers as far as he could see toward the Correr Museum and the Napoleonic Wing in one direction, the Basilica in the other. The piazza was all sound and movement, and now, with the coming of dusk and the turning on of the lights, it had an even more festive air than it had a short time before.

*Carabinieri* seemed to be everywhere in their distinctive uniforms. Two of them were reprimanding a group of drunken teenagers who were trying to climb on each other's shoulders outside a jewelry shop.

Something tugged at the edge of Urbino's mind, wanting attention. What was it?

The image of the woman he had seen a short while ago came to him, the woman who had resembled Croy, the woman whose head had been transformed into a death's head by some trickery of the dying light.

What was it about the scene that was troubling him? He kept playing it over and over again in his mind.

People bumped against him. Someone pushed him, not too gently. But he was almost oblivious to everything except the scene he was replaying in his mind.

The red-haired woman might have been Croy. She might have been Croy, the woman with a painting kit of cadmiums and cobalts, Croy of the battered gondolier's hat and scratched arms, the woman with the sharp eyes who had noticed the German words on Hollander's ring and the intertwined gold 'A' and 'B' on the contessa's bracelet, the woman whose watercolor of the Ponte dei Pugni was hanging in Zoll's apartment on the Grand Canal.

What was it about the scene he had just witnessed at the café?

Sometimes all it takes to find an answer and a pattern – to find *the* pattern – is one event, one sound, one sight, one object that brings everything together.

In Urbino's high school chemistry class, he had always enjoyed forming a precipitate in a liquid by adding one small dose of a chemical, not too much, not too little.

He did that now. He added a small dose of something stored in the vial of his memory. It gathered together scattered specks and pieces, and the precipitate formed.

He needed to reach Claudio's apartment as soon as possible.

The police would be no help. It would take too long to convince them to go to Claudio's apartment – if he *could* convince them.

Claudio was in possession of the one thing that would probably have got them moving quickly, if they could see it.

Urbino went back inside Florian's to call a water taxi.

Night had fallen by the time the taxi finally came. Urbino had waited impatiently for it by Harry's Bar, and had almost considered jumping on the next vaporetto to San Tomà.

And now, to add to his anxiety, they were making slow progress up the Grand Canal. Urbino wished they could go faster but too many boats were in the water, not just public transportation and taxis, but more gondolas than usual, crammed with revelers, and numerous rowboats and small craft in which families and friends were extending the day's celebrations.

Light spilling from the windows of the palaces and from lantern-lit boats was doubled in the dark waters. The Gritti Palace was illuminated, its terrace restaurant busy with diners. The windows of the suite that Urbino believed might be Hollander's seemed to show the glow of light behind its draperies, but like the death's head of the fiery-haired woman it was most likely a deception of the eye.

On the other side of the Grand Canal across from the hotel, the windows of Zoll's apartment were not only dark but also tightly shuttered.

People danced on the Accademia Bridge, and waved and shouted from the railings. Amplified rock music and a laser beam came from the Campo Santo Stefano. From the windows of the palaces beyond the wooden bridge drifted quieter music and softer lights. People stood on balconies. Occasionally their laughter and an odd word or phrase found its way to Urbino's ear despite all the other sounds. It reminded him that most people on this evening, at least for these hours, were far removed from the kind of anxious thoughts troubling him.

The taxi passed the *machina* that had been constructed between the Ca' Foscari and the Palazzo Balbi. The floating platform was now empty of its dignitaries. Its carved and gilded details, its garlands and flags, only reinforced its ghostlike impression, its evocation of how death swept across every person's stage, no matter if it was as sumptuous as Zoll's frescoed and tapestried rooms or as humble as the Gonella apartment.

A few moments later, Urbino was getting out at San Tomà.

The narrow *calle* leading to Claudio's apartment was dark. None of the celebration had spilled into it.

Lights showed behind the windows of the apartment.

The broken entrance door gave Urbino access without any trouble. Two dark rectangular spaces along the hall marked where doors had led into the former apartments, which were now gutted.

He started to walk carefully – and quietly – up the staircase to the first-floor landing. He remembered the damaged steps near the landing and managed to move close to the wall where the steps were intact.

The building was silent.

Urbino went up to Claudio's door. It was slightly ajar, as if it hadn't been closed properly. Muffled voices came from inside, but Urbino couldn't identify them.

Suddenly, a woman's high-pitched laughter shattered the silence. Urbino started. It sounded exactly like Perla Beato's laughter. Urbino couldn't tell if it had come from Claudio's apartment or through the broken window that opened on to a well.

He pushed the door inward as carefully as he could. Light showed at the end of the dark hall.

Framed in the doorway of the living room, with his back toward Urbino, was Claudio. He was still wearing his white trousers and striped T-shirt. All Urbino could see of the person he was staring at was a hand. In the hand was a small, delicate pistol, the kind preferred by women.

'I'll give it to you,' Claudio said in his heavily accented English.

'Get it!'

The voice was Nick Hollander's.

Urbino knew that as soon as Claudio gave him the envelope, Claudio would be dead.

Urbino stepped into the living room.

'Take it and go, Hollander. I'll get it.'

'If it isn't Venice's resident sleuth,' Hollander said. 'Worming your way into one place after another.' It was a new tone for the man, snide and cold, but Urbino detected fear and insecurity beneath it. 'And how might *you* know where it is?'

'Because Claudio keeps everything valuable in the bedroom. And the envelope has something valuable, doesn't it? Your stepfather's last will. With Luca Benigni as the main beneficiary. But I may be wrong. Why don't we see?'

Hollander stared back and forth between Urbino and Claudio, moving the pistol from one to the other. Perspiration bathed his bald head and made his weather-beaten cheeks slick and shiny. He seemed dazed.

Hollander was a murderer, and a calculating one. But he wasn't as sure of himself this evening as he needed to be. Urbino's sudden appearance could only have destabilized him.

'Stay where you are, Macintyre. *You* get it,' he waved the pistol at Claudio. 'And no tricks or your meddling friend here will suffer.'

Urbino exchanged a look with Claudio. Urbino hoped he understood what he should do.

Claudio moved toward the bedroom. Hollander watched him sharply. Claudio stepped into the dark room. He turned to the left along the wall. Moments passed. No sound came from the bedroom.

'What's going on?' Hollander was breathing heavily.

He edged sideways to the empty doorway. With rapid movements of his head he tried to keep on eye on both Urbino and the bedroom.

He entered the bedroom, looking toward the left, where he trained the pistol, seeking out

Claudio.

He emitted a sharp cry as he stepped on one of the rotted, exposed beams. The pistol went off as he fell to the stone floor below.

# Epilogue

### Florian's Ribbon

A few days after Nick Hollander fell to his death, Urbino and the contessa were in the Chinese Salon at Florian's. It was their first opportunity to discuss what had happened.

The Piazza San Marco beyond their windows had regained a less frenetic rhythm. The tourist wave that had crested during the weekend of the regatta had fallen back, leaving something resembling whirlpools and eddies. People had more time and certainly more space to appreciate the beauty around them, and the Venetians, who had partied themselves out, had settled back into the far more placid manner that was characteristic of them.

Urbino watched two elderly Venetian ladies pass by the windows. They moved slowly, talking in a quiet manner. With an air of patience they regarded the tourists taking photographs and feeding pigeons on the stones of the square. It wouldn't be long before their walks under the arcade skirted a much more serene and sociable space. They only had to wait a little while longer.

Urbino turned his attention to the contessa,

dressed in royal blue knits that set off her honey-blonde hair and the gold of the bracelet that the conte had given her.

On most occasions, she had a keen appreciation for food, but this afternoon she was ravenous.

She had already devoured almost an entire plate of tea cakes, except for the one that he had taken when he saw them disappearing so rapidly. She had then gone on to scones, marmalade, and clotted cream, and was now giving the *Coppa Fornarina* no chance to begin to melt. Delicately but determinedly, she took spoonfuls of the macaroon-and-cherry-garnished *gelato*.

'Are you all right, Barbara?'

'I've decided not to restrain myself these days if that's what you mean. I intend to get my fair share, and more than that. Look at poor Zoll – and Albina and Luca Benigni. Just a month ago, they were alive, and thought there would be a tomorrow. Maybe even Zoll did.'

Urbino couldn't disagree with the contessa's philosophy. He remained silent. She finished the ice cream. The waiter brought her a pot of first flush jasmine tea and a Campari soda for Urbino.

'How did you know, *caro*?'

'It turned out to be quite simple. Tables and chairs, for one thing. Not the ones here. The ones at Da Valdo. But they would have meant nothing without the circumstances of Albina's restoration of your bracelet.'

Urbino explained how the chairs upturned on the table tops in the café on his way to Florian's after the regatta had finally made things fall into place. He had remembered Albina doing the same at Da Valdo the night she died. It had been the dose that formed the precipitate.

'I noticed that the bottoms of the chairs at Da Valdo had loosely intertwined slats. You could put your fingers through in places.'

'What does it signify?'

'Everything. According to the waiter at Da Valdo, Luca Benigni was there on the night of the first storm – the one he died in. He must have had the new will with him. He probably had just had an argument with Hollander. He had to keep the will out of his hands. If anything happened to it, Luca would have had nothing.'

'And Hollander almost everything.'

'Exactly.'

'Hollander must have pursued him through the streets. Luca stopped at Da Valdo, could easily have slipped the will in its envelope between the slats of his chair, and left. He figured that when Hollander accosted him, he'd have no way of getting the will from him. Luca could go back after getting rid of Hollander, collect it from under the chair, and put it in a safe place, where it should have been to begin with.'

'But all of this is speculation. All three are dead – Zoll, Luca, and Hollander.' Then the contessa added, 'And Albina.'

'But we have the will. Albina must have found it between the slats of the chair when she was cleaning up. Because Zoll had written it in German, she couldn't make any sense of it. She might not even have known what language it was. She turned it over to Claudio as she did everything else she found – or rather she left it at Florian's for him. She figured he would know what it was, what it meant.'

The contessa nodded.

Urbino then explained how Hollander, who assumed Luca had the will on his person, must have struck him with a brick or a stone after pursuing him from Da Valdo into Dorsoduro.

'It could have been with any of the bricks at the building site,' Urbino said. 'Or maybe it was even with a piece of the parapet stone if it had already fallen from the building. One way or another, if the parapet stone fell before or after Luca was dead, it was something that played nicely into Hollander's hands. As for the will, a quick search after he had Luca didn't turn it up.'

Urbino paused and took a sip of his Campari soda.

'And then Hollander knew he was really in trouble,' he went on. 'As long as the will was in existence, it could link him to Luca's apparently accidental death during the storm. He had to find it. He probably backtracked along Luca's route to Da Valdo and then to Zoll's apartment. But of course he found nothing. He was tortured by the thought that maybe the will had blown away and was waiting to be found somewhere. He must also have turned Zoll's apartment upside down – on more than one occasion. When I was in the apartment the day you went to Torcello with him, I noticed how books and letters and other things seemed to have been taken from their places and haphazardly put back.'

'And he thought that Luca had given it to Albina or that she had found it at Da Valdo.'

'As I see it, he accosted her the night of the second storm after she went out again. I sensed that someone was following us earlier. Maurizio felt the same thing the night of the first storm. Hollander must have been stalking her both times. On the night she died, he approached her, threatened her, perhaps pushed her around a bit. She might have mentioned that she found something at Da Valdo, but I doubt she had time to tell him she had left it at Florian's for Claudio. She collapsed. It was all too much for her weak heart. He left her dying in the storm. But the will was still out there somewhere.'

'And it was only logical for him to assume it was in the Gonella apartment. So he was the one who broke in.'

Urbino nodded.

'But what he found was Giulietta's little pistol,' he said. 'He pocketed it just in case he might need it. The man was desperate. It wasn't only a question of the money. He was now responsible for two deaths. It wasn't the sale of Zoll's apartment that kept him here, but finding the evidence of the will and destroying it. It was your regatta party that showed him the last step he had to take, the one that could save him.'

'My party? What do you mean?'

'Your bracelet. Perla mentioned how Albina restored it to you through Claudio after you had lost it.'

'And so he went after Claudio.'

'And found him easily enough. Any of the

waiters could have told him where he lived. Florian's was very proud of him. Still is.'

Not only was Claudio the hero of the scene at Florian's these days, with his photograph displayed in the entranceway, but also Urbino. He had saved Claudio – not to mention himself – from probable death at Hollander's hands. Giulietta's little pistol could have disposed of them both after Hollander had got what he was looking for.

'Claudio says that when he returned from Florian's after the regatta, he fixed himself a drink, and then opened the envelope. Inside, he found two pages written in what he knew was German. With the signatures on it, he figured it was a contract of some kind. He decided he'd call me in the morning. I would look at it and decide what should be done. He had just put the will between the pages of *Regate e Regatanti* when there was a knock on his door. Hollander rushed in, took out the gun, and demanded the envelope.'

'If you had arrived any later than you did, you might have known Hollander had killed Claudio, and even why, but you would have had no proof.'

'It would have been a terrible situation.'

'You and Claudio aren't going to have any problem with the police, are you?'

'There will be an investigation, but depending on how you look at it, it was either self-defense or an accident.'

'I feel guilty saying this, *caro*, but it's a good thing he died the way he did.'

'Don't feel guilty. It's possible that he might have escaped any punishment. After all, the will doesn't prove that he was responsible for Luca's and Albina's deaths but only that he had motivation. With a good lawyer...'

The contessa stared at him.

'And Zoll's death?'

'There was no reason to kill Zoll. Hollander had to wait for only a short time.'

The contessa eyed a wedge of chocolate cake being carried on a plate by their waiter to a French couple in the corner.

'Who will get what Zoll left Luca?' she asked.

'First of all, the will has to be authenticated. There most likely will be some legal wrangling by Zoll's relatives, maybe even Hollander's mother. The witnesses to the will are Germans, a married couple, it would appear, since their last name is the same. They were probably tourists Zoll met. The police are going through their records to see where the couple was staying.'

All tourists had to be registered with both the police and the Ministry of Tourism. It would only be a matter of time before the two Germans were located, and their signatures verified.

'Once that's done,' Urbino said, 'Clementina will get everything. It doesn't seem as if Luca had a will of his own. Not that he would have thought about it at such a young age. Clementina is his only living relative. She'll be able to give her shop a big infusion.'

'Luca and Clementina had as much of a motive for murder as Hollander had.'

Urbino noted that she no longer used his first

name.

'Actually you could say that Clementina would have had a motive for two murders. First Zoll, then her brother if she had known about the will. She still says he never told her. He might have wanted to keep it to himself for a while. She believes he had no ulterior motives in befriending and taking care of Zoll.'

'What do you think?'

'We're all only human. It must have occurred to him that he had something to gain. But I keep thinking of the two of them out there under the arcade' – he indicated the precise spot where they had seen Zoll and Luca in late July – 'and I say to myself, Zoll had someone looking after him at the end.'

The two bronze giants on the top of the clock tower started to strike the fifth hour. The eyes of the two friends, as well as those of most of the people in the square, were drawn to the tower. Its clock, with its golden stars, Zodiacal signs, and planets against a blue background, looked seaward and glittered in the sun. Beneath it was the entrance to the Merceria, one of the main shopping streets of Venice.

When the Moors had finished, the contessa continued to stare at the clock tower.

'Such a beautiful instrument to measure the inevitable passing of the hours.'

'But since their passing *is* inevitable, isn't it better when it can be beautiful as well?'

'Yes, and I know that I'm fortunate. We *both* are.'

Urbino couldn't disagree with this.

'How is Claudio doing?' the contessa asked. 'Isn't he a little cramped with Gildo?'

Claudio was staying with Gildo until he could find another apartment. He didn't want to stay in San Tomà. Urbino had suggested finding him a hotel room but he preferred, for the moment, the arrangement with Gildo.

'He seems fine. And they'll be even more cramped for the next few days. They'll be living in the gondola. They're taking it out into the lagoon. To spend some time on their own, away from everything. No crowds, no competition, no dangers except natural ones, no—'

'No Perla for Claudio,' the contessa interrupted. 'Not that Jill for this Jack.'

'That's over whether Claudio stays in Venice or goes farther away than the lagoon. He's been shaken up enough from his experience with Hollander to make him want to play things safe. And I'm sure that Romolo is going to keep a short leash on Perla for a long time to come.'

'There's something about that part of the story that I can tell you,' the contessa said with a smile of satisfaction. 'Perla and Romolo are through. That's what Oriana tells me. All that love – if it was love – turned to hate, it seems.'

'"All my fond love thus do I blow to heaven. 'Tis gone,"' Urbino recited. He pursed his lips in imitation of a blowing motion.

'You don't make a very good Othello, *caro*, and Perla never was or could ever be a Desdemona. Romolo loved her so much. It's another one of those thin lines though, or it can be, can't it? Love and hate.' Her gray eyes became reflective. 'So what are your plans, now that most of the madness of the season is over?'

'First of all, I'll put together the little book on Albina. I have to make my lie the truth. I've already written some of it.'

'When it's finished and printed, we'll have a memorial reception.'

'And after I finish the book, I'll immerse myself in Goethe. I want to move ahead with the project. I've missed him. He's a tranquil companion.'

'Before you immerse yourself – or maybe you should say *immure* yourself – why don't you spend three or four days in Asolo with Giulietta, Maisie Croy, and me? It might be one of the last times before the spring.'

Giulietta and Croy had become close during the past few days. Giulietta was still at the Ca' da Capo-Zendrini, and the contessa had invited Croy to stay for a while, too.

'Maisie is going to do watercolors. And I've advised her to bring what she considers the best of what she's already done. Perhaps she can sell some of them there.'

As it turned out, the watercolor in Zoll's apartment was one of only two she had sold in Venice. Zoll had seen her at work by the Accademia and had bought her painting. The fact that she spoke good German had delighted him. She had had no idea of his death or that of his Italian companion until the contessa had provided an account of some of the events that had come to a crisis on regatta day.

'Did you and Maisie talk about her health?'

A more serious expression settled on the contessa's attractive face.

'She mentioned that she finished some treatments in London before she came here. But I didn't want to press her for details. She's not comfortable with the topic.'

And neither, Urbino knew, was the contessa.

'By the way, she has something to give you.'

'One of her watercolors. Which one did she choose?'

'The Bridge of Sighs. She said that she thinks of you as a bridge. America and Italy, crime and punishment, art and life – oh, she went on and on! She even said between the living and the dead, but I stopped her there. I didn't want to hear any more.' The contessa shook her head. 'As for Giulietta, some of my Asolo friends might have work for her. So what about you? Will you join us?'

'I'll bring my Goethe and mix business with pleasure.'

'Then it's settled. We'll all go up together in the Bentley on Saturday morning.' She looked over his shoulder. 'My, my, what's this?'

Urbino turned around.

The waiter Marcello, two of his colleagues, and the manager stood a few feet away. They were smiling. The manager handed Urbino a small, dark wooden box, a little larger than a box for a wristwatch. There was no name or inscription on it.

'Whatever could that be?' the contessa asked, with a big smile.

Urbino opened the box. Inside, against the

dark green velvet lining, was a small crimson ribbon looped and crossed, with the Florian logo and the words '*Mille grazie*' woven into it in golden threads.

'It's to thank you for what you've done for Claudio and Albina,' the manager said. 'And for what you've done for Florian's.'

The contessa got up and went over to Urbino. 'Give it to me,' she said.

The ribbon had a golden pin affixed to its back. She pinned the ribbon to the lapel of his sport jacket. The patrons at the other tables fell silent and watched.

When she had finished, she said, 'A little speech?'

Embarrassed, gratified, Urbino said, 'All I can say is thank you. There's nothing more to say.'

The manager shook Urbino's hand. Marcello gave him a kiss on each cheek. A low murmur ran through the salon, followed by light applause.

'The guardian angel of Florian's,' the contessa said. 'Its patron saint.' She reseated herself on the banquette, picked up her teacup, and raised it. 'Sant' Urbino,' she said again.

The other patrons raised their wine glasses, cocktail glasses, water tumblers, and tea and coffee cups, and repeated, some garbling the words, 'Sant' Urbino!' They had no idea what was going on, but they probably thought it was another one of the city's unusual traditions.

Urbino drank down the rest of his Campari soda.

Outside in the piazza, Florian's orchestra

started to play *'Ecco la mia Venezia'* from Verdi's *I Due Foscari*. No one less than Michele Altieri, who had entertained the contessa's guests at her regatta party, started to sing from the platform in the square. It was one of Urbino's favorite arias. Altieri's suave tenor rang out and filled the Chinese Salon as if it were a privileged box at La Fenice:

*Ecco la mia Venezia! Ecco il suo mare!*
*Regina dell'onde, io ti saluto!*
*Sebben meco crudele,*
*io ti son pur de' figli il più fedele.*

These words of the exiled doge as he cast his last glance at Venice always stirred something in Urbino, awakened his melancholy side that both tormented and delighted him.

He looked over at the contessa and smiled his appreciation. Everything had been perfectly arranged.

Everything was in its place – the golden and blue clock face, the stones of the piazza, the domes of the Basilica, the bronze *amorini* in the salon, the tenor's liquid notes, the contessa's loving, healthy face.

Urbino wished the moment could last forever.